We're always told "You can't buy love,"
but these men, created by fabulous writers
Sharon Kendrick and Jennie Lucas,
think differently…

PRICELESS

"Sharon Kendrick transports readers to a
fantasy land with rich, indulgent characters
and an abundance of romance."
—*RT Book Reviews*

"Once this entertaining tale begins, Lucas
does a terrific job of keeping the reader
off-balance right to the end."
—*RT Book Reviews* on
Bought: The Greek's Baby

Hand in Hand Collection

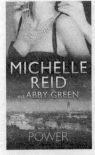

MICHELLE REID and ABBY GREEN

POWER

May 2012

JANE PORTER CAITLIN CREWS

INFAMOUS

June 2012

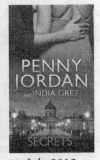

PENNY JORDAN and INDIA GREY

SECRETS

July 2012

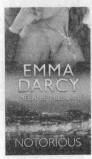

EMMA DARCY MELANIE MILBURNE

NOTORIOUS

August 2012

LYNNE GRAHAM MAISEY YATES

POSSESSION

September 2012

SHARON KENDRICK JENNIE LUCAS

PRICELESS

October 2012

SHARON KENDRICK
and JENNIE LUCAS

PRICELESS

Mills & Boon, an imprint of Harlequin (UK) Limited,
Eton House, 18-24 Paradise Road, Richmond, Surrey TW9 1SR

PRICELESS © Harlequin Enterprises II B.V./S.à.r.l. 2012

Bought for the Sicilian Billionaire's Bed © Sharon Kendrick 2008
Bought: The Greek's Baby © Jennie Lucas 2009

ISBN: 978 0 263 90183 2

010-1012

Harlequin (UK) policy is to use papers that are natural, renewable and recyclable products and made from wood grown in sustainable forests. The logging and manufacturing processes conform to the legal environmental regulations of the country of origin.

Printed and bound in Spain
by Blackprint CPI, Barcelona

BOUGHT FOR THE SICILIAN BILLIONAIRE'S BED

SHARON KENDRICK

Sharon Kendrick started story-telling at the age of eleven and has never really stopped. She likes to write fast-paced, feel-good romances with heroes who are so sexy they'll make your toes curl!

Born in west London, she now lives in the beautiful city of Winchester—where she can see the cathedral from her window (but only if she stands on tip-toe). She has two children, Celia and Patrick, and her passions include music, books, cooking and eating—and drifting off into wonderful daydreams while she works out new plots!

Dear Reader,

When I started *Bought for the Sicilian Billionaire's Bed*, I wanted an unlikely heroine. A poor but proud woman juggling two jobs in order to survive is someone that most people can identify with. And I wanted a powerful and provocative hero who would sizzle off the pages in the way that Sicilian men just do!

Sexy billionaire Salvatore Cardini has hordes of women in hot pursuit—plus some well-meaning friends who are always trying to marry him off. But Salvatore has no intention of marrying and he needs someone to masquerade as his girlfriend. He's the last man you'd imagine dating his office cleaner, yet Jessica has something which appeals to him—not least her petite and curvy body!

I'm a sucker for a Cinderella story. The image of someone poor and downtrodden being whisked off her feet by a powerful man is an enduring fantasy for most women. I hope you enjoy reading this one.

And I'm delighted to be "twinned" with Jennie Lucas whose *Bought: The Greek's Baby* is a crackling page-turner. Jennie writes with all the passion and pizzazz you expect from a Modern™ author—but with her own very distinctive voice. Her heroines are women you can identify with and her heroes are, well…*hot!*

Two fantastic stories in one volume. A bit of a wish come true.

Happy reading,

Sharon Kendrick

www.sharonkendrick.com
Twitter: @Sharon_Kendrick

To Janet, Barbara and Allen, with love.

CHAPTER ONE

'*MADONNA MIA!*'

The words sounded as bitter as Sicilian lemons and as rich as its wine, but Jessica didn't lift her head from her task. There was a whole floor to wash and the executive cloakroom still to clean before she could go home. And besides, looking at Salvatore was distracting. She swirled her mop over the floor. *Much* too distracting.

'What *is* it with these women?' Salvatore demanded heatedly, and his eyes narrowed when he saw he was getting no response from the shadowy figure in the corner. 'Jessica?'

The question cracked out as sharply as if he had shot it from a gun—taut and harsh and unconditional—and Jessica raised her head to look at the man who had fired it at her, steeling herself against his undeniable attraction, though that was easier said than done.

Even she, with her scant experience of the opposite sex, recognised that men like this were few and far between, something which might account for his arrogance and his famous short temper. Salvatore Cardini—

the figurehead of the powerful Cardini family. Dashing, dominant and the darling of just about every woman in London, if the gossip in the staff-room was to be believed.

'Yes, sir?' she said calmly, though it wasn't easy when he had fixed her within the powerful and intimidating spotlight of his eyes.

'Didn't you realise I was talking to you?'

Jessica put her mop into the bucket of suds and swallowed. 'Er, actually, no, I didn't. I thought you were talking to yourself.'

He glowered at her. 'I do not,' he said icily, in his accented yet flawless English, 'make a habit of talking to myself. I was expressing my anger—and if you had any degree of insight then you might have recognised that.'

And the subtext to *that*, Jessica supposed, was that if she possessed the kind of insight he was talking about, then she wouldn't be doing such a lowly job as cleaning the floor of his office.

But in the past months since the influential owner of Cardini Industries had flown in from his native Sicily, Jessica had wisely learnt to adapt to the great man's quirks of character. If Signor Cardini wished to talk to her, then she would let him talk away to his heart's content. The floor would always get finished when he left for the night. You ignored the head of such a successful company at your peril!

'I'm sorry, sir,' Jessica said serenely. 'Is there something I can help with?'

'I doubt it.' Moodily, Salvatore surveyed the computer screen. 'I am invited to a business dinner tomorrow night.'

'That's nice.'

Turning his dark head away from the screen, he threw her a cool stare. 'No, it is not *nice*,' he mocked. 'Why do you English always describe things as *nice*? It is necessary. It makes good business sense to socialise with these people.'

Jessica looked at him a little helplessly. 'Then I'm afraid I don't really see what the problem is.'

'The problem is—' Salvatore read the email again and his lips curved with disdain '—that the man I'm doing business with has a wife—a rather pushy wife, it would seem. And the wife has friends. Many friends. And…' the words danced on the screen in front of him '"Amy is longing to meet you,"' he read. '"And so are her girlfriends—some of whom have to be seen to be believed! Don't worry, Salvatore—we'll have you engaged to an Englishwoman before the year is out!"'

'Well, what's wrong with that?' asked Jessica shyly, even though a stupidly misplaced pang of jealousy ran through her.

Salvatore gave a snort of derision. 'Why do people love to interfere?' he demanded. 'And why in *Dio's* name do they think that I am in need of a wife?'

Jessica gave a helpless kind of shrug. She didn't think he actually wanted an answer to this particular question and she rather hoped she didn't have to give him one. Because what could she say? That she suspected people were trying to marry him off because he was rich and well connected as well as being outrageously good-looking.

And yet despite the head-turning quality of his looks she thought his face was rather ruthless and cold when you got up close. True, the full mouth was sensual, but it rarely smiled and there was something rather forbidding about the way he could fix you with a gaze which froze you to the spot. Yet somehow, looking the way Salvatore did, he could be forgiven almost anything. And he was.

She'd seen secretaries swoon and tea-ladies get flustered in his presence. She'd observed his powerful colleagues regard him with a certain kind of deferential awe and to allow him to call all the shots. And she'd watched simply because he was a joy to watch.

He was tall and lean and his body was honed and hard, with the white silk shirt he wore hinting at the tantalising shape of the torso beneath. Raven-dark hair contrasted with glowing olive skin and completed the dramatic colour pallet of his Mediterranean allure.

But it was his eyes which were so startling. Bright blue—like the bluest sky or the sea on the most summery day of the year. Jessica had never imagined an Italian having eyes which were any other colour than black. The intensity of their hue seemed to suck all the life from his surroundings and sometimes she felt quite dizzy when they were directed on her. Like now.

And from the faintly impatient crease between his dark brows it seemed that he was expecting some kind of answer to his question.

Distracted by his presence, she struggled to remember exactly what it was he'd asked her. 'Perhaps they think you want a wife because you're…er, well—you're about the right kind of age to get married, sir.'

'You think that?' he demanded.

Jessica felt trapped. Backed into a corner. She shook her head. If he wasn't planning to whisk *her* off her feet, then she thought he should remain a lifelong bachelor!

'Actually, no. Your marital future is not something I've really considered,' she hedged. 'But you know what people are like. Once a man passes thirty—which I assume you have—then everyone starts to expect marriage.'

'*Sì*,' said Salvatore and he ran a slow and thoughtful thumb over the hard line of his jaw where the shadow of new growth had already begun to rasp even though he had shaved that very morning. 'Exactly so. And in my own country it is the same!'

He shook his dark head impatiently. Had he really believed that things would be different here in England? Yes, of course he had. That had been one of his reasons for coming to London—to enjoy a little uncomplicated fun before it came to the inevitable duty of choosing a suitable bride in Sicily. For once in his life he had wanted to escape all the expectations which inevitably accompanied his powerful name—particularly at home.

Sicily was a small island where everyone knew everyone else and the subject of when and whom the oldest Cardini would marry had preoccupied too many, and for too long. On Sicily if he was seen speaking to a woman for more than a moment then her eager parents would be costing up her trousseau and casting covetous eyes over his many properties!

This was the first time he had lived somewhere other than his homeland for any length of time, and it had taken little more than a few weeks to discover that, even within the relative anonymity of England, expectation still ran high when it concerned a single, eligible man. Times changed less than you thought they did, he thought wryly.

Women plotted. And they behaved like vultures when they saw a virile man with a seemingly bottomless bank account. When was the last time he had asked a woman for *her* phone number? He couldn't remember. These days, they all seemed to whip out their cell phones to 'key you in' before he'd even had time to discover their surname! Salvatore had fiercely traditional values about the roles of the sexes, and he made no secret of the fact. And the fact was that men should do the chasing.

'The question is what I do about it,' he mused softly.

Jessica was unsure whether or not to pick up her mop again. Probably not. He was looking at her as if he expected her to say something else and it wasn't easy to know how to respond. She knew exactly what she'd say if it was a girlfriend who was asking her, but when it was your boss, how forthright could you afford to be? 'Well, that depends what choices you have, sir,' she said diplomatically.

Salvatore's long fingers drummed against the polished surface of his desk, the sound mimicking the raindrops which were pattering against the giant windows of his top-floor office suite. 'I always could turn the dinner invitation down,' he said.

'Yes, you could, but you'd need to give a reason,' she said.

'I could claim that I had a cold—how do you say, the "man-flu"?'

Jessica's lips curved into a reluctant smile because the very idea of Salvatore Cardini being helpless and ill was impossible to imagine. She shook her head. 'Then they'll only ask you another time.'

Salvatore nodded. 'That is true,' he conceded. 'Well, then, I could rearrange the dinner so that it was on *my* territory and with *my* guest-list.'

'But wouldn't that be a little rude? To so obviously want to take control of the situation?' she ventured cautiously.

He looked at her thoughtfully. Sometimes she seemed to forget herself—to tell him what she thought instead of what he wanted to hear! Was that because he had grown to confide in her—so that some of the normal rules of hierarchy were occasionally suspended?

He realised that he spoke to Jessica in a way he wouldn't dream of speaking to one of his assistants, or their secretaries—for he had seen the inherent dangers in doing that before.

An assistant or secretary often misjudged a confidence—deciding that it meant he wanted to share a lifetime of confidences with them! Whereas the gulf between himself as chairman and Jessica as cleaner was much too wide for her ever to fall into the trap of thinking something as foolish as that. Yet she often quietly and unwittingly hit on the truth. Like now. He leaned back in his chair and thought about her words.

He had no desire to offend Garth Somerville—nor to appear to snub his wife or her eager friends. And what harm would it do to attend a dinner with such women present? It wouldn't be the first time it had happened, or the last.

Yet he was in no mood for the idle sport of fending off predatory females. Like a child offered nothing but copious amounts of candy, his appetite had become jaded of late. And it didn't seem to matter how beautiful the women in question were. Sex so freely and so openly offered carried with it none of the mystique which most excited him.

'*Sì*,' he agreed softly. 'It would be rude.'

Almost without him noticing, Jessica plucked a cloth and a small plastic bottle from the pocket of her overall and began to polish his desk. 'So it looks like you're stuck with going after all,' she observed, and gave the desk a squirt of lemon liquid.

Salvatore frowned. Not for the first time, he found himself wondering just how old she was—twenty-two? Twenty-three? Why on earth was she cleaning offices for a living? Was she really happy coming in here, night after night, wielding a mop and a bucket and busying herself around him as he finished off his paperwork and signed letters?

He watched her while she worked—not that there was a lot to see. She was a plain little thing and always covered her hair with a tight headscarf, which matched the rather ugly pink overall she wore. The outfit was loose and he had never looked at her as man would automatically look at a woman. Never considered that there might be a body underneath it all, but the movement of her arm rubbing vigorous circles on his desk suddenly drew attention to the fact that the material of her overall was pulling tight across her firm young breasts.

And that there *was* a body beneath it. Indeed, there was the hint of a rather shapely body. Salvatore swallowed. It was the unexpectedness of the observation which hit him and made him a sudden victim to a heavy kick of lust.

'Will you make me some coffee?' he questioned unevenly.

Jessica put her duster down and looked at him and wondered if it had ever occurred to the famously arrogant boss of Cardini Industries that his huge barn of an office didn't just magically clean itself. That the small rings left by the numerous cups of espresso he drank throughout the day needed to be wiped away, and the pens which he always left lying haphazardly around the place had to be gathered up and put together neatly in the pot on his desk.

She met the sapphire ice of his piercing stare without reacting to it. She doubted it. Men like this were used to their lives running seamlessly. To have legions of people unobtrusively working for them, fading away into the background like invisible cogs powering a mighty piece of machinery.

She wondered what he would say if she told him that she was not there to make his coffee. That it wasn't part of her job description. That it was a pretty sexist request and there was nothing stopping him from making his own.

But you didn't tell the chairman of the company that, did you? And, even putting aside his position of power, there was something so arrogant and formidable about him that she didn't quite dare. As if he were used to women running around doing things for him whenever he snapped his fingers and as if those women would rejoice in the opportunity to do so.

She walked over to the coffee machine, which looked as if a small spacecraft had landed in the office, made him a cup and carried it over to his desk.

'Your coffee, sir,' she said.

As she leaned forward he got the sudden drift of the lemon cleaning fluid mixed with some kind of cheap scent and it was an astonishingly potent blend. For a second Salvatore felt it wash unexpectedly over his senses. And suddenly an idea so audacious came to him that for a moment he allowed it to dance across his consciousness.

Imagine if he took someone with him to the dinner party. Someone who might deflect the attention of women on the make. Wouldn't a woman on the arm of a known commitment-phobe send out a loud message to the world that Salvatore Cardini might be taken? Especially if that woman was so unlikely as to take their collective breath away and give them something to gossip about!

The sound of the rain continued to lash against the windows of the penthouse office and Salvatore watched as Jessica picked up her cloth and began to attack a smear of dust. It was as if up until that moment she had been nothing but a piece of paper onto which the outline of a woman had been drawn and only now had the fine detail begun to emerge. Salvatore had an accurate and swiftly assessing eye where women were concerned and for the first time he used it on the woman who was dusting behind a lamp.

Her bottom was curved and her hips were womanly, that was for sure. For the first time he allowed himself to notice the indentation of her waist—and a tiny little waist it was, too.

And yet, although he could be a maverick in business, he liked as many facts as possible at his disposal before he made a decision. He never acted on instinct alone. She might be unsuitable for the task, in so many ways.

'How old are you?' he questioned suddenly, and as she turned round he could see that her eyes were grey and amazingly calm—like the stones you sometimes found at the bottom of a waterfall.

Jessica tried not to show her surprise. It was a very personal question from a man who had always treated her as part of the furniture in the past. Her hand fell from the lamp and the cloth hung limply by her side as she looked at him.

'Me? I'm…I'm twenty-three,' she answered uncertainly.

He stared at her bare fingers. No ring, but these days you could never be sure. 'And you are not married?'

'Married? Me? Good heavens—no, sir.'

'No jealous boyfriend waiting for you at home, then?' he questioned lightly.

'No, sir.' Now why on earth had he wanted to know *that*?

He nodded. It was as he had thought. He gestured to her bucket. 'And you are contented with this kind of work, are you?'

Jessica looked at him from between narrowed eyes. 'Contented? I'm afraid I don't really understand the question, sir.'

He shrugged, gesturing towards her mop and her bucket. 'Don't you? You seem intelligent enough,' he mused. 'I would have thought that a young woman would have had horizons which lay beyond the confines of office cleaning.'

It hurt. Of course it hurt. Apart from being completely patronising he made her sound like some kind of mindless robot in a pinny! Yet surely his damning judgement showed just how arrogant and completely lacking in imagination he was.

Silently, Jessica counted to ten, knowing that several options lay before her. She could pick up her bucket and upend it over that dark head and handsome, mocking face, imagining the water soaking through that fine silk shirt—and his look of dismay and of shock. That would surely be the most satisfying reaction of all. Except, of course, she wouldn't dream of doing it—because that really *would* be professional suicide.

Or she could answer calmly, intelligently and maybe, just maybe, make him eat his judgemental words.

'I'm not a full-time cleaner,' she said.

'You're not?'

'No. Not that there's anything wrong with cleaning,' she defended fiercely as she thought of all her fellow workers at the Top Kleen agency, some of whom squeezed in as many hours as they could while juggling life and work and babies in the most adverse conditions imaginable. 'As it happens, I actually have a day-job. I work for a big sales company and I'm training to be an office manager, but...' Her words tailed off.

'But?' His voice was silken as he prompted her.

She forced herself to confront the dazzling sapphire blaze of his eyes. 'My job isn't particularly well paid. And living in London is expensive. So I top up my salary with a little cleaning work on the side.' Jessica shrugged. 'Lots of people do it.'

Not in his world, they didn't—but didn't her relatively impoverished state make his idea a little less audacious? Maybe they could both do each other a favour.

His eyes flickered over to the rain-splattered window which overlooked the glittering lights of London as he began to wonder what her hair was like underneath that hideous scarf. It might, he thought, be shorn close to her head and coloured in a variety of shades. In which case his suggestion would never be made—for it was inconceivable that Salvatore Cardini would ever be seen out in public with a woman like *that*!

'How do you get home from here?' he questioned idly.

How did he think she got home? By helicopter? 'By bus.'

'You'll get wet.'

She followed the direction of his gaze. Droplets were

scudding down the window and the rain was so thick that you could barely make out the distant buildings beyond. It really was the foulest of nights. 'Looks that way. But that's okay—I'm used to it. Don't they say that rainwater is good for the skin—counteracts all the bad effects of central heating?'

Salvatore ignored the attempt at small talk. 'I'll get my driver to drop you off home. He's waiting outside for me to finish.'

Jessica found herself flushing. 'No, honestly, sir— that's fine. I've got my brolly and a waterproof—'

'Just accept it,' he clipped out. 'What time do you finish?'

'Usually around eight—depends how quickly I work.'

'Make it seven-thirty,' he instructed.

'But—'

'No arguments.' Salvatore glanced at the expensive gold timepiece which gleamed against his wrist and his mouth hardened into an odd kind of smile. 'Consider it done,' he drawled.

And punching out a number on his telephone, he began to speak rapidly in Italian before turning his back on her—as if she was of no real consequence at all.

CHAPTER TWO

JESSICA carried on working at an increased pace in order to get everything done in time, but something had changed and it wasn't just because she was alone in the office with Salvatore. Reserve and shyness had entered her body along with the rapid thunder of her heart as it suddenly occurred to her what she had agreed to. It was like every wistful daydream come true—her gorgeous boss was insisting on giving her a lift home in his chauffeur-driven limo!

And what, Jessica?

You think this is the powerful Sicilian's not-so-subtle attempt to get you, his office cleaner, alone away from the office? Maybe so that he can try to *seduce* you? Yes, sure he is—and he won't really be collecting you in a car at all, but in a glass carriage!

Just accept his generosity with good grace, she told herself as she removed a smear from the coffee machine with a fierce wipe. Enjoy the novelty of a trip home in a luxurious car—it'll make up for all the patronising remarks he made earlier.

At seven thirty on the dot, she picked up her bucket and cleared her throat. 'I'll go and get changed then, sir,' she said, feeling faintly foolish. 'Er, shall I meet you downstairs?'

'Mmm?' Salvatore glanced up at her, his eyes narrowing as if he'd forgotten she was there. 'Yes, sure. Where?'

'Do you know where the back entrance is? It's a bit tricky to find.'

There wasn't a flicker of reaction on his rugged features. 'Not really, but no doubt I can manage without a map,' he said drily. 'The car will be waiting and I don't like to wait. So don't be long.'

'I won't,' said Jessica, and sped off.

But her heart was thundering as she pulled off her pink overall and untied the scarf, wishing that she were wearing something other than a plain skirt and jumper with a great big waterproof coat to put on top.

Yet why should she? This wasn't the kind of job that you dressed up for—dressed down for, more like. She took off her flat black shoes and put them in the locker along with her overall and scarf, then set about brushing her hair—which was her one redeeming feature. It fell to her shoulders and, although it was a rather boring shade of brown, it was good and thick and nearly always shiny.

Jessica squinted into the mirror. Her face looked pale and drained without make-up but she found the end of a tube of lip gloss at the bottom of her handbag and her fingers hovered over it with hesitation.

Would it look a little obvious, as if she might be *expecting* something, if she applied some make-up? But suddenly, Jessica didn't care. A woman had her pride, and even if she happened to be wearing cheap clothes then surely it wasn't a crime to want to make the best of a very bad job.

Fortunately, because she had knocked off slightly early, there was no one else around. None of the other cleaners offering to walk to the bus-stop with her—or, worse, witness her sliding into the back seat of a fancy car.

Why, to any other member of staff it would look... Jessica went pink around the ears. It would look highly suspicious and throw a not very flattering light on her character.

But there was no time for any further doubts. He had specifically told her not to be late, so she grabbed her bag and hurried out. And sure enough there sat a long, low limousine purring like a mighty cat by the back entrance.

Jessica gulped down the dryness in the back of her throat. It was odd to think of someone regarding this kind of car as normal—when in her world it was the type of vehicle which was usually used for weddings.

Convulsively, her fingers clenched around the strap of her handbag. Weddings? *Weddings?* Now what on earth had made that thought pop into her head? Probably because Salvatore had rather surprisingly asked her whether she was married. And why had he wanted to know *that*?

But there was no time for further thought because a uniformed chauffeur was actually opening the door of the luxury car—for *her*!

'Thanks very much,' she said hurriedly, trying to

slide into the back of the car as decorously as possible—something which wasn't especially easy since Salvatore was sitting on the other end of the soft leather seat, his long legs sprawled out in front of him. His arms were crossed and she couldn't make out the expression on his face because the interior of the car was shadowed, but she saw the glint in his narrowed eyes as he watched her.

'So here you are,' he murmured, though his initial thought was one of disappointment. His crazy scheme was just that, he realised. Crazy. With her cheap and bulky coat concealing her slight frame and her pale face she looked just what she was. Ordinary. There was *no way* that this young woman could accompany him to anything, other than perhaps to help carry his shopping in to the apartment. Who would believe that a man like him was dating a woman like her? Nobody with more than one brain cell, that was for sure. 'Where do you live?'

Jessica sat bolt upright. 'Shepherd's Bush.' She gave the name of the road to the driver, who then closed the interconnecting glass so that she was left alone with Salvatore. The last time she had felt as out of place as this was her last day at school, when she'd forgotten that it was a 'no uniform' day.

Salvatore's mouth curved with wry amusement as he registered her stiff frame and uptight body-language. She was nervous, he realised. Did she think that he was about to leap on her? If so, then she clearly had an over-inflated view of her own appeal! 'Relax,' he said softly.

Jessica leant back in the seat—though the leather was so soft and squishy that it was hard to believe that she was actually sitting in a car.

'This is really very kind of you,' she said.

'Not a problem.'

'Where…where do *you* live?' It seemed like a very personal question to ask—but what *were* the rules for a situation like this? She couldn't spend an entire journey asking him if he was satisfied with the level of cleanliness in his office!

'Chelsea.'

Of course he did. Rich, glamorous Chelsea with its glorious white villas and springtime trees daubed with cherry blossom.

'I don't want to take you out of your way, sir.'

The 'sir' seemed oddly inappropriate under the circumstances, but she was a thoughtful little thing, he realised. Salvatore smiled as he leaned back and glanced out of the window.

'I can easily have the driver drop me off first if I choose,' he said coolly. 'But there are parts of your city with which I am unfamiliar—and so I shall see this place Shepherd's Bush for myself.'

Don't hold your breath, Jessica wanted to say, but instead she smiled back. She half wondered if she should chat and ask him about whether he was enjoying his time in England, but he seemed to have an aversion to small talk. And besides, he was the kind of man who liked to lead a conversation—not to follow it.

Salvatore felt oddly soothed by the silence which

filled the car and which—surprisingly—she didn't try to fill with inane chatter. Why could women never see the value in peace and always insist on shattering it with unnecessary words?

They drove through a rainy city and for once he felt completely cocooned within the purring warmth of the car. It was all too easy to take luxury for granted, he found himself thinking as the limousine slowed to turn into a road featuring a row of terraced houses.

'It's that one on the end,' said Jessica, glad that the journey had passed without anything going wrong. But she also felt strangely reluctant to leave the sumptuous cosiness in exchange for the cold reality outside. 'Just here.'

'You own this, do you?' questioned Salvatore as the car came to a halt in front of a small house.

Jessica turned to him. Was he crazy? No, he was just rich and the rich were different—everyone knew that. It wasn't his fault that he had no comprehension of how people like her lived their lives. She shook her head. 'Property's hugely expensive in London. I rent—in fact, I share this house with two other girls. Willow works in the fashion business and Freya is an air stewardess—though she's away a lot.'

But Salvatore wasn't really listening. Maybe it was because the rain had finally stopped. Or maybe it was because the moon had appeared from behind the dark curtain of a cloud. It was amazing what a little light could do.

He found himself looking down at her face, at skin

which looked impossibly pure and clean. Her grey eyes were illuminated by that same light and so was the subtle gleam of her mouth. Unexpectedly, she looked all eyes and lips and her pauper-like appearance suddenly crumbled to dust in his memory.

'Are you busy tomorrow night?' he questioned suddenly.

Jessica blinked. 'No. Why?'

'How would you like to accompany me to that dinner I was telling you about?'

'You mean, as your *guest*?' she queried, her voice quivering on the brink of astonishment.

What did she imagine he wanted—that he was taking his own personal cleaner? But at least with Jessica, Salvatore knew that he could be upfront. A girl like her was unlikely to read anything into the situation, but he'd better make it clear.

'Yes, of course,' he said impatiently. 'But what I really want is for you to act like my girlfriend—'

'Your *girlfriend*?' she interrupted, even though everyone knew you should never interrupt your boss but this was so bizarre that the normal rules had gone flying out of the window.

'It's just a little role play,' he murmured. 'Nothing too demanding. Gaze into my eyes a little. Look at me adoringly once in a while. Think you could manage that without too much trouble?' His eyes mocked her with the question because Salvatore knew that there wasn't a woman alive who would find *that* an impossible task. 'Get the predators off my back once and for all, and let them know that if I want a woman, then I'll do the choosing myself.'

'But there must be a million women you could ask!' exclaimed Jessica.

'Oh, at least a million,' he answered, with cool and mocking humour. 'But none of them suitable for all kinds of reasons.' The main one being that they saw him as husband-material, something which this little thing would never be guilty of.

'But won't...?' Jessica bit her lip. Wasn't it more than a bit humiliating to have to ask the next question? But ask it she needed to. 'Won't it be slightly unbelievable...someone like me going out with someone like you?'

'Possibly,' Salvatore conceded, his eye flicking disparagingly over her bulky waterproof. 'If you were dressed like that it might be very difficult indeed.'

'Oddly enough, it didn't occur to me to put on my best party dress for work,' she said, hurt.

'You mean you might have something suitable tucked away?'

For a moment she felt like saying no, she didn't, because surely that would get her off the hook? But somehow she didn't think that Salvatore would let it rest now that he'd made up his mind about this strange assignment. If she said that she *didn't* have anything to wear, then mightn't that look as if she was angling to be given something? Just because she cleaned his office didn't mean that she couldn't scrub up well!

And besides, there was an undeniable part of her which

was thrilled at the thought of accompanying Salvatore Cardini to a party. Didn't life sometimes throw opportunities at you which would be a crime to turn down?

'Of course I've something suitable to wear,' she said proudly, and then a sudden, heady sense of her own power swept over her in a way it had never done before. 'But I haven't said I'll go yet, sir.'

The preposterous statement made him smile, but it made a pulse begin to beat heavily at his temple, too. She would be very foolish indeed if she began to tease him—she was dealing with a man and not a boy. He could bend her to his will with the mere whisper of his fingertip.

Fractionally, he leaned forward, his face closer, his voice soft. 'But I think you will, won't you, Jessica? And while we're at it, I think you should lose the "sir", don't you? In the circumstances it might be a bit of a giveaway.'

He was so close that she could see the moonlight glinting in his sapphire eyes and sense his animal warmth, the tangy scent of soap and raw masculinity. This close he was…Jessica felt her heart give an irregular skip. He was irresistible.

Was she playing with fire?

'Yes, I'll come,' she said, and then stumbled out of the car before either of them could change their minds.

CHAPTER THREE

'You're going *where* tomorrow night?' demanded Willow in a voice of sheer disbelief.

'Out to dinner,' said Jessica faintly as she took off her bulky jacket. The limousine had just driven away and it was almost as if she needed to repeat the words to herself to believe that they were true. 'With Salvatore Cardini.'

Willow's eyes widened. 'That's *the* Salvatore Cardini? The Italian billionaire playboy who owns that company where you play Mrs Mop in the evenings?'

'That's right.'

'Let's make sure we're talking about the same man here, Jessica. Black-haired, blue-eyed, sex-on-legs but with a mean, dangerous look about him?'

'Well, yes—that just about sums him up.'

Willow brushed a lock of dead-straight blonde hair out of her eye. 'You do realise that he's an international playboy with a reputation as a heartbreaker?'

'I sort of guessed that for myself.'

'And that every glossy magazine worth its salt has

been trying to gain access to do a feature on him? Jessica, what are you *like*?'

Jessica shook his head. 'I didn't know *that*—and I don't care and it's no good you looking at me that way, Willow. I know you work for one of those glossies and I know you'd love an exclusive, but you're not getting it via me. Salvatore is my boss—one of the reasons I have that job is because I'm discreet.'

'But it's a rubbish job!'

'Which means I can pay my bills here!' Jessica retorted, thinking of the steep sum she had to shell out for the tiny boxroom of the three-bedroomed house. But then, unlike Willow and Freya, she wasn't cushioned by the comfort of family money if her finances ran into real trouble.

'Perhaps some time you could tell him that your friend would love to do a sympathetic interview and he could even have say on the final copy? I'd be eternally grateful.' Willow shook her elegant head. 'And he's taking you out,' she said. 'Unbelievable!'

Jessica could understand her incredulity only too well. Her housemate lived up to her name—she was tall, blonde and stylish and legions of men were always attempting to beat their way to her door. Yet not even Willow had managed to attract a man of Salvatore's calibre—and here was mousy little Jessica doing just that.

'It *is* a bit incredible,' she admitted.

'So why has he done it, Jessica?'

Jessica dipped a teabag into a mug of boiling water so that her face was partially hidden. Wouldn't it be humiliating to have to tell the whole truth—that essentially she was being taken out as some kind of deterrent to other women? Wouldn't it be acceptable to allow herself the fantasy, just this once—especially as it was just going to be once?

'I think he just wants company,' she prevaricated.

'Yes, but—'

Jessica turned round as suddenly the reality made her heart sting. 'But what, Willow? You mean what's a rich bloke like him doing with a poor, plain girl like me?'

'No, I didn't—'

'Yes, you did,' interrupted Jessica gloomily. 'And what's more—you're right. Don't you think it was the first thing which occurred to *me*?' She walked back into the sitting room and sat down on the battered sofa, her fingers clutching at her steaming mug of tea. How could she have been naïve enough to think about maintaining a fantasy like this for more than a second? Who would ever believe it?

'These people he's having dinner with are trying to set him up and he's fed up with people trying to marry him off,' she explained. 'So he's taking me as a defiant gesture, in the hope that word gets out and they'll stop trying.' She saw Willow's face and knew that further explanation was indeed necessary. 'And presumably he'd picked me and not someone else more glam because I won't get any false hopes in my head. Because I know my place and I'll just accept the evening for what it is.'

'Is he paying you?' asked Willow sharply.

Jessica put her mug down with a shaking hand, her

cheeks flushing. 'You're making me sound like some kind of...of...hooker!'

Willow shook her head. 'That's not what I meant at all. But it seems to me that you're doing him a pretty big favour—so what's in it for you?'

Jessica bit her lip. Honesty not only made you vulnerable, it also made you weak and in a modern world you needed all the bolstering defences you could get. But suddenly she didn't care. 'I just fancy a glimpse into a different kind of life for a change. I've certainly been on the outside looking in for long enough. The only trouble is whether I can fit in and what I'm going to wear.' She looked up at Willow hopefully. 'I was hoping you might be able to help.'

Willow, who was at least four inches taller and several pounds lighter, smiled. 'Oh, I think I can help. Don't worry, Jessica Martin—we're going to make sure you knock his sizzling Sicilian socks off!'

The next day Jessica skipped lunch so she could leave the office early and spent far too long in the bathroom. She nicked her ankle when she was shaving her legs and her nerves built up as the bathwater grew cold and the sky outside the window darkened.

Under Willow's critical eye, she must have tried on twenty different outfits before finding one that she felt comfortable enough to wear, automatically rejecting anything too tight or too low because she thought that would make her look cheap.

By the time eight o'clock arrived her hands were

shaking with nerves and when the doorbell rang it didn't surprise her when she heard Willow yelling: 'I'll go!'

She sprayed on some perfume, took one final glance in the mirror and went to find her boss, who was standing by their rather tatty velvet sofa talking to Willow. And the moment Jessica looked into the narrowed sapphire eyes she knew that her nerves had been justified. In the office he was distracting enough—but tonight he looked as if he should be carrying a government health warning.

His immaculately cut dinner suit emphasised the long legs and the narrow, sexy hips. He looked expensive, urbane, and so totally out of her league that Jessica's heart began to race and she felt the hot pin-pricking of nerves at her forehead. Suddenly she felt daunted. What the hell was she going to *talk* to him about?

'Hello, Jessica,' he said softly.

'H-hello.'

'You look very…different,' he said slowly.

'Well, that's a relief!' she said quickly and caught Willow's warning glance. If she spent the whole night emphasising the differences between them, then the evening was going to be a disaster. 'Er, thank you,' she amended.

Salvatore watched while she picked up her coat. The fitted black silk dress was a little conservative, it was true, but he liked that—and it accentuated a figure which was really very good. His eyes narrowed. Very good indeed. Her hair was thick and shiny and it swung in a healthy bell around her neck. She looked better than he had anticipated—though she was still light years away from his normal type.

But wasn't it strange how your whole opinion of someone could alter in a single moment? Suddenly he was seeing more than the clear grey eyes and the pure skin—now he found his gaze drawn irresistibly to the way the black silk skated so tantalisingly over her pert bottom. His breath was a little unsteady as he took the coat from her and held it open. 'Here, let me.'

Jessica had grown up in a world where men and women considered themselves equals. No man she knew would ever dream of holding open a door or a coat for her, and as she slid her arms into the garment she thought how stupid it was that such a simple little gesture should be so disarming. Was she imagining the lingering brush of his hands and the corresponding quickening of her heart? Had he *meant* to touch her like that?

'Come on,' he said. 'My car is outside.'

'Bye, Salvatore—nice to meet you,' said Willow, with a megawatt smile. 'Hope to see you again.'

They walked out to the waiting limousine, but as the driver opened the door Jessica looked up at the Sicilian and his face looked shadowed in the moonlight.

'Did you…did you tell them you were bringing someone?'

'I did.'

'And what did they say?'

Shaking his head, he placed his hand at the small of her back and propelled her into the car, suddenly wondering if this was such a good idea after all. Was she too unsophisticated to cope with the evening ahead?

'It doesn't matter what they said,' he said softly as

the car pulled away into the traffic. But then she crossed one leg over another and all he could think about was whether the sheer, dark silk which covered her slender legs was tights, or stockings.

Maybe you'll find out later, taunted a voice inside his head as they drove through the darkened streets, and Salvatore cursed silently and shifted in his seat as unexpected and unwanted desire again began to tug at his senses.

It was just at that point that his phone rang and he pulled it out with a feeling of relief and began to speak.

Jessica stared out of the window as Salvatore spent the entire journey conducting a telephone conversation in rapid Italian, which seemed to magnify her feeling of not belonging. And that feeling only intensified when the car drew up outside an enormous house in Knightsbridge, which looked like something you might see in a film.

'Oh, my goodness—it's *huge*,' she breathed.

He glanced at her. 'It's just a house.'

To him it might be just a house—but to Jessica it was the kind of place for which you'd normally have to pay an admission fee. Inside were uniformed staff who whisked her coat away and someone else who guided them through to the murmuring guests, who all looked up as she followed Salvatore into the glittering room.

She was aware of a blur of names and faces as they were introduced, but Jessica's overwhelming feeling was that the women looked like birds of paradise in their jewels and bright dresses and that she had been a fool to come in black—because wasn't that what all the waitresses were wearing?

Their host and hostess were Garth and Amy and there were two other women called Suzy and Clare—neither of whom seemed to be attached to a rather bloodless-looking man named Steve and a wiry individual with light brown hair who introduced himself as Jeremy. And that was it.

So it really *had* been a set-up, thought Jessica as the redhead named Suzy shimmied over to stand directly in front of Salvatore.

'Hi, Salvatore—do you remember me?' she was asking him, with a coy smile. 'We met in Monte Carlo and I told you that Sicily was my favourite place in the whole world.'

Although she was straining to hear while trying to look as if she weren't, Jessica didn't quite catch Salvatore's response, but she turned away with a sudden pang, telling herself that feeling jealous about her partner certainly wasn't on tonight's agenda.

'Champagne?' questioned Garth, offering her an engraved flute with pale liquid foaming up the sides. 'It's rather a good vintage.'

'Yes, please.' Jessica smiled as if she drank vintage champagne every day of her life. She took a sip and began to chat to Jeremy, who—despite his unlikely appearance—turned out to be something very powerful in the City.

'And what about you?' he questioned. 'Do you work?'

Jessica supposed that this was a world where women *didn't* have to work. 'Oh, yes, I'm…I'm…' Oh, *why* hadn't she prepared something? Jessica looked up to find Salvatore watching her.

'Jessica is training to be an office manager,' said the Sicilian smoothly and she blinked at him in surprise. Had he really remembered that?

'Oh, is that how you two met?' butted in Clare. 'In the *office*?'

Jessica's gaze locked with his. Say what you want to say, those blue eyes seemed to tell her.

'Kind of,' said Jessica, and blushed.

Salvatore hid a smile. Oh, but she was perfect for the role! *Perfetto*. The way the blush of rose crept into her cheeks made her look coy and sweet—as if she were embarrassed about a supposed office romance. So that no one, not even the woman Clare with her heavy eye make-up and brazen cleavage—would have had the guts to interrogate her any further.

'Let's go in to dinner, shall we?' said Amy sharply.

A table was laid up with gleaming crystal and silver and studded with tightly bunched white roses in small vases. As she unshook a giant napkin over her knees Jessica found herself wondering whether she was going to be presented with any unfamiliar foodstuffs which she wouldn't have a clue how to eat, even though Willow had given her a crash course in posh dining while she'd been getting dressed. Oysters and artichokes were apparently the biggest hurdles to clear, but thankfully neither of them made an appearance and so she was able to concentrate on what was being said around the table.

Which was easier said than done. Most of the conversation went right over her head and she noticed that most of the food remained uneaten—though everyone seemed to drink plenty of wine.

She forced herself not to feast her eyes on Salvatore—whose black hair and blue eyes and formidable physique seemed to dominate the entire table. Maybe everyone else was aware of him, too, Jessica thought—because the women certainly didn't seem to be intimidated by the fact that he had brought a partner with him. They flirted with him as if flirting had just been invented.

Did he ever get bored with such a gushing reaction? she wondered suddenly as she turned to talk to the man beside her.

What she knew about banking and takeovers could be written on the back of a postage stamp, but she gently quizzed Jeremy about what he did to relax. It turned out that he was mad about fishing and real enthusiasm entered his voice as he told her about digging for bait.

'Rag worms or lug worms?' she enquired and a silence fell over the table.

Jessica looked up to find Salvatore's gaze on her, the bright blue eyes narrowed in mocking query.

'They're talking about worms—*ugh!*' shuddered Clare theatrically, her breasts pushing against the fine silk of her pink dress as if they were fighting to get out.

'You like to fish, do you, Jessica?' questioned Salvatore softly.

For some stupid reason, colour stole into Jessica's cheeks and she shrugged her shoulders a little awkwardly as she answered him. 'Oh, I did a bit, when I was a child.' In that faraway time when her parents had still been alive and the days had always seemed full of sunshine and games. Her mother would take her down to the riverbank and Jessica would sit solemnly with a hook and line dangling from an old gardening cane.

'Presumably you must have been a tomboy,' observed Suzy.

It was like being in one of those awful nightmares where everyone was staring at you waiting for an answer and you couldn't speak. Except that this wasn't a nightmare and she *could* speak. So stand up for yourself, Jessica, she thought. Don't let this woman intimidate you just because she's crazy about Salvatore.

'I liked climbing trees and fishing and swimming in the river, yes,' she said. 'But I never considered them pastimes which were exclusively for boys—why should they be when they're such fun?'

'Bravo!' said Jeremy softly, and laughed.

She felt on a bit of a high for the rest of the meal, especially when Jeremy offered to take her fishing in Hampshire, where apparently he owned a stretch of the river—and he pressed his card into her hand as she was leaving.

But her exhilaration evaporated the moment the car door closed on her and Salvatore and they were enclosed in their own small, private world.

Slowly, he let his eyes drift over her as if reassessing her potential. 'So I have seen the little English mouse in action,' he murmured.

'What…what's that supposed to mean?'

In the darkness his eyes gleamed. 'Quiet. Unassuming. Then she throws off her overall and becomes the unlikely temptress—'

'Temptress?' echoed Jessica. 'I don't think so.'

'Ah, but you tempted Jeremy—that much was plain,' mused Salvatore silkily. There was a pause. 'And you're tempting me. Right now.'

Too late she sensed the danger in the air and too late she read the sexual intent in his eyes.

It was too late for everything, because Salvatore Cardini had pulled her into his arms and started to kiss her with a passion which took her breath away.

CHAPTER FOUR

For a moment Jessica thought that this must be like drowning—when they said your life flashed before you. As Salvatore's lips covered hers she saw the past speed by—with its good and bad, its sadness and joy. But it was as if she had been only a shadow of herself before and his powerful kiss was awakening all her senses.

He tasted of wine and desire and promise and Jessica's lips opened beneath his, her fingers reaching up to clutch at his broad shoulders as if she was afraid that she might collapse. But that was just how it felt— as if a sudden gust of air might blow her clean away.

'Salvatore—' she breathed into his mouth, shockingly aware that it was the first time she had ever used his Christian name, but surely such a situation demanded it.

'Sì?' Groaning, he caught her by the waist, his hands moving beneath her coat to rest proprietorially on the silk of her dress. He slid his palms up to her breasts and cupped them, as if he were examining their weight, before fingering their peaking points through the straining silk.

'*Oh!*' she gasped, in shock and delight.

He stroked her hips. Her bottom. The curve of her thighs—his hunger for her tempered by a sudden shaft of objectivity. This was crazy, he told himself. This was not what he had intended—not at all. Was that why it suddenly seemed unbearably exciting—because he liked to control a situation and here was one which seemed to have blown up in his face? 'Tell me what you like to do, *cara*,' he whispered. 'Show me what you like.'

She touched her lips to his neck; she couldn't seem to stop herself as her every dark fantasy sprang to life. 'Salvatore...' she whispered again.

Her hand had fluttered down to alight like a butterfly on the tensed muscle of his thigh and his head jerked back as it moved away again. 'I live not far from here,' he bit out. 'Come on—we're going. *Adesso*!'

His hungry words wove themselves into her consciousness as her fingers wove into the silken tangle of his dark hair. Jessica felt as if she had stepped on an escalator which was hurtling her towards a shockingly unexpected pleasure. But even while her body gave itself up to the sensations which were washing over her with such sheer, sweet allure she felt the first unwelcome stir of protest in the back of her mind.

'Salvatore—'

'Mmm?'

His lips were at the base of her neck now, drifting in a tantalising path down towards her breasts. And she held her breath, not wanting to break the moment nor the feeling even as some stubborn resistance reared again its unwanted head. Go away, she told her doubts fiercely—but somehow those doubts refused to die. 'I mustn't—'

'*Sì*, you must.' He smiled against her skin as the tip of his tongue flicked against her skin. 'You want to. You know you do.'

Jessica felt herself slipping under—as if sensual dark waters were lapping over her. Her eyelids fluttered open and all she could see was the ceiling of the luxury car. The *car*! He was seducing her in the back seat of his car! 'You…you…oh, *oh*!'

But, ironically, it was as his hand began to slide its way up her thigh that reality hit her like a sudden spray of ice-water and Jessica tore herself out of his arms, wriggling over to the corner where she surveyed him as if she had found herself alone with an unknown and deadly predator.

Her fingers reached for her neck and she could feel the rapid rise and fall of her breast as she struggled to cope with her ragged breathing.

'What…what on *earth* do you think you're doing?' she breathed.

'You know exactly what I'm doing—I'm going to make love to you.'

Jessica swallowed. 'You are *not*!'

'But you want me to.'

Oh, the arrogance and the assurance which was printed all over that gorgeous face—but even worse was the glaring truth which underpinned his words. She *did* want him—more than she could ever remember wanting anyone, but, oh, at what price? Her dignity? Her *job*? She tugged at the black silk dress which had ridden up round her thighs. 'Maybe for a moment I did—but this certainly wasn't supposed to be part of the plan tonight!'

'No?' he drawled, infuriated now by the sudden, abrupt ending and by the growing feeling of disbelief that a woman should be turning him down. And such a woman as this! 'I wasn't aware that we had drawn up some kind of itinerary for the evening.'

'That's not what I meant and you know it!' she flared.

'No?'

'No!' And suddenly Jessica was angry—not just with herself but with him, too. 'Did you think that I'd jump into bed with you at the drop of a hat?' she demanded.

He wanted to say that it was far more likely to be a drop of her panties, which—unbelievably and infuriatingly—he had yet to see. 'I think you were pretty close to it, Jessica. *Si*.'

'You think that all you have to do is to whisk me off to a fancy dinner in a chauffeur driven car and I'll be so…so…*grateful* that I'll capitulate to you!'

Salvatore was beginning to grow bored now. 'I hadn't actually given it that much thought,' he told her damningly. 'It wasn't a situation I'd anticipated.'

Stupidly enough, this only added to her anger. So now he was saying that he hadn't even considered he might find her attractive enough to make a pass at her! Was that why he had chosen her—because she was too plain to provide any temptation? Well, thank heavens she had seen sense before it was too late.

Imagine if she'd gone back with him—let him make love to her, and then what? Would he have sent her on her way in the middle of the night—to be taken home by his driver, like a toy he had grown bored with playing with? Or, even worse, being given money for a taxi to conveniently disappear from his bed?

'We are just a man and a woman,' he mused, when still she said nothing. 'And sometimes passion comes along when you are least expecting it. It is the way of these things.'

As he spoke he reached out to brush a stray strand of the thick, shiny hair which had fallen over her face and that one innocent, almost tender gesture was almost Jessica's undoing. Because that was the kind of thing that a real lover might do—especially if he was trying hard to seduce you. Not that Jessica was the world's biggest expert on lovers, but she knew what was considered acceptable by most women with a degree of self-respect and what was not.

If she allowed Salvatore to make love to her now, then it would be tantamount to telling him to treat her like a disposable cloth—to be thrown away when he'd finished with her!

And by tomorrow, his desire would have died. Why, he might even thank her for having been level-headed enough to put a stop to things before they got out of hand. True, facing him again in the workplace wasn't going to be the most comfortable option, but there were ways of dealing with that.

She pulled her head back from the enticement of that touch. 'Maybe it's the way of things in the world *you* live in,' she said pointedly. 'But not in mine.'

He searched her face for a teasing look, the telltale expression on her face which would indicate that this was merely female playfulness, but to Salvatore's disbelief there was none. Just the kind of jutting-chinned certainty which women often assumed when they meant something, and which made his heart sink.

This was worse than being back in Sicily! Did she really imagine that he was going to start courting her? That she would allow him certain privileges each night? One night the kiss, the next the breasts—until she breathlessly allowed him to take her whole body, as she would have been hungering for from the very beginning?

Did she really think he had the time or the inclination to waste on a leisurely pursuit of a woman for whom his desire was already waning—someone who should have been *thanking her lucky stars* to be here with him in the first place? His mouth twisted. What a little fool she was—to have called time on what would have been the best experience of her life!

'If you think that such resistance will elevate you to a truly irresistible status in my eyes, then I am afraid you are sadly mistaken, *cara*. Do you not think that I have been privy to every devious game played by women? I know them all—and it won't work, for I am immune to them all.'

Jessica sat bolt upright. She hadn't been so angry since…well, actually, she couldn't *ever* remember being as angry as *this*!

'Oh, don't worry, Signor Cardini,' she retorted, trying to match his withering tone with one of her own and in that hot moment of fury not caring that she might be jeopardising her job. 'I really hadn't given any thought to game-playing—why would I? I thought I was coming out to act as some kind of decoy—not to be leapt on in the back of your car! And now, if you don't mind—I'd like to be taken home.'

There was a moment of brief, stunned silence as the impact of her words sank in, until in the shadowed gloom Salvatore's mouth curved into a cruel and mocking smile. 'I think you forget yourself, *cara mia*,' he drawled damningly. 'You will certainly be dropped off—but only after the car has taken me home.'

He pressed a button by his seat, tersely issued the instruction to his driver and drew a sheaf of documents from one of the side-pockets. And then, clicking on a reading light, he leaned back in his seat and began to flick through them, as if he had simply forgotten she was there.

CHAPTER FIVE

BUT the craziest thing of all was that Salvatore couldn't get Jessica out of his mind—and the irony of this didn't escape him. How could one short, bogus date have resulted in him thinking almost non-stop about his damned cleaner? Unable to shake from his mind the memory of her grey eyes, that pure skin and the decadent delight of those luscious breasts.

The light glinted on his razor as he stared in the mirror, his dark jaw half shaved and his blue eyes narrowed. Intellectually he recognised that her improbable attraction was *because* she had turned him down. He was used to women fawning. Plotting. Enticing and scheming. Why, it was not unknown for a woman to *beg* him to make love to her!

Jessica intrigued him because in a world where one thing was predictable—his effect on the opposite sex—the unexpected would always have the power to tantalise him.

So had she been playing games with him? Knowing that precisely the right button to press was not to let him press any buttons at all? To let him touch a little, but not too much. To give him a taste to whet his appetite but leave him hungering for more?

He went to his club and swam for an hour, had a breakfast meeting in a chandelier-lit room overlooking Hyde Park and took a conference call from an Australian banker before most of the world was awake. Yet still he was restless.

How could some plain and mousy little cleaner know how to handle any kind of man—but especially a man like *him*?

All day long he was distracted, though he was astute enough not to make any major decisions until her infernal perfume had left his senses. Some scent he was unfamiliar with—which had reminded him of springtime and softness and clung to his skin last night until he had viciously washed it off beneath the jets of a cold shower.

'*Maledizione!*' Damn her!

Giovanni Amato—an old friend from Sicily—was flying in from New York and Salvatore had arranged to meet him for dinner. Yet he found himself strangely relieved when Giovanni's secretary rang to say his flight had been delayed, and that he was running late.

'Get him to call me,' Salvatore said to her. 'We'll change it to another night.'

As he slowly put the phone down Salvatore felt the stealthy beat of excitement combined with the strong tang of self-contempt. Surely you aren't hanging around the office waiting to see whether that pale little nobody will dare show her face here tonight? he asked himself furiously.

But as he cleared his desk of paperwork he recognised that maybe he was. He glanced at his watch. That was if she was going to bother to turn up.

He had signed the last of a pile of letters and was just putting his gold pen down on the blotter when he heard the door click open behind him. Salvatore felt himself tense, though he didn't move. He didn't dare move. He hadn't felt this kind of hot, instant lust for a woman for a long time and he wanted to prolong it— knowing that the second he turned round, his fantasy would crumble into dust. He would no longer be looking at the woman who had made him feel so deliciously hard all night, but at some mousey little office worker.

He swivelled the chair round to face her. 'Hello, Jessica,' he said softly.

Clutching her bucket and her mop, Jessica froze as she stared across the huge office in horror.

He was still here!

Despite her leaving his office until the last possible moment—until she was certain that he had gone— Salvatore Cardini was still at his desk, his icy blue eyes mocking her with memories of what had almost happened in his car last night! She bit down on her lip so hard that she risked cutting it and the hand which wasn't holding onto the mop clenched into a tight fist by the side of her pink overall. Of all the nightmare situations, this had to be the very worst.

Hadn't she hesitated about coming in here at all, tempted to phone Top Kleen and tell them she was sick?

And hadn't there been a tiny part of her which had wondered about leaving the agency altogether—to sign on with someone new? Someone who might not have a prestigious client like Cardini, but who would guarantee a peaceful working environment where she would be untroubled by ridiculous fantasies.

But Jessica had a strong work ethic, which made her baulk at such behaviour, as well as a stubborn streak of pride which insisted that she had done nothing wrong. Nothing to be ashamed of.

So where was that strong conviction now? Staring across the vast space, she could see the sardonic glint in Salvatore's eyes. Her mouth as dry as parchment, she drank him in. His black hair, his broad shoulders and outline of that amazing hard body. The image of that same body pressing itself close into hers in the back seat of his car drifted tantalisingly into her mind and fiercely she tried to block it.

What the hell was she going to say to him when their last meeting had ended in a frozen silence?

Just act normally. As if nothing happened. Wipe it from your memory—as he has probably wiped it from his.

She cleared her throat. 'Good evening…' she hesitated. '…sir.'

Salvatore gave a slow, mocking smile. So they were back to 'sir', were they?

His eyes flicked over her. She was wearing the same pink overall which she always wore and her hair was almost completely concealed by the hideous pink scarf. Her face was bare of make-up and her grey eyes were wary, watchful. She looked exactly the same as she always did and yet something had changed.

In him?

Was it because he had kissed those bare lips and tangled his fingers in the glossy hair which now lay covered from his gaze that made him so acutely aware of her presence in a way he had never been before? Was it because he now knew the luscious curves and unexpected temptations of the body which lay beneath the unflattering garment?

'Sleep well?' he questioned softly.

Infuriatingly, Jessica blushed. No, of course she hadn't slept well! She'd spent the entire night tossing and turning and bashing her pillow into shape and then getting up to make herself a cup of camomile tea, unable to get Salvatore out of her mind.

It had been the memory of his kiss which had troubled her more than anything. Because wasn't it rather shaming that in all her twenty-three years—the one kiss which had sent her heart soaring was delivered by a man for whom she'd been nothing but a convenience?

She wondered if he was astute enough to notice how awful she looked. Wouldn't the dark circles beneath her eyes show her to be lying if she claimed to have slumbered like a baby?

'Not really, no,' she answered briskly.

'Me neither. I tossed and I turned all night.' His lips lingered on the words as he leaned back in his chair and studied her. 'But I guess that isn't really surprising, is it, *cara*?'

She wished he wouldn't dip his voice like that—as

if he were dipping a rich, ripe strawberry into a bowl of thick, melted chocolate. And she wished he wouldn't stare at her like that, either. As if it were his unalienable right to arrogantly appraise her, with the kind of slow scrutiny of a man performing an imaginary striptease. So just blank all his sensual allusions. Behave as you normally would and sooner or later he'll tire of the game and leave you alone.

'No, not surprising at all,' she said, deliberately mis-understanding. She picked up a plastic bottle which appeared to show two lemons going into battle against an army of germs. 'The food at dinner was very rich.'

'But you hardly touched a thing all evening,' he reminded her.

'I'm amazed you noticed,' said Jessica.

'Oh, I noticed all right.' His blue eyes gleamed with provocation. 'Just as I noticed that Jeremy Kingston seemed to think you were the most fascinating thing to come into his life since his last tax break.'

'Only because I asked him about fishing. He says he gets fed up with people always wanting to know which bank he's taking over next.'

'Are you aware that he's one of the most powerful financiers in Europe?' questioned Salvatore coolly.

'No, of course I'm not,' scoffed Jessica. 'Finance not only doesn't interest me—it also confuses the life out of me. Now, do you mind if I start working?'

He linked his long fingers together. 'You don't usually ask.'

She wasn't usually remembering just what it felt like

to have his lips all over her neck, his hands splayed over her silk-covered thighs. 'So I don't,' she agreed tightly. 'But under the circumstances, I thought I'd make an exception.'

Clutching her bucket, she walked across the office to the cloakroom, horribly and yet skin-tingling, aware that he was watching every step as she passed him, like a clever cat before it leapt onto a helpless little mouse. She reached for the tap. Hadn't he called her a mouse last night? And wasn't that an insult?

Salvatore could hear the sound of running water and he screwed his eyes together. He had been expecting— what? That she would have prettied herself up for him this evening? Flirted a little? Undone a few buttons and flaunted a little cleavage? Or acted in that deliberately coy way that women sometimes did, and which men could rarely resist, even when they knew they were being manipulated.

Yet here she was, behaving as if nothing had happened!

But nothing *did* happen, his aching body reminded him, and his natural sexual arrogance made his fists clench with anger that frustration imposed on him from such an unlikely source. Noiselessly, he rose from his desk and followed her into the cloakroom. 'You don't usually run away from me either, do you, Jessica?'

She turned round, her face flushed, heart-thumpingly aware of his proximity and the way that he seemed to dominate the space around them. Suddenly, her bravado seemed to have deserted her. 'No, I don't,' she agreed unsteadily.

'Just like you don't usually stare at me all wide-eyed like that, as if I'm the big, bad wolf.'

Jessica attempted to make her face look normal—but how the hell did you do something like that when all you could think of was how utterly irresistible the man was? 'Don't I?'

He smiled, but it was a hard edged smile. 'You know you don't.'

He seemed to be deliberately misinterpreting the situation. Didn't he have any inkling how difficult she was finding this? Didn't he realise that she had feelings for him but was sensible enough to know that such feelings were totally inappropriate? Jessica frowned, but part of her felt a sudden sadness, too.

Usually they had an easy rapport, which sometimes happened when two people of completely different social standing came together. You sometimes heard about very rich men confiding in their driver, or a billionairess divulging all her secrets to the girl who painted her toenails. But it didn't *mean* anything—not in the grand scheme of things.

Because such unlikely relationships only worked on the basis that both parties knew their place. That there were strict boundaries which neither should attempt to cross.

And so it had been with her and Salvatore—until last night. Last night they had broken the rules, big time. The taking her to dinner could have been classified as nothing but a minor transgression—but what had happened afterwards could not.

She couldn't deny what she'd done—or nearly done.

And although she had called a halt to that blissful bout of passion she couldn't deny that her body had been crying out for him.

She looked at him. If she allowed herself to sink further into stupid fantasy, then her body could very easily start crying out for him right now. His black hair was ruffled, the bright blue eyes narrowed and the hard and autocratic line of his jaw was shadowed with new growth. He looked imposing and almost magisterial and a whole universe away from her. Standing here now, it seemed almost impossible to believe that they had briefly been so intimate.

Jessica knew that she had a choice—and the only sane one which lay open to her was not to rise to his teasing remarks or the sensual light which lurked in the depths of his sapphire eyes. He's only playing with you, she told herself, and she knew she couldn't afford to join in—neither financially, nor emotionally. That if she wanted to keep her job and carry on as before, then she had to forget the rapport they used to share. Forget everything except doing what she was paid to do, which was to clean his office.

'I'd better get on with the floor,' she said awkwardly, turning the hot tap on full and then jumping back as the red-hot water splashed onto her hand, and she gave a little yelp of pain. 'Ouch!'

'*Sollecita!*' Salvatore made a clicking noise with his tongue as he walked over to her. 'Here.' And he calmly turned on the cold tap and held her flaming fingers beneath it.

The water was deliciously cool and soothing but his touch was even more unsettling than the stinging pain. Jessica tried to pull away but he wouldn't let her.

'Leave it under the running water,' he ordered. 'I said, *leave* it, Jessica.'

She didn't have the strength or the inclination to disobey him and yet this was just too odd. He was here, in the most inappropriate of settings, administering hasty first aid to her. She felt dizzy with shock and pleasure. Everything was all wrong and yet through all the confusion of her thoughts came the overwhelming sensation that she liked him touching her.

She swallowed. Of course she liked him touching her—who wouldn't?

After a couple of minutes, he turned the hand over and examined it, tracing a light fingertip over the still-heated flesh. 'I think you'll live,' he said softly.

The surprising gentleness of the contact was completely disarming, as was the sudden deepening of his voice.

'It's okay. I mean, I'm okay,' she amended, trying to pull her hand away.

'Maybe you are,' he objected as he drew her towards the warmth of his body. 'But I'm not.'

Her eyes opened wide, startled by pleasure and shock. 'What…what are you doing?'

'This,' he said, his voice distorting savagely as he stared down into her pale face. 'I have to do this.'

She knew he was going to kiss her—she could read it in the fractional dilation of his eyes. She could sense it in the sudden tension in his body and in the raw tang of masculine desire which made her forget everything she had vowed last night as she'd listened to the ticking of her bedside clock and waited for the alarm to ring. He was going to kiss her and, although she knew she should stop it, she could no more have stopped it than willed the earth to stop turning.

'Salvatore…' she whispered.

The 'sir' had gone once more, he thought, with grim satisfaction. '*Sì*,' he agreed arrogantly, her breath warm against his lips. 'That is my name.'

With a groan, he drove his mouth down on hers. She tasted sweet and minty, as if she had just brushed her teeth. Had she done that specially, hoping that he would kiss her? The thought that she had been anticipating this—wanting this—made him harder still.

He pulled her closer, his hands reaching down to cup her buttocks, and for the first time he appreciated how small she was. Positively tiny. In the car their bodies had been on a level, but now she seemed to slip into his arms and disappear into them, melding into his body like a pocket Venus.

Jessica clutched onto his shirt as his lips beguiled her, the palms of his hands skating with arrogant possession over her bottom. On and on his mouth continued to plunder hers until suddenly her knees threatened to give way—and perhaps he also sensed too that things were getting out of hand because he stopped kissing her, though he didn't let her go. She gazed up at him uncertainly, in a daze.

His blue eyes looked almost black and his breathing was ragged and there was an odd kind of expression on his face, as though he liked what he was doing but despised it all at the same time.

'We can't stay here,' he said flatly. 'Come back to my apartment.'

Jessica swallowed. Stay focussed. Don't behave like you're expendable. You may have a lowly job but that doesn't mean you don't have pride. 'No,' she answered stubbornly. 'I can't.'

He shook his head impatiently. 'Forget the cleaning for tonight.'

Jessica almost laughed. He thought that her refusal was solely about some loyalty to the dust levels in his office! Was that the only kind of thought he believed her capable of? 'That wasn't what I meant.'

Salvatore stilled as he heard the note of determination which had crept into her voice. He had allowed her a token show of defiance last night—but she was trying his patience now. Was she daring to *bargain* with him?

'What *did* you mean?' he demanded dangerously.

But Jessica was not going to be bowed or bullied simply because he was in a position of authority. She lifted her chin up and stared at him. 'You think I'm just going to come back with you to your flat and let you make love to me?'

'Why, are you planning to go all demure on me when we both know that's what you want, *cara mia*?'

Jessica took a step back, needing the space and looking at him with a kind of defiance. 'Life isn't just about doing what you want, Salvatore, it's about doing what's right, too.'

Dark eyebrows rose in haughty surprise. 'Don't tell me we're going to start talking morals now?'

Jessica shook her head, hurt now, but impatient, too. 'Is it because I clean your offices that you think you can just pick me up like an ornament and put me down again? Do you treat all women like that? No, of course you don't! If I were someone else—you'd at least do me the courtesy of going through the motions of normal behaviour. You might ask me out to the theatre, or take me out to dinner. You might at least *pretend* that you're interested in getting to know me as a person, rather than how quickly you can get me into your bed!'

Her breathing was all over the place and she stared at him with a boldness he had rarely seen directed at him, and certainly never by a woman.

'Finished?' he questioned.

Go on, then, thought Jessica. Sack me, and see if I care! 'Yes,' she said.

Salvatore's lips twisted into an odd kind of smile. 'I think I get the drift. You're objecting not because I want to go to bed with you, but because I have not gone through the necessary rituals which society demands?'

'Are you making fun of me?'

'Not at all. For who am I to argue in the face of such a passionately put plea?' Such passion boded well for the bedroom, he mused as he looked down at her flushed cheeks with some amusement. 'What is it they say? The mouse who roared. Very well—I have heard you, my little mouse, and we shall play the games according to your rules.' He glimmered her a mocking look. 'So will you have dinner with me, Jessica?'

She swallowed. 'As another pretend date, you mean?'

He shook his head and this time his tone was almost gentle. 'No. As a real one this time.'

She was so taken aback that for a moment words completely failed her. 'When?'

He gave a low laugh. 'How about Tuesday?'

Jessica stared at him. How could he go from such urgency to a day which seemed ages away? 'Tuesday?' she questioned tentatively.

'*Sì*, that is the first evening I have free. I'm flying to Rome for the weekend.'

'*Rome?*'

'Mmm. Ever been there?'

'No. Never.' She wanted to ask him who he was going to Rome with, but that was none of her business.

He moved a little closer and he could see the sudden wild darkening of her eyes, the instinctive way that her lips parted. He should kiss her now, take her here and have done with it—it wouldn't be hard to overcome her coy reluctance.

Yet he had never been forced to wait. Nor to dance attention to a woman's demands, and it was oddly exciting. Why not let her enjoy her brief moment of power while it lasted? Soon he would have her exactly where he wanted her. 'So are you going to see me on Tuesday?' he murmured.

'Yes, I can do Tuesday,' she whispered.

He stared down at her for one long moment, drifting a contemplative finger over the outline of her lips and feeling them tremble beneath his touch. He read her silent plea to have him kiss her once more, to seal the agreement in another traditional way—and with a brief, hard smile he turned away. Let her simmer. Let her wait as she had forced him to wait.

'Until then, *cara*,' he said softly.

And holding onto her stinging hand, Jessica was left weakly staring after him as he walked out of the room without another word.

CHAPTER SIX

THE restaurant took Jessica's breath away. She'd heard of it, of course—but never actually imagined eating there. It was right in the middle of London's theatreland and so anonymous from the outside that you wouldn't know it was there. A secret door opened straight onto the pavement. You stepped in from a crowded and busy street and it was like entering a different world.

It was a large yet intimate space with stained glass windows filtering in coloured light while keeping it private from prying eyes outside. Although it was a Tuesday evening, it was packed out. One of those places where it was impossible for mere mortals to get a table at short notice, though Salvatore had managed it without any trouble.

He seemed to be known here, thought Jessica as they were shown to their table. The waiters beamed. The sommelier nodded at him with a smile. Were staff in places like this taught to remember the names of all their influential customers, she wondered—or was it Salvatore's bright blue eyes and dark, towering presence which would always stamp him indelibly on people's minds?

She had never felt more self-conscious as they wove their way through the linen-draped tables. She saw a couple of faces she recognised from TV and spotted a well-known author who had won a literary prize last year and whose book she had at home.

The women all looked very thin and very beautiful. A couple of them glanced up as they passed and Jessica was certain she wasn't imagining their faint frowns. They looked as if they were trying—and failing—to place her.

What's a guy like him doing with a girl like her? their carefully made-up eyes seemed to ask—or was that just her own insecurity talking? All the same, she wondered what they'd think if they knew the truth!

'You are amused by something?' questioned Salvatore as she sat down.

Jessica let the waiter unfold a giant napkin onto her lap. 'I'm just hoping I don't pick up the wrong fork.'

Salvatore gave a low laugh. 'I remember the first time I left Sicily. I went to stay in France and one of my uncles took me out to eat in the most famous restaurant in Paris. I could see what looked like fifty pieces of cutlery at each setting, and the very *crème* of Parisian high society surrounding me.'

'And were you scared?' asked Jessica, for a moment forgetting all her nerves, the anxieties which had plagued her all day, about how the evening was going to end and whether she looked okay.

Salvatore shrugged. He supposed that it wouldn't be

particularly helpful to her to know that nothing ever really scared him. That men were there to be strong and doubts were for women—but he wasn't going to invent a timid persona just to make her feel better.

'No. I watched my uncle and copied exactly what he did. The only difference was that he left food on his plate. It was a thing that people did then, to show that they were not peasants, but I had the hunger of youth, and finished mine. Every scrap.'

Jessica nodded, eager to hear more. The unexpected glimpse into his past made him seem less daunting somehow. More like the man who usually chatted to her in the office before this whole sexual attraction thing had blown up in their faces. It made it easier to forget what this evening was about and to pretend that they were alone in this gorgeous restaurant for no other reason than that they liked one another.

'And don't tell me,' she teased, 'that no food has ever tasted as good as the meal you ate that night?'

He shook his dark head. 'On the contrary,' he demurred softly. 'They had messed around with the menu so that everything I ate was almost unrecognisable as the original ingredient. The best food of all is simple, and fresh—the fresher the better. The fish you pull from the water yourself and throw onto the flames. The rabbit whose blood is still warm and which goes straight into the pot. And no orange is sweeter than the one plucked from the tree.' But other appetites had been satisfied that night, he recalled, with an ache of nostalgia.

He remembered the beautiful waitress who had

slipped him her phone number while his uncle was paying the bill. Later, he remembered sneaking out to her tiny room close to the *Sacre Coeur* and the long, sensual night which had followed. The sound of the church bell striking the hour and voices shouting in the street outside as she had moaned her pleasure beneath him. The bowl of strong, sweet coffee he had drunk amid the rumpled sheets in the morning. How sharpened his senses had been then.

He stared at Jessica, at the way her hair hung in two shiny wings by the side of her face, and he felt an unexpectedly savage kick of lust. He wanted her, he realised, with a sharp hunger he had not felt in a long time.

All weekend he had thought about just how much he wanted her and how her sweet, flowering perfume had invaded his senses. He felt a pulse beating deep at his groin. Maybe he just liked the kind of woman who would never make any demands on him.

The waiter came over with two glasses of champagne and made as if to leave them alone with their menus, but Salvatore waved him back, eager for the formality and constraints of the meal to be over. 'Shall we order?' he questioned unevenly.

'Yes, of course.' He might as well have announced, Let's get it over with! Jessica knew exactly why he wanted to speed through the meal—she could read it in the way he was looking at her and the sudden tension in the air. The way his face had changed. The sudden tension in his body.

This whole occasion was a formality, she reminded

herself painfully—it wasn't real, it was phoney. And suddenly the nerves which had been simmering away came bubbling up to the surface. She forced a smile, clasping her hands together so he couldn't see them trembling. 'What would you recommend?'

'Let's have steak, and salad, oh, and a half bottle of Barolo,' he added, glancing up at the waiter and then leaning back in his chair to study her once the man had gone. 'So where do you usually go to eat?' he questioned politely.

'Small independents, mainly,' she answered, horribly aware that they were now going through the motions of having a conversation. As if Salvatore really cared where she normally ate! 'Though it's hard when there are so many chains. I'm not really mad about—'

'You're looking very…delectable tonight,' he cut in softly.

'Am I?'

'Yes, you are. Almost unrecognisable. That colour suits you.'

'Thank you.' Nervously, Jessica licked her bottom lip as she responded to a compliment she wasn't really sure she merited. It was another borrowed outfit, loaned once again by Willow, but given more grudgingly this time.

'He's taking you out *again*?' Willow had demanded in disbelief when Jessica had arrived back from work, pale-faced with shock as she'd shared her news.

'That's right. For dinner.'

She hadn't said why. She hadn't dared. She found it hard to believe it herself—that she should be pursuing something which had the power to wreck her admittedly dull, but relatively ordered life. *She* had been the one who had wanted this evening to happen and yet now it had arrived she felt as flat as a punctured balloon.

And that was the trouble. When Salvatore had taken her to that dinner party she'd had nothing to lose—she had been there acting as his girlfriend. She had been given a role and known how to play it. But tonight was different. The meal was one that *she* had demanded in order to put a gloss of respectability over something which wasn't respectable at all. She was contemplating going to bed with her boss.

Tonight she was here as herself and never had the differences between them seemed so glaringly obvious. Had she really thought that they could just sit through a meal together and then go off to have sex as if it were the most natural thing in the world? Didn't matter how much she wanted him or how long she'd had a stupid crush on him—deep down she knew this was wrong. It had to be wrong, surely, when two people came from such different worlds?

Jessica stared down at her plate. 'It was a mistake to come here tonight,' she said unhappily.

Salvatore surveyed the gleaming and neatly parted crown of her head, the way that her silk-covered shoulders were hunched in an expression of defeat. 'Why do you say that?'

'Because…oh, come on, Salvatore—you *know* why,' she whispered.

'I thought you wanted to eat dinner with me.'

'Yes, I did—but maybe I was wrong to want it. Or maybe the circumstances surrounding it were wrong. Are wrong.'

'You weren't being so coy or so dismissive the other day,' he said slowly.

'I know that. And maybe I'm regretting it now.'

'Are you?' When she didn't answer, his voice deepened into a silken caress. 'Jessica, look at me.'

In the background she could hear the distant laughter and chatter of the other diners and the chink of glass and cutlery. Everything sounded as if it were coming from a long way away.

Reluctantly, she raised her head and stared into the bright blue eyes—instantly caught and mesmerised by their sensual light. She could feel the inevitable leaping of her heart, the heavy singing of excitement in her blood as she looked across the table into his ruggedly handsome face.

Had he known that would happen—one look and she would be captivated? Yes, of course he had. He wasn't a stupid man and he must have capitalised on his undeniable power over women time and time again.

Reaching across the table, he took one of her hands in his, turning it over to study it. The nails were cut short and filed down sensibly and the skin was unusually dry. The women he usually dated had silky-soft flesh, buffed and creamed and indulged during their innumerable sessions at the beauty salon.

These were worker's hands, he realised with a start, and suddenly he found himself wanting to pamper her.

He had thought that this place might be a treat for her—but now he could see that it might be something of an ordeal. 'We don't have to stay here, you know,' he said.

'But we've only just ordered.'

'We can cancel it. Go back to my place and have something there, if you're hungry.'

'I'm not.'

'No.' Their eyes met. 'Neither am I.'

Jessica swallowed, because now his thumb was stroking a tantalising little circle on her palm. He was weakening a resolve which was already terminally weak. She looked at the sensual curve of his lips, scarcely able to believe that they had kissed her so passionately, and yet just the touch of him was making her shiveringly aware that they had. 'Won't it look…strange if we just walk out?'

Salvatore smiled. 'Who cares what it looks like? I don't spend my life seeking the opinion of others.' He gave a shrug and his thumb began to stroke a bigger circle, and then to trace a slow path up the length of her middle finger. He smiled as he saw her eyes darken at the unconscious eroticism. 'Come on,' he ordered huskily.

In a way, it was the craziest solution of all. If Jessica had felt out of place before, then choosing to leave just as the waiter was bringing out the red wine and salad was guaranteed to focus attention on them.

But even in spite of that, she felt an overwhelming sense of relief that they were going—because anything was better than trying to maintain a façade that this was like a normal date, when clearly it was anything but. Of having to try to chew her way through a piece of steak, no matter how tender it was, when food was the last thing she wanted right now.

When they got outside she could tell him that the whole thing had been a bad idea and that it had all been a stupid mistake on her part. She should never have asked for this. But at least if she called a halt to it now, she wouldn't get hurt.

The January air which hit them was bitingly cold and Jessica wished she'd remembered to bring gloves.

'I think maybe it's best if we just forget all about tonight,' she said, pulling her coat tighter around her. 'I can make my own way home on the Tube.'

His eyes narrowed. 'Are you crazy?' he questioned silkily. 'You think I'm letting you go anywhere without me tonight?' The limousine purred up to a silent halt beside them and, aware of the paparazzi hanging around, he pulled open the door and quickly pushed her inside.

'Salvatore,' she said as he slid onto the back seat beside her and Jessica's heart began to race. 'You can't take me somewhere against my will.'

'Does protesting and playing the innocent salve your conscience?' he questioned. 'Or does it simply turn you on?'

'That's unfair. And it's not true.'

'No?'

She shook her head. 'No.'

He tipped her pale face upwards, his thumb beneath her chin. Her grey eyes were smokier tonight, he thought, and her lips gleamed at him enticingly and they were trembling. Very slowly, he lowered his head and drifted his mouth across hers, feeling it shiver and hearing the instinctive little escape of her breath. It was a lingering, unhurried whisper of a kiss, the brush of their lips the only point of contact. She had every opportunity to stop it but she did not.

Salvatore could feel his own desire building. He could sense her impatience, could hear the faint flutter of her hands as she tried to prevent herself from reaching out to touch him. Still he teased her with the merest whisper of a kiss until, with a small cry of her own surrender, Jessica reached up to clasp his face between both her hands.

'Oh, Salvatore,' she whispered brokenly. 'Salvatore.'

He stared deep into her eyes and nodded. 'Yes, *cara*. You have proved it to yourself. You want me, and I want you. It is so simple, isn't it? You are coming home with me,' he said softly, and thought that he disguised his triumph well.

Jessica stared up into the gleam of his brilliant eyes, her lips parting as he lowered his mouth to kiss her properly this time as the car sped off towards Chelsea.

CHAPTER SEVEN

THE front door closed behind them and Jessica stared at Salvatore, unsure of what to do next—out of her depth in a situation like this and weak and dizzy with the sensations which were sizzling over her skin.

She was vaguely aware that Salvatore's apartment was enormous and that there was the indefinable scent of luxury in the air, but luxury was the last thing on her mind as she gazed up at the man in front of her, wondering if this could really be happening to her. Her gorgeous boss staring down at her with the unmistakable look of sexual hunger on his face. What on earth did she do next?

Salvatore cupped her face in between both his hands, one thumb brushing against the pulse which fluttered furiously by the paper-thin skin at her temple. 'You are scared.'

It was an observation rather than a question and it sounded almost gentle. Jessica nodded. 'A little.'

'Am I to take it that you don't do this kind of thing very often?'

She shook her head. 'Never,' she whispered, slightly hurt that he should ask. And yet, who could blame him for asking—she hadn't exactly played hard to get, had she? Hadn't even stopped to think what she was getting into. 'Look, Salvatore, maybe this is crazy—'

But she got no further, for he had lowered his lips to brush against hers and his touch was intoxicating.

'No,' he murmured, breathing in her perfume. 'Not crazy at all. *Perfetto*. Perfect. It will be perfect—believe me, Jessica. Now let us get out of this inhospitable hall and go somewhere where we can be more at ease with one another.'

He laced her fingers with his and led her along a seemingly endless corridor, but inside Jessica's heart was racing. *At ease*, he had said, and yet she had never felt so nervous in her life. He was so confident, so sure of his own sexual power to assure her that this would be '*perfetto*'—but didn't he realise that he was dealing with someone who, while not a complete novice, wasn't exactly seasoned in the ways of making love?

Should she tell him so? And what could she say— that she was afraid she would disappoint him and was completely out of his league? Like a small, scruffy pony used to transporting schoolchildren round a field who had suddenly dared compete with a long-legged and aristocratic racehorse in the biggest race of the season?

But her throat was frozen as he led her into the biggest bedroom she'd ever seen, and no words of protest came.

She was aware of highly polished floors strewn with

beautiful faded rugs in different, muted colours. A silk-covered bed dominated a room which was big enough to accommodate a sofa and a couple of chairs, as well. An arched area led to a large study and she could see big pots crammed with amazing scarlet flowers and dark glossy foliage.

'Ah, Jessica,' Salvatore murmured as he drew her into his arms and stroked a tumble of shiny hair from her face. 'You look as though you are about to be thrown to the lions.'

'D-do I?'

'Mmm. Shall I be your lion? Your big, fierce lion?' his lips whispered to her neck. 'And shall I eat you up, every little bit of you, *cara mia*—would you like that?'

'Salvatore!' she exclaimed, but now she was trembling.

He smiled as he heard the faint shock in her voice, but deep down Salvatore approved of her lack of sophistication. Her relative innocence and reluctance were a welcome change from the lovers he had known in the past.

Unless it was all an act. A wide-eyed sham to make him 'respect' her more.

Pulling her a little closer, Salvatore skated his hands over her breasts and heard her breath quicken. Even if it was a sham—what did it matter? In the end, this was nothing but a temporary pursuit. Something to be enjoyed by both of them—and as long as she was fully aware of the rules, then nobody would get hurt...

He glanced down at her. Tonight she was wearing a purple silk dress with tiny buttons all the way down the front, which he began to undo, one by one.

'So many buttons! Did you wear this to deliberately tantalise me?' he teased.

Jessica could barely think, let alone speak, as he began to pop each one open and bare her heated flesh to the cooling wash of air. She had worn it because it was the most suitable thing that Willow had been able to find in her wardrobe.

His finger brushed along the edge of her bra—a plain and functional bra, he noted with an element of disapproval. But maybe there would be a lick of lace beneath.

'Salvatore,' she whispered, because by now the dress was open to her stomach, and he had bent down and was kissing her there—flicking his tongue into the gentle dip of her navel so that she gasped aloud and clutched at his broad shoulders.

And Salvatore gave a low laugh of delight. 'What is it, *cara mia*?' he questioned, his breath warm against her skin.

She wanted to tell him that she was terrified she would disappoint him, but no words came. 'I...I...'

'Just relax,' he murmured. 'Enjoy it.'

Somehow she did as he said, forgetting everything except the pleasure he was giving her as his tongue tracked slowly and erotically down over her belly. Desire began to grip at her in a way she had not experienced before. She felt it gathering pace, like a snowball getting bigger as you rolled it in fresh snow. She wanted him to...to...

But he didn't. The last button freed, he straightened up to slide the shirt-dress away from her narrow shoulders, so that she was left aching and hungry for him.

Salvatore saw the disappointment on her face and sensed her growing frustration, but he took his time. It was always best for the woman the first time if you made her wait. His eyes flicked over her. Despite her surprisingly expensive dress, her underwear was as disappointing as it had promised to be, plain and functional, her panties obscured by a hideous pair of tights. She would not wear those again, he thought grimly. 'Take off my shirt,' he ordered softly.

And Jessica, who was normally so good with her hands, now found that they would not obey this simple command at all. Had she thought he might take pity on her and remove the garment himself? But he did not. In fact, her struggle with freeing the buttons seemed to please him, until at last she slipped the shirt from his silken olive skin.

She swallowed. His golden-olive torso was formidable with not an ounce of spare flesh to be seen. He was all lean and honed muscle. So gorgeous. Too gorgeous, really. And if he asked her to take his trousers off, she would *die*.

But he didn't. He caught her against him, firmly and decisively—tangling his fingers in the thick gloss of her hair. And then he began to kiss her again, until she was soft and melting. He kissed her until her knees started to buckle and her hips began to make their own restless little circling against the formidable hardness of him. And still he kissed her, ignoring the growing clamour of her muffled little pleas for more. Until all her inhibitions had dissolved and she had begun to pluck impatiently at the belt of his trousers.

And only then did he smile, slip his fingers down the front of her panties and touch her with such unerring precision that she gave a loud gasp.

'Ah, *sì*,' he said softly, moving against her sweet heat. 'Now you are ready for love.'

Her blurred and hungry senses agreed, but his words sent questions dashing round her head. Love? Did this really have anything to do with love? wondered Jessica dazedly as he picked her up and carried her over to the bed. No, of course it didn't. Love was a word used to sweeten the act of sex.

She lay and watched him, as clearly he intended her to do. A slow and erotic striptease performed just for her benefit. His hand moved to his belt, and then his zip. He was pulling off his shoes, his socks, his trousers. He was stepping out of dark boxers with lazy elegance and he was aroused. Very aroused.

Their eyes met in one long moment and in that moment Jessica decided that nerves were no longer going to freeze her, because what would be the point of that? She was here and she was damned well going to enjoy every second of it. Every second of him.

'C-come to bed,' she said shakily.

He laughed softly as he joined her on the bed and she reached for him.

'You are hungry for me, little one?'

'I'm absolutely starving, if you must know!'

'Well, then—come here.' With one slick movement he removed her bra, then turned his attention to her naked breasts, first with his eyes and then letting his lips roam over their hard pink tips. He licked her, felt her shiver. 'Mmm. You taste of honey, and desire. You taste good.'

And his words made her *feel* good—so good that she wanted to throw inhibition to the wind. Shyly, she reached down to stroke him, feeling him jerk beneath her hand.

For one second, Salvatore stilled as something in her tentative gesture made a warning bell sound deep in his subconscious. He laid one hand over the fingers which lay so intimately over his flesh, mentally gearing himself up for a scenario which had only just occurred to him. And wondering how he could have been so stupid. For had not one of his beloved cousins been trapped by a woman in such a way?

'Please tell me you are not a virgin?' he demanded, his voice suddenly harsh.

Jessica didn't know whether to laugh or cry. Did that mean he equated her fumbling with a complete lack of experience? 'No, of course I'm not. Would it matter if I was?'

He took his hand away and moved over her, stroking her hair away from her face. 'Of course it would matter! But it is not important. Not now. Only this matters. *This*…'

And he blocked all words and thoughts with his lips. For a moment Jessica struggled against the wall of pleasure which was beginning to build, her thoughts uneasy as something in his attitude troubled her, though she wasn't quite sure what.

Quickly concern gave way to pleasure—how could it not, when Salvatore was the most wonderful lover imaginable? He kissed every inch of her body, she had never known that a man could find so much delight in the discovery of flesh alone.

'You like that?' he questioned silkily as his tongue found a particularly vulnerable area.

'I…' Jessica shut her eyes and shuddered. 'I…'

'Tell me,' he urged.

'No one has ever done that to me before,' she breathed.

'And this?'

'Oh, Salvatore,' she whispered. 'Yes.'

He took her along familiar pathways of delight and to his astonishment discovered that, for him, she was the perfect lover. So it was not a sham after all. She was not a virgin, but neither was she particularly accomplished. Inexperienced but not innocent—*perfetto*.

But she was also very sweet. Too sweet really, he thought wryly, as she pulled his head towards her and showered him with tiny kisses which made him tingle with delight. Did she not know that a woman should always hold something back in order to completely entrance a man?

'Jessica,' he said, in a voice which was suddenly unsteady, and he could wait no longer, he reached for protection as she writhed beneath him.

'Yes, now,' she whispered. 'Now.'

'Then damned well keep still for a minute!'

'I c-can't.'

'Neither can I,' he groaned as he thrust into her. *'Mia tesoro.'*

It was amazing. She was amazing—and he couldn't work out why. Was it her eagerness to please him? Her breathless pleasure as she worked out what made him moan with delight? Or her sheer joy when the first orgasm rocked her small, curvy body and she clung to him, choking out her pleasure and a few broken syllables which sounded a bit like his name?

Afterwards, Salvatore collapsed back against the disarray of pillows, his skin sweat-sheened, his heart racing like a piston as he stared at the ceiling, gasping for breath, like a man who had been pulled out of the water just before he drowned.

And Jessica snuggled up to him, resting her silky head in the crook of his arm as if that was the place she most wanted to be.

'Mmm,' she sighed. 'That was...*bliss*.'

A habitual post-lovemaking wariness began to creep over him. He was going to have to be very honest with her about the limitations of an affair with him—but surely she was sensible enough to recognise that there could be no future in this?

'Mmm.' He yawned, and edged away from her very fractionally. 'I'm hungry now, aren't you?'

She wanted to say, Not for food, I'm not—the way she would have done a few minutes ago, when they were making love and she seemed to have been given the most delicious freedom to indulge and tell him about every single one of her secret fantasies.

But something had changed—she could tell. Salvatore had withdrawn from her in more ways than one. It was true that in this bizarre situation she was probably being acutely sensitive, but it was quite clear that his mood towards her had changed, become cooler. What happened now—was she expected to get dressed and just go home?

'Shall I go and get us something to eat?' he questioned lazily.

And Jessica hated herself for the overwhelming sense of relief she felt that she wasn't to be dismissed like a servant. Hated herself even more for just accepting it— for allowing Salvatore to dictate the terms of what happened next.

But how could she do otherwise when she felt so blissfully *alive* in his arms—as if up until that moment her life had seemed without direction and the whole reason for being born had just been made clear to her?

'Yes, please,' she said, forcing herself down from the clouds. She'd barely touched a thing all weekend. She'd been to visit her grandmother, who had asked her if she was sickening for something when Jessica had done the unheard of and refused a slice of her famous lemon drizzle cake. But what could she have said to the much-loved woman who had brought her up after the death of her parents? No, I've lost my appetite because I think I'm going to end up in bed with my boss on Tuesday. Wouldn't that go against everything she'd been taught?

He flicked her an amused glance as he climbed out of bed, gloriously and goldenly assured in his nakedness. 'Thank heavens for that,' he murmured. 'A little loss of appetite in the restaurant was understandable— but I can't bear women who do sustained starvation as a matter of course.'

'Er, no. Neither can I.' Maybe she should pass that nugget of information on to Willow—who, of course, would never believe her. 'Should I get up?'

His eyes lingered over her. She looked deliciously tousled with her cheeks flushed pink and her grey eyes huge. 'No. Stay right there. You look enchanting. We'll have a picnic in bed.'

Once he'd gone, Jessica hurried into the bathroom and tried to tame her hair. Then she got back into bed and rather self-consciously sat there waiting for him until he returned carrying a tray loaded with expensive-looking goodies.

Champagne. Grapes. Some crusty-looking bread. And there was a lovely wooden box containing cheese—as well as a box of dark chocolate.

'That all looks wonderful,' she said brightly.

He heard the nerves in her voice and put the tray down and took her into his arms.

'You've brushed your hair,' he observed softly.

'Combed it. I borrowed your comb—I hope that was okay?'

Behind the tentative query, he heard a million other questions. From past displays of post-coital neediness, Salvatore knew that this was the most vulnerable time of all for a woman and the best time for ground rules to be laid down.

'You can borrow anything you like, while you're here,' he said easily.

The words should have reassured her, but they did just the opposite. Silently, Jessica acknowledged that she needed to know where she stood. At work, she might just be his office cleaner—but she had just shared his bed. Surely that gave her the right to know what he wanted from her?

'You asked me a question earlier,' she said.

Salvatore raised his brows. 'Which particular question was that?'

'You asked whether I was a virgin. Why?'

He had been about to trickle a finger from her stomach to the tempting fuzz of hair which lay at the fork of her thighs, but he resisted. If it was the truth she wanted, then he would give it to her. That way he couldn't be accused of having capitalised on sex to make her agree to something she would later throw back in his face.

'Because it would make a difference to what happened next,' he said, and went over to open the bottle—wishing now that he had brought something other than champagne, for that too could be misinterpreted. He said nothing until the liquid had foamed up inside the glasses in a creamy cascade, letting it settle before he topped them up. Then he walked back over to the bed and handed her a glass—though he put his own down on the bedside table, untouched.

'Thanks.' Jessica took the drink with a reluctance she hoped didn't show. It looked like ginger ale, and frankly, she wished it were ginger ale, for suddenly she felt peculiar, sitting naked in this billionaire's bed, drinking his champagne.

He sat down on the edge of the bed and looked at her.

'A woman's virginity is the greatest gift she can give to a man—apart from the children she will one day bear him.'

There were two outrageously old-fashioned concepts here, but for now only one concerned her. 'So…so what would the problem have been if I had been a virgin?'

He had hoped that she might have been able to work it out for herself without him having to spell it out. But he must—to do otherwise would be deception, and that he could not and would not tolerate.

'It would have been wasted on me,' he said softly. 'If you had been a virgin, I would have sent you away and told you to save that gift for the man you will one day marry.'

'But—'

'You see…' his blue eyes narrowed as he cut across her words, for there must be no misunderstanding on her part '…you must understand that I am Sicilian, Jessica, and that I have very strict values about life, as well as marriage. I intend to one day go back to Sicily, to marry a Sicilian girl who will be a virgin. That is a given.'

Jessica stared at him. Didn't he realise how that made her *feel* in the circumstances? More than a little bit cheap for having given herself to him so freely. And expendable, too. No, of course he didn't—why should he?

'That's so old-fashioned.'

He shrugged. 'I recognise that, but I don't care. In many ways, I am a very old-fashioned man. For me it is important that the mother of my children has not…how do you say? Been around the block?'

Jessica sat bolt upright, some champagne spilling on the rumpled cotton sheets, but she didn't care as she swung her legs over the bed and put the glass down with a trembling hand. 'How dare you?' she demanded shakily. 'How dare you accuse me of sleeping around, when actually I *haven't*—and you've probably had more women than I've had hot dinners and, oh…*oh!*'

Her furious words were silenced with a kiss, because Salvatore had moved even faster and caught her in his arms as he tumbled her back on the bed, his silk robe falling open and his unashamedly aroused body moulding itself against hers.

'Get off me!' she exclaimed, drumming her fists furiously against his chest. 'Get *off* me!'

'You want me to?'

'Yes! No. *Yes!*' But her words belied her actions because her eyelids were fluttering closed and she could feel the instant clamour of desire.

'Jessica?'

She opened her eyes and stared at him with the caution of a hunted animal which knew it was cornered. 'What?'

'I make you no false promises,' he said simply. 'Nor spin you any false lies. I like you. That's why you are here. I like making love to you. I'd like to do it again. I'd like to spoil you a little. To fly you to Paris and feed you with oysters. To show you a little of the world you do not yet know—and I think you'd like that, too.'

As his words painted a tempting picture Jessica stared at him in confusion, aware of the frantic hammering of her heart and the way that her breasts were peaking insistently against his chest—as if eager to be touched by him. As if her body were impatient with her questions, but she knew she had to ask him.

'I don't understand,' she breathed. 'What is it you want from me?'

Salvatore gave a swift, hard smile, recognising that her inexperience was a double-edged sword. It attracted him—but it made explanation necessary, and he liked to keep explanation to a minimum.

He fixed her in his gaze, staring down at her wide grey eyes and the parted rose-petal lips. 'I want you to be my mistress,' he said softly.

CHAPTER EIGHT

STILL tangled against his naked body, Jessica stared up into the blue of Salvatore's eyes and for a moment thought she might have misheard him. 'Your mistress?' she echoed, because in her world men didn't come out and say things like that. 'But you're not even *married*!' Her eyes narrowed suspiciously as a terrible thought occurred to her and she wondered why it had never entered her mind before. 'Are you?'

He shook his head, a wry smile curving his lips. 'No, I am not married, *cara*—but a man does not need to be married to require a mistress.' He saw the confusion on her face, and he stoked it. 'It is nothing but a title given to a woman who fulfils a special role in a man's life. Mainly, it does away with uncertainty and means that we both know exactly where we stand. And where we stand is to have a wonderful affair while accepting that there is no future in it. That's all.'

She blinked. 'That's all?' she repeated.

'That is over-simplifying it a little, perhaps,' he admitted. 'But essentially that is what it is—and what is more I think that you are utterly perfect for the role, *cara*.'

The word 'perfect' was a verbal caress, accompanied by the whisper of his lips as they trailed along the line of her jaw, causing Jessica to shiver with longing. She was so weak in his arms; she imagined that every woman would be. Yet how could she even consider what he had just proposed? Wasn't such a bald proposition hugely insulting?

He raised his head to stroke the outline of her lips with a questing fingertip. 'You do not answer,' he observed.

She heard the unmistakable surprise in his voice and somehow that irritated her. Did he really expect her to fall upon a suggestion that many women would dismiss out of hand—perhaps even be *grateful* to him for asking?

'It's…it's a lot to take in,' she said, wondering why he'd said anything at all. Why couldn't he have just made love to her and taken her out again? Why couldn't it have just drifted on in the normal way between a man and a woman, if he had really enjoyed it as much as he claimed?

Because then you might start getting the wrong idea, you idiot! You might start thinking that you had some kind of future with him, and he is making it crystal clear from the very start that nothing like that is going to happen.

Without warning, he lowered his head, his mouth replacing his fingertip with a lingering kiss, and Jessica tried for a moment to resist him. But it was just a moment—her body was greedy for him, warm and soft as she welcomed him in.

'*Che voglia,*' he said, his voice suddenly harsh.

She gasped as he entered her, their eyes meeting in a long unspoken moment.

Salvatore looked down at her and felt desire overpower him. 'It's good?' he questioned unsteadily.

'Y-yes,' she trembled.

'You want more?'

'You know I do,' she whispered, as vulnerable then as she had ever been.

Deeply, he thrust inside her, hearing her gasp again, watching her face as passion melted away the last of her lingering doubts and listening as her eventual shuddering little cries pierced the air. Only then did he allow himself to let go, falling over into a place of incredible sweetness—made sweeter still by a victory he should not have had to press for with a woman like Jessica.

Afterwards, they lay spent in each other's arms. Salvatore stroked lazily at her soft skin, still damp with exertion as he inhaled her flowery perfume, which was now mixed with his own raw, elemental scent. His touch was abstracted and his thoughts had drifted far away, for she had surprised him.

She had viewed his proposition with a remarkably cool restraint—weighing it up with all the consideration which he himself might have given to a business proposal. Why, he knew society beauties and heiresses who would have bitten his hand off to grace his bed like this! And she still hadn't given him an answer, he realised.

'You are sleepy?' he questioned.

Jessica opened her eyes. Yes, her body was tired, but her mind was racing, and feigning sleep was easier than having to face up to the uncomfortable reality of the situation. What should she do? 'A little.'

'We still haven't had any supper,' he observed.

'No.' Jessica sat up, seeing his eyes transfixed by her naked breasts, and in a way that helped her make up her mind. He saw her as a body—something that he desired. She fed his sexual appetite just as the bread and cheese would soon feed a more elemental hunger. As long as she didn't forget that, then surely she could protect her heart against being broken? 'So perhaps we'd better have something to eat,' she said softly. 'And then I'll get going.'

Salvatore stilled. 'Going?' he echoed the word in soft disbelief. 'Going where?'

Jessica looked at him. 'Why, home, of course.'

Now he was taken aback, a state of being completely unknown to him. Usually, he could read a woman like a well-thumbed book, but for once in his life he was perplexed. Was the inconceivable happening? Was Jessica Martin *walking out*? He felt the flicker of a pulse at his temple. If she was trying to test him, then she would soon discover that he would not be manipulated!

'Why home?' he questioned silkily.

At least he had managed to tear his eyes away from her breasts and was actually looking at her face! 'Because it's a Tuesday night and I've got work tomorrow morning.'

Salvatore leaned back against the pillows. 'So what's the problem? Stay the night here and I'll have my driver drop you off at your office in the morning.'

Jessica looked at him and, despite the see-sawing of

her emotions, she couldn't help a smile from nudging at her lips. Oh, yes—that was an absolutely brilliant idea. She could just imagine the helpful kind of gossip *that* would produce! Her turning up for work in a chauffeur-driven limousine wearing last night's make-up!

'It's very sweet of you, Salvatore,' she said softly. 'But I don't think it's such a good idea.'

'Why not?' he snapped.

'Well, for a start, I haven't brought a change of clothes with me.'

'And why not? You didn't think you would end up in bed with me tonight? We both knew it was on the cards,' he accused hotly.

Jessica met the furious blaze in his eyes, but she didn't flinch—even though his words were far from flattering. 'Well, yes. I suppose I did.'

'Then why the hell didn't you bring something with you? A change of clothes? A toothbrush?'

Didn't he know *anything* about women? 'Because that would have looked so…so obvious, wouldn't it? If I'd turned up for a dinner-date clutching a small overnight bag! Listen…' she leaned over and kissed him briefly on the lips '…I'll have some supper with you first and then I'll go home. That way, you'll get a good night's sleep, and so will I.'

He glared at her. 'You sound like my nurse!'

Her mouth crumpled into a smile. 'If I were your nurse, Salvatore—then I would just have broken my professional code rather spectacularly,' she teased.

Salvatore frowned. In a way, he couldn't fault her logic

and yet he had never felt quite so wrong-footed in his life. *She* was outlining her plan of action to *him*—instead of hanging onto his every word and waiting to hear what his wishes were? It was unimaginable! His cleaner!

'You are playing the coquette with me?' he growled. 'Is that it?'

Jessica giggled, suddenly feeling more than a little bit high—unsure whether that was the result of the most fantastic lovemaking of her life or drinking champagne on an empty stomach. 'It's a little late in the day for playing hard to get, isn't it?' She reached down for the plate of grapes and popped one in her mouth, holding another up in front of his. 'Here. Have one.'

'I don't want a damned grape,' he growled. Suddenly, he needed a drink. Incredulously, he watched as she slid off the bed. It had not been an idle threat after all. 'So you really are going?'

Jessica turned round, trying not to feel self-conscious in her nakedness—but having no clothes on when you were in bed with a man was one thing, having to walk across the room to retrieve your discarded clothing was another. 'Yes.'

Briefly, he contemplated getting up and going after her, of perhaps pinning her up against the wall and making her gasp his name out loud. But he recognised that, although he could easily delay her, he wasn't going to stop her from leaving. Despite the fact that she must know she was displeasing him, he could see the unmistakable look of determination which had tightened those rose-petal lips of hers.

Jessica picked up her panties and slithered into them, and clipped her bra closed, wondering how on earth strippers managed to do this kind of thing erotically, and in a room full of strangers, too. She picked up the pair of tights. Though maybe it was easier in front of strangers. Just pretend he isn't watching you with that predatory stare, she told herself as she struggled into them.

'Jessica?'

She looked up as the elastic pinged round her waist. 'Yes, Salvatore.'

His mouth curved with undisguised distaste. 'You will not wear those *things* again when you are with me.'

'Tights?'

'Yes. *Tights.*' He shuddered. 'Whoever invented them should be shot. Women should wear nothing but lacy stockings, and suspender belts.'

'I'll bear it in mind,' said Jessica gravely as she picked up the purple silk dress and pulled it over her head, glad of the distraction of doing that for fear that he might read the slightly sad fact in her eyes. That she'd never actually worn stockings and a suspender belt before. Wouldn't that be a shocking admission?

'Make sure you do,' he said coolly as, with the naturally critical eye which most Sicilian men possessed, Salvatore assessed her. The purple silk dress suited her very well, he thought, since it clung enticingly to her curves. But the length was all wrong.

'And why do you wear your dresses so long?' he questioned idly.

Jessica blushed. 'You don't like it?'

His gaze travelled slowly from toe to thigh, and lingered there. 'It hides your legs—your beautiful legs. Why hide one of your best assets?'

She hesitated. Should she tell him? Did he actually want the truth—for her to paint an accurate picture of her life so that he could see her as she really was, warts and all?

'It's Willow's dress,' she said.

'Willow?' He frowned. 'This is the tree, *sì*? It lives along the riverbank?'

'My housemate,' Jessica elaborated and was slightly horrified at the feeling of relief which shot through her. He hadn't even remembered the name of her stunning blonde housemate! 'She's taller than me.'

Still he looked blank.

'It's her dress I'm wearing. Willow's dress. I borrowed it.'

And suddenly Salvatore felt better. Much better—because this was stuff he could deal with, stuff he could understand. He watched as Jessica did up the final button and then ran her fingers through her hair. Maybe she was cleverer than he had given her credit for—or maybe it was just coincidence that she had told him now—but this nugget of information gave him back the familiar feel of power and control.

Had she worn the dress to get precisely this result? That he would take pity on her and shower gifts on her? It wouldn't be the first time it had happened, but at least it made the playing field more level.

He put his empty glass down and got up from the bed,

seeing her eyes darken with desire and apprehension as
he began to walk across the large bedroom towards her.
And when he had reached her, he lifted both her hands
to his lips and kissed each fingertip in turn—like a man
playing a harmonica.

'I don't want you wearing second-hand clothes any
more,' he said silkily.

Jessica opened her mouth to tell him it wasn't as
easy as that. That most of the items in *her* wardrobe
were completely unsuitable for the kind of place
Salvatore frequented, but he forestalled her with a swift
shake of his ruffled dark head.

'I know what you're going to say.' He dropped his
hands to allow his fingers to roam expertly over the
fine, slippery material which covered her bottom. 'That
you can't afford to buy clothes of this quality.'

'Well, I can't,' said Jessica proudly.

'And one of the many advantages of being mistress
to a rich man,' he purred, 'is that I can.'

She shook her head. 'No!'

'Oh, yes. Do not protest, Jessica—for your protests
are unnecessary. You see—' his voice deepened '—it
will give me great pleasure to buy for you, and to
dress you—from the skin up.' He touched the silk,
tracing a light line over her breast, smiling as she
shivered—despite the mutinous look on her face. 'I do
not want you wearing these ugly little bra and panties
any more, either.'

She felt as if he were tearing her up into little pieces
before putting her back together again. 'If how I look

is so disappointing to you, then why don't you go off and find someone whose looks *do* appeal?'

'You appeal to me very much,' he said softly. 'But you are like one of the trees in my orchard back home in Sicily. You need to be pruned before you can blossom properly. Now come here.'

'Salvatore—' But he was teasing her with his kiss, pulling her closer into his warm naked body—hard up against the unmistakable force of his renewed arousal.

'You still wish to go?'

She closed her eyes. How easy it would be to say no. To allow herself to be undressed once more and made love to. But it would be a sign of weakness, surely, showing him that she could be manipulated to his will whenever it suited him. And she would *not* go into work tomorrow resplendent in a gaudy party dress.

'I must.'

His mouth hardened. 'Very well. So be it. I will notify my driver.'

Jessica felt anxious as he picked up a phone and bit out a command—and when he had finished he turned to her, an odd kind of smile on his face, his blue eyes glittering with a message she couldn't read.

'I'll call you,' he said.

She wanted to say, When? But suddenly Jessica felt disorientated. Did any of the normal rules of dating apply when you agreed to become a rich man's mistress, or did he call all the shots? She bent down towards her handbag. Who was she kidding? Of course he called all the shots—in just about every area of his life.

'Goodnight, Salvatore,' she said, and, picking up her handbag, she hurried towards the door before he could see any of the gnawing anxieties which were eating her up.

CHAPTER NINE

'WHAT do you mean—his *mistress*?' Willow demanded.

Jessica stared down at the cereal which was growing soggy in the bowl of milk and stirred at it uninterestedly with her spoon. She shouldn't have said anything to her housemate. *Why* had she opened her big mouth and confided Salvatore's shockingly erotic proposition? Because you had to tell someone or you'd go crazy and burst!

'Oh, it's a kind of arrangement that men make with women all the time,' she said, shrugging her shoulders in an airy manner, as if she were used to dealing with such concepts every day of the week.

'You mean it allows him to behave exactly as he wants to behave without having any responsibilities towards the woman!' flared Willow. 'Why the hell did you agree to it, Jessica? I take it you *did* agree to it?'

'I guess I did,' she said slowly.

'But *why*? Are you out of your mind?'

'Because…because…' Jessica bit her lip. Because she adored him. Because a camaraderie had built up between them since she'd been working for him and that had contributed towards the way she had seized on this opportunity.

'Because what?' prompted Willow.

Jessica pushed the untouched cereal away and stared at her housemate, her blonde hair tumbling all over her shoulders, her porcelain skin flawless without a scrap of make-up. She wondered whether Willow was just being naïve, or mischievous. 'Are you trying to tell me that you *wouldn't* have succumbed to his charms?'

'I'd have made him wait.'

'Yeah, sure you would.' Jessica clamped her lips shut. She would never ever dream of telling another woman of what had gone on behind closed doors, but surely Willow must realise that there were some men who were simply impossible to resist, and Salvatore was one of them.

'But I wonder why he chose *you*,' pondered Willow thoughtfully, and it was only when she saw the expression on Jessica's face that she attempted to take some of the sting out of the question. 'I mean—isn't it a bit risky, Jessica? You work there, and everything.'

'You mean I clean his office,' said Jessica, her cheeks flushing with defiant pride. 'And if you really want to know why I think he chose me, Willow…' Because surely if you forced yourself to face the fundamental truth in a situation, then you removed its ability to cause you pain? It was only when you ran from the truth that you were in trouble.

'I think it's precisely because I *do* clean his office,' she continued slowly. 'I know my place and I'm not a threat. We can have…*fun*…but without him worrying that he might have to make some kind of commitment to me.' She forced herself to remember his stark words about going back to marry a Sicilian virgin. 'Because it isn't going to happen.'

'And did he…' Willow began to fiddle self-consciously with her hair '…did he happen to mention me?'

A crueller person than Jessica might have rubbed it in that the Sicilian hadn't even remembered Willow's name. But Jessica was not cruel, and anyway she doubted that the sunnily confident blonde would have believed her. 'No, he didn't,' she answered quietly. 'Should he have done?'

Willow carefully fielded the question with another of her own. 'So when are you seeing him again? Or maybe you don't know. Can he just ring out for you at a moment's notice—like pizza?'

Jessica didn't react. She was *not* going to rise to it. But didn't Willow's taunt only feed her own terrible fears? 'He's been away—on business. He travels such a lot. He's in New York this week.'

'How nice for him. So did you see him before he left?'

'Briefly,' said Jessica. She had been stricken with nerves, terrified about going in to clean his office, not knowing how she would face him or what she would say to him after what had happened between them.

But after all that angsting, he hadn't even been there—the room had been quiet and empty and she hadn't known whether to laugh or cry. Instead, she had busied herself by cleaning up the vast space, scrubbing at the surfaces even more energetically than usual and resisting the temptation to snoop around in his desk— something which had never occurred to her before she'd slept with him. She had just been coming out of the adjoining cloakroom with a damp cloth in her hand when the door had opened and in he'd walked.

He had been wearing a dark suit, which intensified the deep ebony of his black hair, and the blue of his eyes looked unbelievably bright—set like sapphires in his glowing olive skin. He had put his briefcase down, and looked at her for a long moment.

'Jessica,' he said.

She really didn't know how to react. She wanted to run into his arms, to stroke his glowing skin, to touch him wonderingly as if she couldn't quite believe he was real. But she didn't dare do anything except stand there in her stupid pink overall.

'Come over here,' he ordered softly.

The cloth must have somehow slipped from her fingers by the time she reached him, but he lifted up her hands and looked wryly at the bright yellow rubber gloves she wore.

'I've never been able to understand the sexual allure of rubber,' he said, almost conversationally, as he began to pull off the gloves which had stuck unflatteringly to her fingers. When he had peeled them off, he tossed them aside and took her into his arms, his blue eyes dancing. 'Have you?'

'N-no. I've…never really given it any thought.'

He lifted her chin and frowned. 'You are nervous,' he observed.

Jessica nodded. No point in denying it when it was as obvious as the huge moon which looked like a stage prop shining outside the penthouse window. 'A little bit,' she whispered.

'And yet we have been deliciously intimate with each other,' he mused. 'With the promise of so much more. Are you angry because I haven't rung you?'

'You haven't got my phone number,' Jessica replied, more pointedly than she had intended.

His blue eyes gleamed. 'You think that would be a problem, *cara*? That I could not find you if I wished to find you?'

She supposed not. But it gave Jessica an insight into the kind of man she was dealing with. The kind of man who could get just about any information with a click of his powerful fingers.

'Now kiss me,' he murmured.

Had she been afraid—and half hoping—that he would sandwich in a bout of fast and furious sex with her, before he left for the airfield where his plane was waiting?

But to Jessica's surprise, he did not. Maybe he didn't have time for a shower in the luxury cloakroom which adjoined the penthouse office, or maybe he didn't want to crease his immaculate suit. Or maybe, unlike her, he didn't allow a lover to dominate his thoughts. Whereas she had been able to think of nothing but him, it seemed that she had barely even crossed his mind.

Yet the kiss was sweet. Unbearably sweet. Kisses could be more poignant than anything else, she found herself thinking, her heart aching. His kiss made her wish that he weren't Salvatore Cardini, boss of one of the biggest corporations in the world. It made her wish he were just an ordinary man—not a glittering star who was way out of her reach. If he were an accountant, say, that she'd met at one of the city's bars, wouldn't that have been just so much easier? They would go back to her flat, or his—and she would cook spaghetti bolognese and they'd drink a bottle of cheap plonk.

There would be no unrealistic expectations, no worries about what to wear or whether she would say the wrong thing if he took her out somewhere. And no fears already creeping in as she wondered just how long this would all last.

'When are you back?' she asked him in spite of having vowed not to do any such thing.

'I'll be back by the weekend.' His mouth curved in a smile as he looked down into her eyes 'Are we going to see one another?'

'I hope so,' she said shyly.

Her words made him halt, stroke her hair almost reflectively. 'Okay, Jessica—I'll be in touch.'

And with another brief and tantalising kiss, he disappeared, leaving her looking after him with a feeling of longing and realisation that she would never be anything but a peripheral person in his life.

'So when are you seeing him?' Willow's words prompted Jessica back to the present with a jolt and with a blink she looked up at the bright yellow clock which was hanging on the kitchen wall.

'He's collecting me any minute now.'

'Then oughtn't you be getting ready?'

'I *am* ready.'

Willow's face froze. 'Oh.'

But Salvatore had criticised her borrowed clothes and Jessica had decided that she wasn't going to borrow any more of them. Consequently, she was wearing her favourite pair of jeans. They were old and rather faded, but a perfect fit, and with them she'd put on a soft grey cashmere sweater bought in last year's January sale. A black velvet ribbon caught her hair back in a loose ponytail and she wore the minimum amount of make-up.

Outwardly, she was trying to project a calm exterior, but inside she was quaking with nerves and exhilaration at the thought of seeing him again.

There was a loud knock on the door and Jessica opened it to Salvatore's driver. Behind him the limousine dominated the small road and through the smoked glass she could see Salvatore talking into his cell phone.

'Signor Cardini is just finishing a call from Milan,' explained the driver.

Jessica picked up her jacket, her expression just *defying* Willow to make some smart comment, but she said nothing.

'That's fine,' she said brightly, and walked out to the waiting limousine.

Salvatore was sprawled in the back seat and when he saw her he said something very quickly in Italian, and terminated the conversation.

'*Ciao, bella,*' he murmured silkily. 'Come over here and say hello to me.'

His eyes were glittering over her in an unashamedly sexual appraisal, making her feel a little like a trophy. But suddenly Jessica didn't care. Wasn't this what she had been dreaming about since the last time she'd been out with him? She scrambled into his arms like a puppy reunited with its master as the driver closed the door behind her.

'Mmm.' Salvatore felt the kick of lust as he lowered his mouth to kiss her. She tasted of toothpaste, as if she was fresh from the bath. She tasted clean and pure—with that strange innocence which was all her own. He gave a little groan as he drove his mouth down on hers, his hand skimming down over one denim-clad hip—and when eventually he broke the kiss, it was to raise his head to look down at her with smoky blue eyes.

'I'm taking you straight home because I've spent the last five days imagining making love to you,' he promised unsteadily.

'I can't wait,' she breathed, locking her arms tightly around his neck.

'I can tell,' he mocked, but she simply lifted her lips to kiss him again and he gave a low laugh of pleasure. He had chosen his mistress well. In his arms she was utterly inhibited—like a wild little foal eager to be trained. He wanted to touch her now, maybe to bring her to climax within the private world of the dark-windowed limousine, but she was wearing jeans.

He let his fingers splay into a possessive star at the very top of her thigh, hearing her breathing quicken, but his eyes mocked her. 'These jeans are so inhibiting,' he observed caustically.

'But so practical.'

'On the contrary,' he said. 'They are extremely *impractical* for lovers who are being reunited.'

Suddenly Jessica felt about eighteen years old.

'You have never had instruction on how best to dress to please a man?' he persisted softly.

'It's not usually part of an English education.'

'Then I shall teach you,' he promised. 'And I shall take you shopping.'

'To kit me out as befits the mistress of a wealthy man?'

'Precisely that, *cara mia.*'

'And what if I tell you that I won't let you buy me anything?' she questioned proudly.

'Then I will ride roughshod over your wishes,' he murmured throatily, his finger fixed on the tip of her chin so that she couldn't escape the erotic question in his eyes. 'Do you think you'd enjoy me riding roughshod, *cara*?'

Predictably, she blushed, and just as predictably that made him kiss her again.

'Oh, oh, Salvatore…*you*…*you*…!'

'Oh, you what, *cara*?' he breathed back as he put his hands underneath her sweater and began to caress her.

She wanted to tell him that she was here, in his arms, because she wanted to be—not because of what she could get out of him. But by then the car had reached the pretty Chelsea street where he lived.

By daylight it looked quite different. It was exquisite, lined with trees which would soon bear blossom in the springtime. Would he have flown away by then and gone off to warmer climes? she wondered. Back to Sicily to choose his pure bride, leaving Jessica with nothing but sweet memories and an empty future?

The apartment looked bigger by daylight, too—and far more luxurious than Jessica remembered. Every piece of furniture looked as carefully chosen as a work of art, every surface gleamed with attention. Who cleaned his apartment for him? she found herself wondering.

'Did you choose these pieces yourself?' she questioned, running her finger along the curving line of a small sofa which looked far too beautiful to sit on.

His eyes narrowed. Had she started taking an inventory of how much he was worth? 'I had someone buy them for me,' he said casually. 'Someone who is an expert in antiques and interiors. I spoke to her on the phone, told her what I liked and disliked—she flew to Milan to take a look at the apartment I owned there and from that she came up with this.'

'And you like it?'

'I love it.' His voice was smooth. 'Don't you?'

'Oh, yes,' said Jessica, feeling a little unsteady. It was such a weird way to live your life, she thought—and so different from hers. You could buy anything, she realised. Expertise. Tables in exclusive restaurants.

Quickly, she walked past a beautiful painting she would normally have spent ages looking at, and went instead to the window and the pale expanse of the winter sky. The view of the river was beautiful and calming—though even that too carried a very expensive price tag.

Salvatore came up behind her, his hands on her shoulders as he pressed his body against her back and whispered his lips to her neck.

'What's up? Your shoulders look all tense and you were miles away,' he murmured.

A whole world away, she thought, but what would be the point in spoiling it? That would be like someone failing to appreciate the beauty of a rainbow, on the grounds that it didn't last long enough!

She turned round in his arms and lifted her face up to his. 'I'm here now,' she whispered.

But through the heavy beat of building desire, Salvatore felt a faint sense of misgiving, even as he slid his hands underneath her grey sweater and cupped her soft breasts. Did those shining eyes of hers reproach him, or was that his own, guilty conscience?

But you've got nothing to be guilty for!

They were both consenting adults who had gone into this with their eyes open—and if Jessica was a different breed from the city-sophisticates he ran across in his daily life, then why not just lie back and enjoy the difference?

But as he guided her hand towards his belt he felt a sudden fleeting wish that she was one of those women, with their experienced eyes and experienced hands. Someone who wouldn't look at him with that crazy mixture of tenderness and enthusiasm. Didn't she realise that such feelings were a total waste of her time and that he would not be swayed by them?

His mouth hardened. He must teach her how he liked his women to behave.

CHAPTER TEN

'WE OUGHT to think about getting up.'

Lazily, Salvatore opened his eyes and yawned. 'Why?'

'Because…' Jessica tried to put her thoughts into some kind of coherent order, but it wasn't easy when there was a naked man in bed beside you who possessed her Sicilian lover's impressive physique. One golden and muscular thigh lay sprawled over one of hers, pinning her to the bed, making her achingly aware of the strong, warm weight of his body. 'Because we've been in bed nearly all day,' she blurted out. 'That's all we ever seem to do.'

He smiled, whispering a finger with idle precision over one breast and seeing her automatic shiver of delight and desire. 'And what is wrong with that, *mia cara*? In bed we can talk, we can sleep, eat—and of course make love. Can you think of a place you would prefer to be?'

Jessica stared into the bright blue eyes, feeling her stomach turn to water as he stroked her so expertly. 'Well, no. I suppose when you put it like that, I can't.'

'So what's the problem?'

The problem was that Jessica felt as if she was building up an addiction to her Sicilian lover and she couldn't see how she was ever going to conquer it. Like someone who had never tasted chocolate and had then been given a huge boxful and told to eat as many as she liked—she couldn't seem to stop herself. The lazy days they spent in each other's arms only intensified her perception of the two of them as a unit; the two of them in their own little world. And two months as Salvatore's mistress had only increased her desire for him to a dangerously high pitch.

'I can't really think properly when you're touching me like that,' she complained weakly.

'Then don't think. Just feel. Just like that. And that feels good, doesn't it, Jessica?'

'You…you know it does.'

He made love to her slowly, luxuriously—revelling in the way she reacted to him. She did not shy away from showing her delight, or her thanks. Each time he gave her pleasure she behaved as if she had just been given a precious gift. She was the sweetest lover he had ever known, he reflected.

He kissed the tip of her nose and stared down into her face. Her cheeks were flushed and her thick, shiny hair lay spread all over his pillow—her parted lips always looking as if they wanted to be kissed. Her eagerness had captivated him in a way he had not expected to be captivated—and yet he was naturally wary. 'You have not slept with many men, I think?' he questioned thoughtfully.

Jessica stilled. Was that supposed to be a criticism—that she had in some way disappointed him? And what had made him come out with it now?

'You mean I'm no good?'

He shook his head. 'Most emphatically I did not mean that, *cara*.'

'Then how? How can you tell?'

He shrugged as he circled his hand over the flat of her belly, ignoring her wriggling little unspoken request that his hand travel down further still. 'It is difficult to put into words,' he said slowly. 'You are quick to learn and eager to please and yet you are not as so many women are—so experienced that they treat the act of love as if they were eating a meal, that they always do *this* first, and then they always do *that*. You understand?'

Jessica nodded. 'I think so.' She bit her lip, suddenly shy. 'It makes me aware of how many different women you must have had.'

His smile was indulgent as his fingertips continued their tantalisingly slow journey. 'Probably not as many as you would imagine—but, *sì*, of course there have been women. What else would you expect, *mia tesoro*—when I am a man of thirty-six years?'

'I suppose.'

'How *many* lovers?' he demanded suddenly, his fingers halting.

For a moment Jessica looked at him blankly, not knowing what he meant.

'How many lovers have you had?' he questioned.

She wanted to say that he had no right to ask her a

question like that, but deep down she knew she wanted to redeem herself in his harshly judgemental eyes—to let him know that there had not been a long line of men in her past. 'Only one,' she admitted.

His eyes narrowed as he took in the implications of her words. 'You were in love with him?'

She shrugged. What she had felt for William had been a pale imitation of what she felt for Salvatore. 'I thought I was at the time.'

'Ah.' He nodded. 'It is a pity,' he said slowly, 'that you did not wait—that you wasted your innocence on a man who is now in your past.'

Jessica blinked. *'Wasted?'*

'Sì. Of course. Then you would have had the perfect gift to offer to your husband on your wedding night.' His lips curved into a soft smile. 'But then, of course, you would not be in bed with me, *cara mia.'*

Jessica counted to ten, trying to remind herself that at heart he was a Sicilian—hard and unyielding and uncompromising. She wouldn't ever change him—so what was the point of having this kind of insulting conversation again and again?

She had to keep her face from crumpling as his cruel words brought home just how temporary this arrangement was. And if you keep allowing your emotions to get involved, then you are going to end up very badly hurt, Jessica.

The trouble was that she suspected it was already too late. She was already in much too deep. And where was it going to lead her? Precisely nowhere. She might be spinning all kinds of foolish fantasies about him, but he sure as hell wasn't doing the same thing about her! In fact, he would be horrified if he could read her mind and her dreamy thoughts about him.

So start behaving like a mistress should, instead of some weak little victim who's desperate for a crumb of love he will never throw in your direction.

Putting her arms above her head, Jessica stretched and yawned, knowing that the movement extended her body like a taut bow and seeing from the darkening of his eyes that the gesture had not escaped him. Surely playing out the kind of fantasy a man like him would expect couldn't be *that* difficult?

'Didn't you say something about shopping?' she questioned in a lilting voice.

Salvatore's eyes narrowed. Yes, he had—but her comment took him completely by surprise. In the past, she had brushed off his suggestions that she allow him to buy her some clothes—and since they had spent most of their time in bed, there hadn't been the necessity to do so.

Had that simply been a clever ruse on Jessica's part, he wondered—to lull him into thinking that she was uninterested in his money? Had she played the oldest trick known to man—of first ensnaring him with her body before moving in for the financial kill? And had he, Salvatore Cardini, been stupid enough to fall for it?

'*Sì, cara*—I should love to choose your wardrobe for you,' he said silkily.

Jessica thought she heard a flicker of warning in his voice. But wasn't this what he wanted—to dress her up like a doll, so that she would be fit to enter the finest salons in London? Hadn't he been on about it for days now? 'Didn't you say that there was a big dinner next week that you wanted me to attend?'

Salvatore propped himself up on his elbows. 'Indeed I did,' he agreed slowly, his eyes travelling over her pink and white curves. 'So why don't you put your clothes on, and we'll go out and buy you something to wear?'

But, disconcertingly, his voice had a new, hard edge to it. Jessica slid her legs over the side of the bed, aware that his blue eyes were watching her with unsmiling scrutiny— as if she had just agreed to some unspoken transaction and now she was expected to play her part in it.

Nervously, her tongue flicked out to moisten her lips as she pulled on her functional panties and the plain bra, trying to make it look as erotic as possible, but her nerve was evaporating like water spilt on a hot pavement.

How could she possibly compete with all those women he'd known in the past? Women of his own class—rich women—who could afford to clothe their bodies in the finest silks and satins, the kind of underwear of which he had spoken so longingly the first time they'd been to bed together.

Salvatore felt his body stir yet again as he watched her and it was as if someone had just removed the blinkers from his eyes. Oh, but she was good. The way she snaked her tongue out to make her lips gleam at him so provocatively. That innocent little flutter of her eyelashes. The coy way she half turned her back to make him achingly aware of the high swell of her bottom.

'Come over here,' he said.

'But…but you said—'

'I said, come over here.'

Despite the sudden harshness in his voice, she couldn't resist him even though she could see exactly what he wanted from the smoky look of desire in his blue eyes as he looked at her. You're just an object in his eyes, she told herself—but knowing that didn't stop her.

He reached up and pulled her down on top of him and instantly she could feel his arousal pressing against her as his fingers began tugging impatiently at her underwear.

'Salvatore,' she whispered. 'I've only just put them on.'

'Then let's get rid of them once and for all. Didn't you say you wanted new ones?' His voice was as rough as his gesture as he hooked the panties between his hands and ripped them apart.

'S-Salvatore—' It should have felt just like erotic play, but it did not. Suddenly it felt very different indeed, and as Jessica gazed up into his eyes they became hooded, guarded. But he caught her by the hips, brought her up close, and then he was thrusting into her and it was too late to do anything other than to bite out her pleasure.

It was fast and it was highly charged and Jessica found herself sobbing out her fulfilment just before Salvatore followed her with a strange, almost bitter cry.

Afterwards she lay beside him, gulping air back into her starved lungs as she became aware not just of the rapid thundering of her heart, but that he was not cradling her against his chest, nor stroking her hair as he usually did.

How strange sex could be, Jessica thought. Sometimes it could make you feel so close to someone, and sometimes it could make you feel completely distant.

Like now.

She turned her head to the side as she felt him move. Salvatore was getting up, uncurling his body like a large and very elegant cat—but he didn't say a word, just headed for the shower, and she lay there wondering what it was that had made him so suddenly moody.

Well, don't, she told herself firmly as she got out of bed and went to use one of the other bathrooms. Sensitivity isn't going to get you anywhere.

She showered and dressed and when she reappeared Salvatore was waiting for her. And although he still had that rather forbidding look on his face, she went straight over to him and looped her arms around his neck. Because, otherwise, what was the point in all this?

'I had the most gorgeous shower,' she whispered.

He could tell. She smelt of violets and jasmine and her shiny hair was still faintly damp. He tried to tell himself that now that she had a shopping trip in her line of fire, there was going to be no stopping her—but he hadn't counted on that soft way she spoke when she was in his arms, and something about her tenderness made him bite back his discontentment.

Why not give her the benefit of the doubt? After all, *he* had been the one to bring the subject of a new wardrobe up in the first place. And she certainly hadn't been demanding that he take her to fancy and impressive places, had she? In fact, last week when he had asked her if she wanted to go along with him to meet a visiting member of the Italian government, she had blushed and said that she'd probably be in the way.

In fact, she had been right—it had not been a suitable occasion for partners. But Jessica was unusual for her gender. She didn't swoop on every opportunity to be seen with him—to make the world aware that she was the woman sharing his bed at night.

That had not been why she'd turned the invitation down, of course. It had been because she was insecure about not having the right clothes to wear. His mouth hardened. Well, not for much longer.

The car dropped them outside one of the city's swishest department stores and he led the way past the frothy rails of lingerie towards the clothing section with assistants fluttering around him like moths.

'Can I help you, sir?' questioned an elegant Frenchwoman, dressed entirely in black, who was clearly in charge of the department.

Salvatore rested his hand with lazy possession at Jessica's waist. 'I want to buy my girlfriend some clothes,' he said.

Lucky girlfriend, the Frenchwoman's eyes seemed to say. 'Is there anything in particular you're looking for, sir?'

'Everything,' he said softly.

They were taken to a private section at the back of the store, where Salvatore was given a chair and coffee while Jessica was shown into a huge changing room with horrible unflattering mirrors everywhere, and the Frenchwoman began to bring in outfit after outfit.

'Sir, he is very particular about what he likes.' The woman beamed as the zip was slid up the back of a gown of silk chiffon so fragile that Jessica wondered how it could possibly have been sewn into such a flattering shape.

'You could say that,' said Jessica, feeling rather dazed by the swift efficiency of the expedition. This was so well choreographed that it felt more like opera than shopping, and the moment where a lacy suspender belt and several pairs of fine silk stockings were added to the purchases was the moment when she really *felt* like a mistress.

It seemed like hours later that other assistants were dispatched to help load the packages in the boot of the car, with Jessica walking rather self-consciously at Salvatore's side. She was wearing some of her new clothes—a fitted day-dress in silk jersey which swirled around her knee. Underneath the whole ensemble was the most outrageously sexy underwear she had ever seen.

Her old clothes had been bundled into one of the shop's carrier bags and lay somewhere amid the new, shiny bags—all but forgotten. And Jessica couldn't quite decide whether she felt like a butterfly emerging from the chrysalis—or whether it wasn't just a little bit frightening to have cast off her old persona quite so completely.

'I'll get the car to drop you off at home,' said Salvatore, with a yawn. 'And I will see you on Wednesday.'

She couldn't help herself. He had just spent a fortune on her and yet he wasn't going to see her for four days? 'Not…not tonight?'

There was a brief silence while she looked at him in surprise and disappointment.

But Salvatore's mind was made up. He needed some space. He needed to put her into her proper place in his life and to show her that he was the boss. He closed his mind to the lure of her skimpy new garments with a hard, glimmering smile. 'No, not tonight, *cara*. I have to make a trip to Santa Barbara—didn't I mention it?'

No, he had not mentioned it—but why would he need to? Mistresses didn't qualify for any of the normal, common courtesies which existed between a man and a woman, did they?

So show a little pride, she told herself.

'I don't think you did,' she said, with a slow kind of dignity.

When the car drew up outside her house, she somehow managed to turn to him with a smile. 'Thanks for all my lovely new clothes,' she said, even though his rebuff made her want leave them all behind in his car, untouched.

But where would that get her? The proud Sicilian would only see it as an unforgivable snub to his pride and she simply wasn't prepared to risk it. Not yet.

'Have a good trip, Salvatore,' she said, and leaned over to kiss him briefly.

Her lips were cool—as cool as her attitude. He hadn't seen her like this before and, perversely, it made him want her all the more. Sensing her dismissal, he brought her closer into his body, his fingers feeling the unaccustomedly soft luxury of the silk and cashmere she now wore. Had indulging her begun to spoil her—to corrupt her in the way that new riches sometimes did? Would her sweet eagerness now be replaced by a kind of bored dissatisfaction?

He spoke against her mouth. 'Maybe I've changed my mind, *cara*,' he murmured. 'Maybe I'll take you home after all.'

His proximity enticed her as much as the sultry promise in his voice—even though it shamed her to admit it. But Jessica recognised that something far more important than desire lay at stake here. Being a mistress was one thing and of course that inevitably meant she would be at Salvatore's beck and call.

But allowing him to move her around as if she were some little pawn in a game of chess he wasn't particularly interested in playing—well, that was something else. First he pushed her away and then he pulled her back—and she was supposed to just fall in with his every whim? His allure was powerful, but how would she feel if she allowed him to turn the car round and drive back to Chelsea, leaving her lying there in the morning feeling somehow *used*?

'You have to get ready for your trip,' she said demurely, drawing away from him and seeing his eyes narrow.

Salvatore studied her, watching as she picked up her bag—a new squashy crescent of a thing which matched the sexy boots she wore. Money gave a person power, he recognised. Put his sweet little cleaner in costly clothes and she could be as much of a diva as the next woman.

Should he insist that she bow to his will? he wondered idly. Kiss her until she complied? But he could see the fierce look of pride which had darkened her grey eyes and made them look positively stormy, and he sighed.

Let her enjoy her pointless little victory. One day he would be gone and she would ask herself how she could have possibly turned down a night with him.

'I'll see you next week,' he drawled softly.

CHAPTER ELEVEN

THE doorbell pealed loudly an hour before it was supposed to and Jessica looked at her half-dressed figure in horror. He was early—and Salvatore was *never* early!

Hanging on the front of her wardrobe was a floor-length gown of white silk-satin so beautiful that she was almost scared to put it on. Salvatore was driving straight from the airport to pick her up and not only had she been ticking off the seconds since he'd been away—but she had wanted to look her very best.

It had been a horrible week. She'd regretted her decision to let pride stop her from spending that last night with him and she had begun to realise just how dull her jobs were. It was as if every time Salvatore went away his absence threw a spotlight on her life and emphasised all its deficiencies. And that wasn't a very positive aspect of the relationship either, was it?

Pulling the soft silk-satin over her head, Jessica strained her ears for the sound of his deep baritone but heard nothing—until there was a tap on her door and she opened it to find Freya standing there.

'You've got to come and sign for a parcel,' she said, her voice growing wistful. 'And that's the most gorgeous dress I've ever seen, Jessica.'

'A parcel?' said Jessica distractedly, smoothing the delicate fabric over her hips and walking rather self-consciously into the hall, where Willow was chatting to the delivery man.

After she'd signed for it, her two housemates crowded round her and for some reason Jessica's fingers were trembling as she slit open the padded envelope containing a small box. Was that because there was only one person who would send her a package by special delivery?

'It's a box,' she said.

'We can see that for ourselves, stupid—go on, open it!'

She untied the dark green grosgrain ribbon and flipped open the lid of the box and the three of them gasped in shocked unison.

'Oh, my word!'

'Jessica!'

Jessica swallowed. 'There must be some kind of mistake.'

'Read the card and see what it says.'

Her fingers were trembling as she pulled the card out of the accompanying envelope. 'I couldn't find stones to match your eyes,' it read, 'but these should go with most things.' She stared at the brilliant circlet of diamonds and swallowed. 'They can't possibly be real.'

Willow snatched the bracelet out of the box and held it up to the light with the skill of a prospector. 'Oh, they're real all right. My word, Jessica—what on earth did you do to make him buy you these?'

Jessica flinched, taking the bracelet back, even though the cold and beautiful stones now felt somehow tainted by Willow's words. But hadn't she been wondering the same thing herself?

Freya was staring at them curiously. 'They must be worth an absolute fortune,' she said. 'Better put them on your insurance.'

'But I haven't got any insurance!'

'It's about time you did—particularly if there's going to be more of this kind of thing arriving.'

Jessica slid the bracelet on and stared at it as it caught and reflected the light. It was beautiful. Utterly beautiful—but she found herself wondering why had he bought it for her—apart from presumably wanting her to wear it this evening. A suitable and costly accompaniment to an expensive dress.

Her heart lurched from the ever-present fear which was never too far away. Or was it a goodbye gift? Quickly, she took it off and put it back in the box just as the doorbell rang.

'He usually sends his driver,' confided Willow as Jessica slipped the box in her bag and picked up her wrap and the overnight bag which contained her work clothes and toothbrush.

But tonight he hadn't sent the driver. Salvatore stood there on her doorstep, looking more gorgeous than Jessica could ever remember.

He was dressed in a formal black dinner jacket and

bow tie, the suit emphasising his height—the powerful thrust of his thighs and the broad shoulders. Freya had never met him before and as Jessica introduced him she registered her housemate's dazed expression. And hadn't Jessica felt much the same way herself, the first time she'd ever run across him? Didn't she feel a little like that now, as if this were all some kind of dream which would soon evaporate?

Salvatore's eyes swept over her. The pure white satin coated her curves like cream, giving her an expensive and almost unrecognisable look. He felt the flicker of a pulse. This was a Jessica he had never seen before—a Jessica he had helped create with his money.

'You look beautiful, *cara*,' he said softly, once they were in the car. 'But why aren't you wearing my bracelet?'

Jessica knew she would never be beautiful, but she was aware that the white dress seemed to do remarkable things to her figure. She took the box from her bag and opened it.

'*This* is beautiful,' she said quietly. 'Is it on loan?'

He looked surprised. 'Of course it's not. It is a gift—from me, to you. Put it on.'

'But it's not my birthday, Salvatore—and even if it was, I couldn't possibly accept something as valuable as this. Thank you, but no thanks.'

He searched her face. Another game? The refusal of a gift with the intention of making him believe she was uninterested in his money? Knowing, of course, that such a proud gesture would guarantee the purchase of an even more expensive trinket. But Jessica's expression was set and determined, and there was a defiant look of pride flashing from her grey eyes.

'I don't want your refusal. I want you to wear it tonight,' he said softly as he lifted the bracelet from its velvet base.

'But it's not—'

'No buts. *No*. Listen to me, Jessica. I am a wealthy man—and it pleases me to buy you diamonds.' His eyes gleamed at her. 'Surely you would not deny your Salvatore such simple pleasure as that?'

She tried to tell herself fiercely that the *your* Salvatore was simply a slip of the tongue. He wasn't *her* Salvatore any more than she was *his* Jessica. But he was managing to make her refusal seem crazy and wasn't there a tiny voice in her head urging her to accept the gift? Wasn't she discovering that she rather *liked* the costly gems—and wasn't that a rather inadvisable and dangerous liking to acquire, given her circumstances?

'I suppose…if you put it like that.'

He smiled as he sensed her capitulation and began to slide the glittering bangle over her tiny wrist. Didn't they say that every woman had her price?

'Wear it for me, and then kiss me and tell me how much you have missed me.'

Her lips brushed against his. 'I've missed you,' she whispered truthfully.

But her head was spinning as they kissed. She felt as if she had put herself in some kind of catch-22 situation—unable to refuse his gift, but her acceptance of it making her feel as if she had crossed some invisible line and sold out in some way.

And suddenly she saw with remarkable clarity what she had become. She was there to warm his bed when he desired her and to be kitted out with costly clothes and expensive pieces of jewellery which were supposed to make her look like she belonged to his world when she did not. And she never would. She was nothing but an imposter. A cleaner masquerading as the legitimate partner of a billionaire. A cleaner who had fallen in love with him somewhere along the way.

Suddenly the bangle felt as cold and heavy as her heart, a manacle which hung around her slender wrist. I've fallen in love with him, she realised, and a terrible hopelessness clenched at her heart.

'You are cold?' Salvatore questioned as he felt her tremble in a way that was more frozen than desire.

'A little.' She pulled the stole closer around her bare shoulders. 'There isn't very much to this dress.'

'Which happens to be its appeal,' he commented drily as the car drew up directly outside the Natural History Museum.

Jessica looked startled as she stared up at the huge building, where her grandmother had once brought her during one of the school holidays. 'Don't tell me we're eating dinner in *here*?' she questioned nervously.

'We are. It is often hired out for charity and corporate events.'

Inside, the place had been transformed with glamour on a scale Jessica hadn't believed existed. Tight scarlet roses were bunched into tall, dark vases which were placed everywhere and starlike lights twinkled against an indigo backdrop. Crystal laid tables were dotted beneath the impressive form of a giant dinosaur, which towered over the evening's proceedings.

But tonight Jessica couldn't seem to get rid of the gnawing sensation that she had no real place here. That in Salvatore's car was her overnight bag with her neat office clothes, which were a world away from the slippery silk-satin she was wearing.

Their table was right at the top of the room and, in the dazzle of introductions made, a wiry, red-headed man she half recognised shook Salvatore by the hand.

'I didn't expect to see you again so soon!' he exclaimed, and then appeared to notice Jessica. 'Salvatore and I bumped into each other in Santa Barbara earlier in the week,' he explained as they took their seats, and then added, 'Hi, nice to meet you. I'm Jeremy, by the way.'

Jessica nodded as it all came back, remembering the keen fisherman who had been so kind to her on that first, rather nerve-racking evening when she'd been Salvatore's pretend date at the dinner party. And an unexpected feeling of relief washed over her. She actually *knew* someone here! Already she had a bit of a history with Salvatore, despite all her fretting. Maybe she could fit in, after all.

'We've met before,' she said, with a smile. 'I'm Jessica. Remember?'

Jeremy's eyes remained blank. 'I don't think…'

'At that lovely house in Kensington. Garth and Amy's.'

Jeremy's eyes cleared, but his look of comprehension was quickly replaced by one of confusion. 'Yes, of course. You asked me about fishing. But what has happened to you?'

Jessica gave a look of mock-surprise. 'What do you mean?'

He shook his head. 'Oh, nothing. Silly mistake.'

'Please.' She lowered her voice. 'What do you mean?'

He gave her an odd kind of smile. 'Just that you used to look so…different.' He cleared his throat as he reached for his wine glass in a gesture which was unmistakably intended to close the subject. 'That really is a magnificent bracelet you're wearing.'

Jessica went through the motions of eating the meal, but inside her stomach felt as if it had been turned into a tight steel drum. Despite his best diplomatic attempts, Jeremy couldn't have made it plainer if he'd tried. The woman he'd met that night—the one he'd clearly liked and enjoyed talking to—had vanished.

And in her place was a new woman—one created for and by Salvatore. Clothed in white silk-satin and dripping in diamonds, she had been transformed. All traces of the real Jessica ironed away to enable her to become the stereotypical mistress.

Somehow she managed to endure the endless courses and then an auction for which it seemed that Salvatore had donated the top bid of an all-expenses holiday in a luxury Sicilian villa. Images of the island were flashed up on a giant screen—a place of seemingly unimaginable beauty with its lemon trees lining amazing beaches, exquisite old towns and dark green mountains.

Jessica stole a glance at his profile, seeing the faint

smile which curved the edges of his lips as the slide-show finished.

Was he imagining his permanent return to his island home, and the day when he married his virgin bride? A pang ripped through her, and as they were leaving she found herself wondering if he would ever remember Jessica Martin—or whether she was just one in a long line of anonymous mistresses, all interchangeable in their costly clothes and jewels.

Laden with designer goodie-bags, they stepped into the waiting limousine and as the car purred away Salvatore turned to her.

'You were very quiet tonight, Jessica.'

'Was I?'

'Any particular reason?'

She looked out of the window, at the glittering night which was flashing by. 'Not really.'

'You were perhaps a little disappointed that Jeremy was less amenable to your charms than last time?' he questioned.

He was more perceptive than she sometimes gave him credit for, but of course he had completely missed the point. 'He didn't recognise me,' she said.

He stroked the silk of her gown reflectively. 'But that is a good thing, surely? Isn't the whole idea of a brand-new wardrobe to give the wearer a brand-new look?'

'Is it?' She felt like a flower plucked from a simple country garden who had changed into a forced, hothouse bloom and left without fragrance or freshness.

'Of course it is,' he said softly. 'It would be naïve to expect your experience with me not to leave its mark on you, Jessica.'

She felt as if she'd sold out to his money and that Jeremy had noticed and disapproved of it in some way—but what was the point in telling Salvatore that? He was just back from a long trip. He didn't want to hear about her crushing insecurity—it wasn't actually going to *change* anything. Mistresses weren't supposed to become emotionally involved, were they? That was the number one rule. And I've broken it, she thought unhappily as she turned to stare into his handsome face. I've broken it big time.

'Oh, it would have been nice to have been alone with you,' she said instead.

'*Nice*, Jessica?' he mocked as he pulled her into his arms. 'What have I told you before about lacklustre words which say nothing?' He put his mouth close to hers. 'Come on, think of a more accurate description, *mia tesoro*.'

Jessica closed her eyes and swallowed. This was easy. Too easy. 'Incredible. It would have been incredible to have had you all to myself,' she whispered. 'Is that better?'

He touched her breast. 'Much better.'

'And…how was Santa Barbara?'

'Oh, cold. Busy. Predictable.' And filled with glamorous women, it seemed—most of whom had wasted no time in letting him know that a Sicilian billionaire was very desirable indeed.

But, inexplicably, he had missed Jessica, despite her stubbornness just before he'd left. Not just the sex—because he always enjoyed sex with the appetite of a man who enjoyed food when his belly was empty, or fine wine when he wanted the luxury of relaxation.

He had missed the ease he enjoyed with her. Her ability to listen to him and her refusal to say what was expected of her, simply because of her inferior social position. He had felt her absence keenly and that had alerted him to danger. Because missing someone meant that you were in some way dependent on them—and he was dependent on no one. He ran the flat of his hand against the silky surface of her hair. 'Have you missed me?' he questioned idly.

'Yes.'

'How much?'

She wanted to cling to him, to shower every inch of his autocratic face with soft, butterfly kisses—hug him with a poignant and heartfelt embrace for what could never be. But mistresses didn't do that, either. He had bought her the dress and the diamonds—she knew exactly what was expected of her. Instead, she trickled her fingernails over one taut thigh and heard him groan. 'This much.'

'Do that some more,' he urged softly. 'Ah, *sì*.'

They barely made it in through the front door. Their hands and lips were frantic—with Salvatore removing the white satin from Jessica's trembling body with the dexterity of a man peeling a banana.

He took her against the wall—wild and urgent—her gasping cries inciting him as he drove into her.

But afterwards, Jessica felt shaken, not just by that stormy coming together, but by the certain knowledge of how much she was going to miss him.

They barely slept at all. She wondered if it was absence which made the sex seem much more intense than usual. As if it had moved on to a different dimension. Or was that simply wishful thinking on her part? A woman conjuring up a fantasy because she had fallen in love with a man who was out of bounds. Well, falling in love with Salvatore was about as sensible as diving into the sea from a cliff-top when you could barely swim. And he had warned her that this was going nowhere—so there was no one to blame but herself.

Next morning, she slipped quietly from the bed into the shower so as not to wake him, but when she returned to the bedroom to put on her office clothes she found him staring at her.

'That was some night,' he observed softly.

Jessica swallowed. 'Yes.'

The blue gaze didn't waver. 'Let's do it again tonight. I have an early evening meeting out by the river—come with me, and we'll have dinner together afterwards. We could stay over if you like—there's a beautiful hotel.' He smiled. 'Wake up in the morning in the countryside for a change.'

'Salvatore, I can't—'

His invitation had been impromptu but her ready refusal irritated him. 'Can't?'

'No. I'm sorry. It's too short notice.'

Suddenly he felt angry, with her and with himself, and he couldn't work out why. He leaned back against the pillows, his dark features assuming a bored expression. 'Jessica—I thought we'd already established the ground rules. We're way past that stage, *cara*. And if you think that refusing me like a sixteen-year-old virgin is going to make you more desirable, then I am afraid that you are very much mistaken.'

Jessica froze. Not only had he forgotten—and dismissed—her *real* life, the one which involved regular work for a regular wage-packet to pay her rent, but he had turned round and accused her of emotional manipulation. And it hurt. Hadn't he learned *anything* about her in the time they'd been together? No, of course he hadn't. He wasn't interested in finding out anything about her as a woman—that kind of knowledge didn't even register on his radar.

Just because he had made love to her with such passion during the night didn't actually *mean* anything, did it? The supposedly tender way he had held her had nothing to do with emotion. Because Salvatore hadn't changed. Nothing had changed—except maybe *her* feelings.

So stop it right now. Remind him of the reality.

'I've got my job to do tonight,' she said quietly. 'Cleaning in your office. Remember that, Salvatore? It happens to be how we met.'

There was a pause. 'Well, I'm absolving you of the responsibility. Leave it. Don't do it. For heaven's sake—you can easily miss a night.'

'I can't do that.'

'You can and you will. I'm the chairman of the damned company, Jessica—and what I say goes!'

She shook her head, clinging onto this last piece of independence like a drowning woman scrabbling at a slippery rock. 'But I don't work for *you*, Salvatore. I work for Top Kleen who won't be very happy if I make a habit of missing work. For a start they might begin to wonder *why* I've been given the evening off by the boss—and we wouldn't want them knowing that, would we? And then…' She paused, before drawing a deep breath. Remind him of the reality.

'Then there's the money,' she finished painfully. 'I need that money, Salvatore—that's why I do the job.'

Salvatore smiled. This was language he could understand. Reaching for his wallet, he pulled out a thick wad of notes and peeled off several before holding them up. 'How much do you need?' he questioned carelessly.

Jessica's cheeks stained with anger and embarrassment. 'That wasn't what I meant at all. I don't want your money.'

'Oh, for goodness sake—it's no big deal,' he snapped. 'I want your company. I don't want you cleaning my office. Surely if you take emotion out of the situation, you can see the logic in my offer? It makes perfect sense. I have more than enough and you don't. So take the damned money, Jessica.'

She shook her head.

'Please, Jessica.'

It was the 'please' that did it. Who could deny

Salvatore when he asked her like that? Reluctantly, Jessica nodded.

'You'll take it?'

The truth was that she *could* see the logic in his words—but that didn't stop the feeling of shame which washed over her. Knowing she was trapped. Knowing that there was no other solution than to accept an offer which he didn't even realise was so insulting.

'Yes, I'll take it.'

With trembling fingers she walked towards him and removed two of the notes, shaking her head when he extended the pile towards her again. She would take exactly what she would have earned, and no more.

'Jessica—'

'I'll see you later,' she said quietly, and, bending to plant a swift kiss on his lips, she turned and left.

Outside, it was raining but Jessica barely noticed the bus which splashed icy water over her legs. She bought a cup of coffee from the office vending machine, which tasted pretty disgusting, but at least it was hot.

Forcing herself to try to concentrate, she sat down at her desk to survey the mass of emails which had accumulated, but she had only been working for a couple of minutes when the phone rang.

It was the hospital—and the call that she took seemed to put all her problems into perspective.

CHAPTER TWELVE

'YOUR grandmother's going to be fine, Miss Martin—it's the shock as much as anything.'

Jessica nodded, her eyes filling with tears as she clutched at her grandmother's hand, thinking how unbelievably pale and small she looked lying in the hospital bed. But she supposed that was what happened when someone you'd thought of as indestructible all their lives managed to injure themselves. For the first time she realised that her grandmother was getting old. That nothing ever remained the same.

She looked up at the orthopaedic surgeon. 'Thank you so much, Doctor. I really appreciate it.'

'She's a very interesting patient,' he said, giving a quick smile.

After the surgeon had left, Jessica turned to her grandmother with a mixture of love and exasperation. 'But you shouldn't have *been* dancing the salsa!' she exclaimed. 'Not at your age!'

Her grandmother smiled. 'Oh, rubbish, Jessica. There's far too much of "don't do this" and "don't do that" once you pass sixty. I've always enjoyed dancing, as well you know—it was that clod of a partner who made me fall.' She held up her wrist, which was covered in a bright pink plaster, and pulled a face. 'The trouble is that it's my right wrist. So no lifting. No carrying. I'm going to have to get someone to do my shopping.'

Jessica nodded, her mind spinning. 'And someone to do the cleaning,' she pointed out as she picked over the possibilities of how she could possibly help. She could stay here tonight, of course; she'd have to. She'd already rung a rather distracted Salvatore, interrupting him at the office, which was something she'd never done before, and told him she'd be staying away.

'What's happened?' he demanded.

'Oh, my grandmother took a tumble. She's broken her wrist, but is fine otherwise.'

'That's good,' he said distractedly, but Jessica could hear the sound of a telephone ringing and the low hum of voices in the background and knew that he wasn't really interested in the fine print of her family troubles.

And work wouldn't give her indefinite leave to look after her grandmother—why, they'd only let a girl from the finance department have two days off to fly to Ireland when her father had died.

'We need to get someone to come in and help you,' she said slowly. 'There's that agency in the next town, of course.'

A look of concern crossed her grandmother's face. 'But they're expensive, Jessica—everyone says so, and we haven't got—'

'Oh, yes, we have—and you're not to worry about a thing. Not a thing,' Jessica told the old lady fiercely. 'I can sort something out.'

Jessica knew exactly what she was going to do, even though the thought of it was daunting. She had the bracelet in her handbag—she kept it close to her at all times, terrified to leave something so precious in the house. Yet, in a funny kind of way, the thought of getting rid of it was a relief. It represented both too much and yet nothing at all. It had not been given as a token of love, but as a token of worth. Its price was its value— so why should she hang onto it when it just taunted her of what she would never have from Salvatore?

The sum which the jeweller offered sounded ridiculously high. 'This is a simply fabulous piece,' he breathed as he stared at it for ages through his eyeglass.

He seemed surprised when Jessica accepted the price he offered without demur—but what did she know about diamond prices in the current market? She needed money, and quickly. And for once local hearsay hadn't been exaggerated—the agency she was drafting in to help really was expensive.

'I've arranged for someone to come in twice a day to help you,' she told her grandmother once they were back in the tiny cottage where Jessica had spent most of her childhood. 'Someone who'll do any washing, or cooking or shopping. Whatever you like, really—you just have to tell them.'

'Gosh—I'll have to fracture my wrist more often.'

'Just you dare!'

Jessica was exhausted. It felt strange to sleep in her little bed that night, in the back bedroom which overlooked the apple trees. The skies were pitch black and lit only by starlight, and a car-less hush settled over the place once the only pub had shut, cloaking it in a comforting kind of silence. A village which had always seemed frighteningly quiet and lacking in any kind of life now seemed to offer a soothing balm to her troubled thoughts.

Jessica woke up next morning to the sound of birdsong, and she lay there wondering whether she had done the right thing in going up to London to try to make something of herself. Had her ambition overreached itself? True, she'd ended up living in an okay house with the very real chance of promotion in her office job. And, yes, she happened to have an amazing lover—but that bit was only temporary, and she was having to work round the clock for the rest.

She left her grandmother playing a slow game of one-handed poker-dice with an elderly neighbour and then headed back to London, where she was back at her desk by lunchtime.

From time to time she glanced down at the handbag by her feet, knowing that she needed to bank the thick wad of cash which the jeweller had given her. And surely she needed to tell Salvatore what she had done?

Jessica bit her lip.

How could she? Wouldn't that essentially be saying to him that she needed his expensive presents to support her lifestyle? And mightn't it look as if she were hinting for more?

After all, Salvatore didn't care whether she actually *wore* the jewels—it was the gesture of giving them which counted, and clearly giving diamonds to your mistress was de rigueur.

But later that evening she flew into his arms as if she had been separated from him for a year, rather than an unexpected night, and he laughed softly as he kissed her.

'Missed me?'

'Yes.'

'How is your grandmother?'

'She's fine.'

He took her on an overnight trip to Paris, where they stayed in an amazing hotel on the Place de la Concorde. They bought frothy lingerie in a little shop on the Avenue Montaigne and Jessica insisted on taking a boat ride down the Seine. Salvatore laughed and accused her of making him feel like a tourist.

'But we *are* tourists!' she retorted. 'And, besides, I've never seen you looking quite so relaxed before.'

It was true, he thought as they queued for tickets at the Musée d'Orsay. He hadn't stood in a queue for years—and for once in his life he felt utterly free.

He found himself watching her as they strolled around the famous Flea Market. Left to her own devices, Jessica seemed to like pottering among the junk, lifting a perfect moonstone on a silver chain which had caught her eye and holding it to the light.

'Look, it's the *exact* colour of the Seine,' she observed.

Salvatore frowned. Was she hinting for another

present? But surely not something as commonplace as that cheap little necklace?

'Where's your bracelet?' he questioned later, over lunch—as he trickled raspberry vinegar onto an oyster and held it in front of her lips.

Jessica froze as obligation hovered over her—but how could she possibly destroy this perfect moment with such mundane reality? 'I've...I've left it at home,' she lied as he slid the oyster into her mouth.

On Monday she gave into sweet pressure and again cancelled her cleaning job so that Salvatore could take her to the Festival Hall to listen to a visiting violinist who tore at her heartstrings.

On Tuesday, she dashed up after work to see her grandmother, who, it seemed, was quickly becoming used to her new leisurely life and the fuss being made of her.

On Wednesday she deliberately turned up late at Cardini's—because Salvatore had told her he was having a meeting which might run over and she couldn't face turning up in front of him and all his colleagues in her pink overall and scarf. And as she'd told herself time and time again—as long as she did the work, then no one was any the wiser if she ran over her appointed hours.

But when she walked into his office it was not empty, as she had expected. And there was no sign of her Sicilian lover. Instead, her supervisor was waiting there for her.

'Perhaps you'd like to explain yourself,' said the woman grimly.

There was no explanation which would satisfy even the most reasonable of people, and, judging by the look of simmering rage on the face of the supervisor, reasonable was the last thing she was feeling. It seemed that a whole catalogue of complaints about Jessica's behaviour had been building up.

'It's gone round the building like wildfire!' the woman began, her words barely coherent as they poured out in a torrent of venom. 'A member of Top Kleen having an affair with the company chairman. I've never heard anything like it!'

Some rogue instinct made Jessica want to retort that it said a lot for the calibre of Top Kleen employees that the boss should *want* to have an affair with one of its employees at all! But she could see that such a remark would inflame an already inflammatory situation and half an hour later she was leaving the building with Salvatore's car on its way to fetch her.

For a moment she wanted to laugh at the irony of the sacked cleaner being collected by the boss's limousine, and the next she was slumped in the back seat, speeding towards Chelsea and feeling as if her life were being slowly dismantled, piece by piece.

Salvatore was talking on the phone when he answered the door to her, and waved her in the direction of the drinks tray. All Jessica wanted to do was to hug him, to wrap her arms tightly around his neck and have a little moan about her job and the aggressive supervisor. But comfort was not part of his role, just as seeking emotional reassurance was not part of hers.

So she hung up her coat and poured herself a drink and waited until he finished the call.

He looked up at her. *'Ciao, bella,'* he said softly.

'Important?' asked Jessica automatically, for she had noticed him frown.

'Just a deal in the Far East which is worth looking at. You remember the hotel on Phuket I was telling you about? Well, one of my cousins—Giacomo—is thinking of buying it. But I think the price is too high and the trouble is that he is hot-headed and impulsive.' His gaze swept over her. 'I was wondering why you wanted the car to collect you so early and how pale you looked,' he said softly. 'Are you ill, *cara*?'

Jessica swallowed, the term of endearment spoken in that deceptively gentle tone making her feel even more wobbly than she already did. 'No, I'm not ill. I've been sacked, actually. Sacked from my cleaning job,' she elaborated.

The frown deepened. 'For what, precisely?'

The laugh she attempted fell flat. 'Unprofessional behaviour is the phrase they used. Somehow my agency have found out that I've been…that we've been… They know about us, Salvatore,' she said, aware even as she said it that there was no *us*. 'They think that my affair with you has made me abuse my position, and in a way they have a point. I'm sorry if your reputation is going to suffer as a consequence of that.'

There was a pause. 'You think that anything would reflect badly on *my* reputation?' he challenged softly. 'Or that I seek the good opinion of others through the way I live my life?' His blue eyes hardened into chips of sapphire as he walked towards her. 'And you want to know something? I am glad that you have lost that stupid job, Jessica—it ate into too much of your time. Time you should have been spending with me.'

Jessica looked at him incredulously. Now he had dismissed a chunk of her life as if it were of no consequence! 'Of course it did—it was a *job*! I wasn't doing it for fun, you know.'

'I know that. You were doing it for money—but money is not a problem, is it, *cara*?' he questioned silkily, and pulled her into his arms. 'Since I have more than enough to go round. I thought that we established that the other day. So can we please stop pretending and just accept that?'

Of course she was tempted. Who wouldn't have been—especially when he was touching her like that and his breath was warm against her cheek? But something prevented Jessica from taking the easy way out that he was offering her. She remembered how cheap she'd felt as he had peeled those notes from his wallet. She thought of the costly diamond bracelet now languishing in the jeweller's and the lie she had told him about it, because she had panicked in Paris. And because you knew he'd go crazy if you told him the truth.

Jessica bit her lip. 'I'm not taking any more money from you,' she said. 'I've taken enough.'

'But I insist.'

'You can insist all you want, Salvatore—but I'm not accepting it.'

He studied her for a moment, but could see she meant it. And although it riled him to have his wishes thwarted—wasn't it admirable in a way that she had turned down his offer? She was a stubborn, sometimes proud woman, he thought, a reluctant smile curving his lips. Even though it was futile, he rather liked her determination to maintain her independence—it was almost worth the occasional disruption to his social life. But enough was enough. She had made her point and now he would make his.

He lifted her chin, fixing her in the blaze from his eyes. 'Refuse my money if you must,' he said softly. 'But I don't want you getting another part-time job— not while you are with me. Is that understood?'

How formidable he sounded in that moment, she thought. Some rebel streak urged her to tell him that he had no right to dictate the terms of her life. Yet as Jessica gazed up into the unyielding glint in his eyes she registered that maybe he did. Because wasn't another function of the mistress to be always available? Not to have to turn down your lover because you had to rush off to clean and polish.

She laid her head against his shoulders and closed her eyes and suddenly she didn't care if he was dictating terms or not. Because this was where she most wanted to be—in his arms. These precious moments which were ticking away all too quickly.

Surely it *was* slightly crazy for her to be cleaning offices—forcing her to cancel dates and leave her billionaire lover cooling his heels. And surely she *could* manage without an additional job—at least until the affair finished.

'Is it, Jessica?' he repeated silkily.

How could she resist him anything? Snuggling into his hard body with a sigh, she turned her face upwards and gave a little shrug of her shoulders. 'Okay, then,' she agreed softly. 'Just this once, I'll let you insist.'

But as Salvatore looked down at her, a strange kind of feeling twisted in his gut. All he was aware of was the quiet grey light from her eyes, the pale oval of her face and the petal-pink lips. As those lips parted unfamiliar feelings began to tug at his senses and in that moment he felt completely perplexed.

He shook his head—as if he could shake away the sensations which were creeping over him like unwelcome intruders. He didn't want to *feel*—and certainly not with her. Not until he had decided the time was right and the woman was right—and this woman most emphatically was not.

His mouth hardened. 'I'm glad that's been sorted out,' he purred. 'From now on, you'll be available when I need you. Understood?'

Jessica nodded, telling herself that his use of the word 'available' didn't exactly boost her self-confidence. 'I just wish I could contribute a bit more.'

The twist in his gut became something much more recognisable. 'Oh, but you do,' he said unsteadily, his hands roving over her bottom and beginning to ruck up her skirt. He felt her thighs begin to quiver coolly beneath the hot, seeking heat of his fingers. 'You contribute in the most imaginative way of all, *cara mia*.'

'Salvatore!' she gasped, but her desire was overshadowed by the harsh truth of his words. That sex was her contribution—and that was all he wanted. All he needed—certainly from her. So you'd better start dismantling your fantasies before they get too real, she told herself fiercely, and gave herself up to the plunder of his kiss.

He took her to bed and that night Salvatore dreamt of Sicily, wondering if it was some kind of portent. Were his dreams trying to tell him that his time in England was finished? That maybe he should return to the island of his birth and begin to search for a woman to bear his sons, as he had always intended to do?

The figure beside him stirred lazily. 'Can't you sleep?' she murmured, her hands reaching up automatically to caress his shoulders, the tight muscles relaxing beneath the ministrations of her touch.

'No.'

'Can I help?'

'You can try.' And he made a sound between a laugh and a moan as she began to touch him.

This time the pleasure was stealthy, but the power of his orgasm took him by surprise. How the hell could someone so inexperienced be so good? Because she's passionate, that's why, he told himself.

His thoughts were troubled even as his eyelids began drifting to a close. Tomorrow, he would speak to his cousin, Vincenzo, and discuss returning to Sicily—and in the meantime he would buy Jessica another piece of jewellery. Something bigger this time. It would perhaps make up for the indignity of being sacked because of her relationship with him.

Something to remember him by.

Next day, once his assistant had gone home and the building was quiet, he clicked onto the website of the leading diamond retailer. He liked diamonds—their purity and glittering beauty—and they were always a good investment.

Idly, he scrolled down through the blur of dazzling gemstones until his attention was caught by the unexpected. Eyes narrowing, he returned to the page with a growing sense of disbelief as he began to study the photograph carefully.

There could be no mistake.

He felt the harsh beat of his heart. He tasted the stale flavour of disappointment—but, beneath it all, he was aware of the sensation of having been thrown a lifeline. Something which dissolved all his niggling doubts in an instant. He smiled, but it was a hard, cruel smile. Because this was something he understood almost better than anything. She was nothing but a cheap little gold-digger, after all.

Picking up the phone, he punched out her number. 'Jessica?' he questioned. 'Can you get over to the apartment right away?'

CHAPTER THIRTEEN

JESSICA arrived in a rush. It had been raining outside and her hair was spattered with raindrops which glittered on her shiny head. Like jewels, Salvatore thought grimly. She was wearing a cute coat, a leather trench which clung to her curves and gave her an expensive, pampered look—a look which she wore like a second skin.

How quickly his cleaner lover had adapted to luxury, he marvelled. Salvatore's mouth hardened as she removed the coat to reveal a slither of silk jersey beneath. And pale stocking and killer heels. A pulse began to beat at his temple. She looked like what she'd become—a rich man's plaything. He wondered how she was going to take it when she heard that he would no longer be bankrolling her. That the presents were stopping and so was the lifestyle.

But he would give her one last chance to redeem herself.

'You look beautiful,' he said softly as he hung the coat for her and gestured for her to follow him into the sitting room.

'Do I?' Jessica was trying to get better at receiving compliments—and, to be honest, it was getting easier all the time because Salvatore made her *feel* beautiful. Sometimes, when he was running his hands over her body in bed, stroking her as if she were some sleek racehorse—she felt as good as anybody else. 'Why, thank you,' she said softly and looked at him expectantly. 'Is everything okay? You sounded...I don't know...*urgent* on the phone.'

'Did I? Sit down. Like a drink?'

She shook her head. 'No. No, thanks.'

His gaze flicked over her. 'That outfit looks wonderful, *cara*—but it is a little on the plain side.'

'You think so?'

'I think it could do with a little embellishment, that's all. Why do you never wear that diamond bracelet I bought you? Does it not please you?'

Jessica gave a high little laugh. She had tried to forget all about the wretched bracelet—forced it to the back of her mind so that the thought of what she'd done couldn't haunt her. Because not only had she told a lie—how on earth would it look if she told him that she'd sold it? No matter how worthy the cause— wouldn't that make her look as if she were just out for everything she could get out of him?

'Oh, I...I love it,' she said, and bit her lip. 'In fact, I love it so much that I've put it somewhere safe—and you know what sometimes happens when you do that?' She met the cool expression in his eyes. 'What would you say if I told you I couldn't find it?'

There was a loaded pause while fury erupted within him like a dark, poisonous storm. 'I'd say you were a damned liar and a cheat!' he bit out, unable to keep up the pretence for a moment longer. He saw the alarm which had widened her grey eyes and the stain which pinkened her pale cheeks. Guilty, he thought grimly. Guilty as hell. 'And a stupid little fool to underestimate a man like me!'

'You mean…you've found out?' she breathed.

'That you flogged my gift to you at the first opportunity?' he snarled. 'Yes, I found out, Jessica. Didn't you realise that a piece of that quality would always find its way to the best dealer? How much did you get for it?'

Jessica felt sick. 'Salvatore, please…'

'Oh, please don't act as if the very mention of money is distasteful to you when clearly this was nothing but a *transaction* you were intending to capitalise on from the very beginning! Come on—how much? Nine? Ten?'

Miserably, she shook her head.

'More?'

'No. Half that, in fact.'

His eyes glittered. 'So not only have you sold it—but you've been ripped off into the bargain?' He gave a humourless laugh. 'Clearly you've never done this kind of thing before—'

'Of course I haven't!'

But deep down he knew that there was no *of course* about it. This was Salvatore on familiar and oddly comforting ground—probing with accuracy to try to find an ulterior motive. Because there was always one of those.

Riches and power attracted people who had an eye for the main chance—who wanted something for very little—and *his* big mistake had been in thinking that Jessica was any different from all the rest. He thought how very clever she'd been—at first trying to refuse the gift. All that coy reluctance about letting him pay her not to work. So simple and so clever, and yet he had been sucked right in, thinking her both stubborn and yet charmingly lacking in materialism.

'So why did you do it?' he questioned, almost conversationally. 'Go on, tell me. I'm intrigued.'

She met the resigned expression on his face and somehow that hurt even more than the fierce accusation of earlier—as if he had been expecting something like this all along. It cut right through her so that she had to blink to hold back the tears of remorse. Part of her wanted to tell him to go to hell, and to think the worst of her. Because that was what he wanted to do, she recognised suddenly.

That was the image which would fit in with Salvatore's stark vision of the world and of women in particular—that only virgins were worth marrying and all other women were gold-digging, greedy little tramps!

Well, whatever else came out of this sorry mess, he would know that she *wasn't* one of those women.

'I sold it to pay for my grandmother to have help while her broken wrist was mending!'

He gave a soft, disbelieving laugh. 'Ah, *sweet*! Like Little Red Riding Hood, perhaps?' he questioned with silky cynicism. 'Stealing through the forest with your basket of food for grandmamma? Aren't you a little too old to expect me to believe in fairy tales?'

Jessica stared at him, shaking her head in disbelief. How could she have deluded herself into believing that she loved a man with as warped a view of life as his? 'My goodness,' she breathed. 'It's never occurred to me before. It can't be easy being Salvatore Cardini, can it? Not when all the riches and power in the world can't change a fundamental mistrust in human nature!'

'A mistrust which you have just proved is well founded!' he iced out. 'If you wanted to help your grandmother, then why the hell didn't you tell me? Why didn't you come to me and explain what had happened? Am I such an ogre that you would not dare to do that, Jessica?'

'Why?' he persisted. 'When that is what a woman would normally do.'

'So I'm damned if I do, and damned if I don't? I thought you were fed up with the fact that people always wanted something from you! That's the main reason I didn't ask you,' she said, her voice shaking with rage and hurt as she stared at him.

'But, according to you, I'm a gold-digger whichever way you want to look at it, aren't I, Salvatore? You forced me to take a bracelet I didn't particularly want— presumably because it satisfies some sort of mistress "code". I didn't realise that it came with certain specifications of what I was or wasn't allowed to do with it! I suppose if you'd given me perfume you would have included a list of times when I was allowed to spray it!'

'But we are having a relationship,' he snarled, 'which surely entitles you to ask for my help with your family.'

'Entitlement?' Jessica might have laughed if she hadn't been so angry. 'You're talking about relationships and *entitlement* in the same breath? Relationships are about sharing and caring and being equal—you wouldn't know one if it came up and hit you in the face! In fact, for all your power and wealth and achievements, you really don't have a clue about life, do you, Salvatore? In fact, you're more of a robot than a man!'

'You think so?' It was an insult too far and the anger which had been bubbling away inside him suddenly transmuted into something much more manageable. His arm went out to pull her up against his hips and to press her hard against him. 'Want me to show you how much of a man I am?'

The arrogant boast should have repelled her, but it did no such thing—emotions and temper were running so high that it was like putting a match to a bone-dry timber. He was hot and he was hard. And heaven help her but Jessica's body responded to him with an overpowering greed—even while her mind and her heart battled against his powerful influence. 'No,' she breathed, when—maddeningly—he loosened his grip on her.

Correctly, he read the disappointment which clouded her grey eyes and gave a soft laugh. 'That would drive your point home, wouldn't it, Jessica *mia*? The big, bad wolf who just takes his pleasure when and where he wants it.' He lifted her chin with his finger. 'But you want it, too, don't you?'

Her eyelids fluttered down.

'Yes, you want me badly. You always did and you always will.' And he wanted her, too. Still. His discovery about her lies and duplicity were the perfect get-out clause—giving him the freedom to walk away from her now without a pang. Without all the tears and scenes he had anticipated.

But he didn't want to.

Not yet.

Not until the inexplicable fever she evoked in his blood had vanished once and for all.

'Jessica,' he said softly, and brushed his lips against hers.

The sudden change of mood took her off guard—the soft kiss hinting at a tenderness she secretly longed for. And he knew that. He knew her weak spots. He knew what women wanted because he was a clever man who'd had women throwing themselves at him ever since he'd grown out of short trousers. He's playing with you, she told herself—playing exactly as a cat plays with a mouse before it lures the innocent little creature towards its horrible fate.

So stop him. She wriggled a little—but that had precisely the wrong effect.

'Don't fight me for the sake of fighting me,' he murmured against her mouth. 'Not when you want this just as much as I do.'

And in a way, his cruel perception only heightened her hunger. She had shown herself to be a liar. She had sold his costly gift in secret and, no matter how worthy the cause, didn't that make her look cheap? Nothing would ever redeem her in his eyes and so she had nothing to lose. Nothing.

'Who's fighting?' she questioned throatily, beginning to unbutton his shirt.

Her instant compliance was less surprising than the fact that she had taken the initiative and was slipping the silk from his shoulders. And now she was unbuckling his belt…pulling at it impatiently and sliding down the zip. He choked as she slipped her hand inside, circling him with possessive eroticism as she began to stroke him.

'Jessica!' He choked out her name on a shuddering entreaty, but she calmly finished undressing him and then pushed him to the ground with an authority which was a breathtaking turn-on to watch.

Barely able to breathe for excitement, he watched as she peeled off her dress with a fluid movement and tossed it aside. And now all she was wearing was a frothy concoction of black lace bra and panties with stockings and a suspender belt. His tongue snaked out to moisten a mouth which felt like parchment as she slithered out of the panties and they joined the discarded dress on the floor, and he could see exactly what she was going to do. Exactly. To lower herself down on top of him and to…to…

'*Dio*, Jessica!' he gasped as she straddled him and pleasure surged through him like a high-voltage shock. But that was exactly what it was. She was the sweetest and most teachable lover a man could ever ask for—but usually she bowed to *his* experience and *he* was the one who always took the lead. Yet not this time. Oh, not this time. 'What are you doing?' he gasped.

'Don't you know?' she queried mock-innocently as she moved her hips—and yet she wasn't quite sure herself. All she knew was that he could turn on her with a speed which drove home just how temporary her place in his life really was. So why not give him the kind of treatment he clearly wanted? Why not play the accomplished mistress and leave him with the memory of *this*? She moved again.

'*Donna seducente*!' he moaned.

'What does that mean?'

'Witch!'

'Am I?'

'*Sì*. Ah, *sì*!'

At least the compliment showed that her seduction was working even if it didn't sound like the Jessica she really was—whose heart had been lost to this emotionless Sicilian. It made her sound like a real temptress of a woman, a woman totally comfortable in her own skin who knew how to please her man. But for a moment that was exactly what she felt like—even if the image was simply an illusion, because Salvatore was not *her* man, and he never would be.

She kept her eyes closed as she rode him, not wanting to see his expression for fear of what it would tell her and not daring to let him see what was in hers.

Because he doesn't want your love.

He groaned again as she increased the pace. This was all he wanted, she reminded herself. This, and this, and...

'Jessica!' Her name was wrenched from his lips and she opened her eyes just as the first blissful spasms began to catch hold of her too, and their eyes met in a naked moment of pure pleasure.

'Jessica,' he said again as he shuddered within her, lost in her spell and deep within her body.

Afterwards, she sank down onto his chest as his arms came up to enfold her. And in the aftermath of spent passion it was all too easy to forget what had led to that moment. The bitter words and the recriminations. The realisation of how temporary this all was and her growing recognition of just how badly it was going to hurt once it was over. Jessica screwed her eyes tightly shut to hold the tears at bay. She wanted to hold onto this moment for ever. This man.

'Jessica?'

His voice was sleepy but Jessica didn't underestimate him, not for a minute. He was a master of timing, after all—and the end might come when she was least expecting it. When she was warm and sated in his embrace. Was he going to tell her now? Well, she would be calm and dignified. She'd known what was going to happen when she walked into this—so she could hardly turn round and weep when it did. And yet already she could feel the sharp ache in her heart as she imagined a life without him.

'Yes, Salvatore?'

He caught hold of her hips and deftly turned her onto her back and then rolled on top of her, his blue eyes glittering and hard as they gazed down at her.

'Don't ever lie to me again,' he said softly.

Jessica blinked up at him. She had been mentally preparing herself for the inevitable and now she stared at him, feeling lost and wrong-footed. 'But I thought…' Her voice tailed off in confusion.

'What did you think, *cara mia*? That I would be unable to forgive you?'

The taste of fear felt bitter in her mouth. 'Well, yes.'

He enjoyed her confusion; savoured it. 'On the contrary—I forgive you. Everyone deserves a second chance, my beauty.' Stroking his fingertips over the delicate lace of the bra she had not bothered to remove, he felt her tremble and he gave a hard-edged smile. 'And that was far too good a performance for me not to want to repeat it.'

Performance? 'Is that supposed to be a compliment?' she questioned shakily.

'It's the truth,' he said roughly. 'Now let's go to bed and you can do it all over again.'

CHAPTER FOURTEEN

BUT Jessica soon realised that Salvatore's idea of 'forgiveness' wasn't the same as hers. Not at all. He might have decided it wasn't worth ending their relationship because she'd sold the bracelet and then lied about it—but that didn't make everything magically better between them. How could it? Something had changed—and that something was his attitude towards her.

Before she had felt as though she was getting occasional glimpses at the chinks in his armour. As if he sometimes allowed her to see the living and breathing man beneath the hard exterior—and every time he did it had felt like a little victory. But not any more.

Was it because he no longer trusted her that the shutters had come banging down and now seemed to completely exclude her? That the ease and relaxation she had started to feel in his company had disappeared, to be replaced with an inner ice she could no longer penetrate, nor even dare to. And that while the sex was as good as it had ever been, it was as if he now took a calculated pleasure in demonstrating every skill in his sensual repertoire. Almost as if he wanted to taunt her with it.

Did he mean to make her heart ache? she wondered. During those moments of intimacy, did he intend her to imagine the terrible gap he would leave in her life when he was gone? Because she was getting very good at that.

That carefree weekend in Paris now seemed as if it had happened to another couple. She even found herself longing for those simple days when she'd cleaned his office, when he used to confide in her and ask her advice—sometimes even listen to it. That was *true* intimacy, she thought wistfully. Much more than wearing the fine clothes he bought for her and then having him strip them from her body.

The telephone rang and Jessica jumped as she picked it up, even though she had been waiting for him to ring for the past hour. These days she felt as if her whole life was a waiting game. Some nights he booked ahead with her—especially if it was for some grand dinner, or opera. But others—like tonight—were dependent on Salvatore's mood and how long his meetings ran for.

'Hello,' she said in a strained voice.

'Jessica?'

'Hello, Salvatore.' Pulling herself together, she forced herself to sound interested, to rid herself of the succession of doubts which were spinning around in her head like a washing machine. 'How…how was your meeting?'

'Tedious—I don't really want to talk about it.' He stifled a yawn. 'Can you be ready to go out to dinner in an hour?'

Jessica frowned into the mirror. It would need a small

miracle to get her presentable enough for his exacting eyes in that time. 'But I thought you said you wanted a quiet evening in.'

'Did I? Sorry—change of plan. A friend of mine is unexpectedly in town with his girlfriend and wants to meet up. I thought she'd like a little female company.'

What could she say? That she was delighted to meet his friends? Because it didn't feel like that. It was less of an invitation and more of a command—but Jessica would be there because that was her role. To be available. To be ready whenever her lover snapped his fingers. To mould herself to *his* desires.

'Sure I can,' she said, hating herself for her weakness.

He sent a car to collect her, and when Jessica walked into the restaurant Salvatore was already seated with the guests and rose to his feet to greet her. And, as always, her heart turned over when she saw his dark and imposing figure.

'*Ciao,*' said Salvatore softly as he kissed her on each cheek—the swift, sleek movement of his hand over her hip an indication of what she might expect from him later. 'Meet Giovanni and Maria,' he added. 'This is Jessica.'

'Hello,' said Jessica, wondering what he'd actually told them about her.

Giovanni Amato was a rather daunting and powerful Sicilian and his girlfriend was very sweet, but the three of them kept lapsing into Italian. And even though they switched to English when they realised they were doing it, it only increased Jessica's bubbling feeling of insecurity.

She felt like an alien, an outsider. Staring at the congealing red-wine sauce on her plate, she found herself wondering what the hell she was doing here. At least Giovanni and Maria seemed like a *real* couple, while she felt as disposable as the crumbs from the bread rolls which the waiter was disposing of with a tiny brush.

You're nothing to Salvatore, she thought painfully as she watched his dark and beautiful profile laughing at something Giovanni had just said. Nothing solid or enduring. You're just here to even up the numbers and to satisfy his overwhelming sexual hunger when the evening is over.

And you care for him far more than he will ever care for you.

She said little in the car on the way to his Chelsea home and Salvatore shot her a glance as she stared out at the passing streets. He thought how pensive and pale she looked. And why was that? he wondered. 'You're very quiet tonight, cara,' he observed silkily.

She turned her head. 'Am I?'

He lifted her hand—beautifully manicured and showing none of the roughness of her cleaning days. Was she quiet for a reason? Perhaps it was time to sweeten her up with a gift. Another piece of jewellery, maybe. His mouth hardened. Or maybe he should just give her cash—at least that would save her the trouble of selling it and cut out the middleman!

'You know you are. Maybe you're tired,' he observed, a question in his voice as he lifted her fingertips to his lips, kissing each one in turn.

'Not a bit of it,' said Jessica brightly as she stared into the glittering black coldness of his eyes. Because mistresses weren't supposed to be tired, were they? They had to be pampered and preened and gleaming and sheening and stripped ready for action whenever their lover wanted them to be.

But as the car slid to a powerful halt in front of Salvatore's apartment, Jessica knew that she couldn't carry on with this. Not any more. Her self-respect and her self-worth were being whittled away with every second she remained as his mistress.

It had been wrong from the start and time was only making that more apparent. Maybe the whole diamond bracelet incident had just brought it to a head sooner. And if she didn't get out now, then she was going to suffer unbearable heartbreak. She needed to get out while she still had a choice to recover. She needed to tell him.

But not until the morning. Just one more night of bliss in his arms—surely that wasn't too much to ask for?

Once inside his apartment, she turned to him—suddenly realising just how much she was going to miss him.

'Salvatore,' she whispered, her lips brushing against the hard line of his jaw as she began to unknot his silk tie.

He looked down at her. 'What is it, *tranquilo cara*?'

Knowing that this was to be the last time made her want to reach out to him in a way she knew she never could. So reach out to him in the only way you can. The only way he'll let you. She stared up at him. 'I want…to go to bed.'

'Oh, do you?' He could feel the sudden breathless urgency in her trembling body and, as always, a heady response surged fiercely through his own. 'So do I,' he said unsteadily.

In a way, it was both the best and the worst kind of farewell. It was Salvatore as she would always remember him—at his most tender and passionate throughout the night. But it's just sex, she told herself. And men can do that—particularly men like Salvatore. They can make it seem as though it means something, when it doesn't. Not a thing.

She slept fitfully and, waking early, showered and dressed before collecting her few bits and pieces from the bathroom. Apart from a couple of spare pairs of panties which were stuffed into Salvatore's sock drawer, that was pretty much all she had to show from her time there.

When she came through to the kitchen, Salvatore was also up and dressed, drinking coffee and reading through a sheaf of papers. Automatically, he poured her a cup and pushed it towards her. The smell was tantalising and she gave him a weak smile of thanks. How domesticity could mock you with its false intimacy, she thought, and her heart gave a painful lurch at the thought of what she had to do.

She took the coffee but her fingers were trembling too much for her to dare pick it up and instead she looked up at him, trying not to be affected by the dark, tousled beauty of his face—but it wasn't easy. 'Salvatore, I want to talk to you.'

'Can't it wait?' His fingers flicked over the bundle

of legal documents. 'I have meetings all day and want to read through these first.'

She swallowed, but shook her head. 'No, I'm afraid it can't wait.'

A flicker of impatience crossed his face, but then it was gone. He sighed. 'What is it, Jessica?'

'I just wanted you to know that I'm not…' She ran her tongue over her lips. 'That I shan't be seeing you any more.'

For a moment he thought he might have misheard her, but the uptight expression on her face told him otherwise. He didn't react. 'Go on,' he said softly.

'And I just wanted to say that I've enjoyed—well, if not quite *every* second of being your mistress, then most of it. Definitely.'

Salvatore put his papers down on the breakfast bar. 'And that's it?'

She nodded. 'That's it.'

'Do you want to tell me why?'

It was a measure of the inequality of their relationship that Jessica was almost flattered that he was bothered enough to ask! But she suspected that a man who was so suspicious of feelings and wary of commitment wouldn't really want to know all the nuts and bolts which had brought her to her decision. Would he care if she told him that she felt like an object, that she was in love with him and that she feared her heart would break if she let it just drift on and on until he ended it? No, of course he wouldn't.

Jessica paused. 'I just think our relationship has run its course.'

There was a long, tense silence before his words sliced through it. 'It won't work, you know.' He spoke with silken threat as he met her eyes with a look of pure blue steel. Didn't she realise that *he* was the one who always ended the relationship? That *he* was the one in control?

'What won't?' she whispered.

'If this ridiculous *gesture* of yours is some kind of ultimatum trying to get me to commit to you, Jessica— to get a damned ring on your finger—then I can assure you that you're wasting your time! It's been tried before and it hasn't worked and it won't work this time. I don't bow to pressure—either in the boardroom nor the bedroom; I never have.'

She stared at him in horror. 'It is not a *gesture*, Salvatore!' she returned. 'It's real! And neither is it an ultimatum. It's something I've been thinking about for some time and your reaction is making me question why on earth it took me so long.'

He rose from his seat and approached her with a look on his face that she had never seen there before. Dark and smouldering with anger—with all the slow-burn intensity of a carefully banked fire.

'I shan't change my mind, you know,' he said softly.

'I'm not expecting you to,' she blustered. 'I don't…*want* you to.'

At this he stilled and an odd kind of smile twisted his lips into a cruel and mocking smile. 'Oh, you don't?'

'No.' She should have seen it coming, but she didn't realise what he was going to do until she felt the hard, warm impact of his body. And then she knew he was going to kiss her—and she knew exactly why and it made her shudder. Because this had nothing to do with affection. It was a branding, a stamp—a mark of indelible possession—intended to spoil her for every other man who followed him.

And how bizarre that even while the Jessica who had just finished the affair should dread that kiss—the Jessica who loved him longed for it more than anything else in the world.

His lips were hard and hungry. If sexual excellence could be demonstrated in one brief and utterly arousing display, then Salvatore Cardini should have taken out a patent on that kiss.

It left her reeling and gasping for breath, even after he dropped his hands from her body and turned to walk out of the room. Just by the door he stopped to turn his head and look at her. And suddenly this was not the Salvatore she knew, but the face of a dark and forbidding stranger with icy blue eyes.

'Make sure you clear all your stuff out of here,' he said, with icy precision. 'And leave your key behind when you go.'

Somehow she managed not to react during the time it took him to grab his stuff and to slam the front door behind him. It was after that, of course, that the tears came, without mercy.

CHAPTER FIFTEEN

THE typewritten words danced in a meaningless haze on the page and Salvatore's lips curled.

He should have been a happy man.

Liberated from a relationship which had begun to look tricky. Freed from a low-class little gold-digger who had foolishly overestimated her power over him. The London side of the business was enjoying a record year under his stewardship and his social calendar was as busy as he wished it to be. Yes, he should have been, not merely happy, but *ecstatic*.

So what was it that troubled him? Which made him restless, unable to settle? Which had him remembering those wide grey eyes and pink-petal lips and shiny hair spread all over his pillow? The way her skin felt so soft when he drifted his lips to her neck.

Damn her!

Viciously, he jabbed the nib of his pen into the tail end of a signature and pushed the signed pile of letters towards his secretary, ignoring her perplexed expression. He knew that his mood had been black and that he had been bringing it with him to the office and yet he couldn't quite seem to stop himself—and neither could he pinpoint the exact cause for his discontentment. For a man used to having all the solutions at his fingertips, it was an unwelcome and unusual state of affairs.

Was it because Jessica had been the one who had finished the relationship—was that it? He stared out of the window. Very probably—since he was the one who liked to dominate and control. Maybe it was because such an action had wounded his pride—and to a Sicilian, pride was everything. Salvatore's mouth hardened.

And maybe most of all it was because he still wanted to have sex with her—because the strange, sensual magic she had woven over his body had not yet been exorcised.

So what was he going to do about it?

Leaning back in his chair, he ran a thoughtful thumb over the dark rasp of new growth at his jaw. The answer, it seemed, was ridiculously easy.

Why not get her back into his bed for one night—to remind her just what she'd been missing? He felt the hard curl of lust at his groin. And to remind himself what he'd been missing, too. Salvatore ran his tongue over his lips. To have her sob out her fulfilment once more in his arms as she lay beneath him…wouldn't that help purge her from his system once and for all? Meaning that he could walk away and finally forget all about her?

He lifted the phone and punched out her number, surprised at the wariness he heard in her voice when she answered. His ex-lovers usually gushed like oil wells if he deigned to speak to them, instead of speaking in small, clipped tones like these. Surely she should have sounded a little more *grateful* to hear from him again than that?

Once they had swopped meaningless little pleasantries, she came straight to the point.

'What can I do for you, Salvatore?'

Fractionally, he elevated his brows. Why, for a moment there, she had made it sound almost as if he were disturbing her! 'Remember that trip we'd planned to the opera on the fifteenth?' he purred. 'Well, you were looking forward to it so much that I've decided we should still go.'

In the Shepherd's Bush house, Jessica stared at her paper-pale face in the mirror, trembling with rage as she marvelled at his arrogant assumption. Because concentrating on that was better than allowing herself to focus on how badly she missed him, how much her heart ached just to hear his voice.

'I can't do that,' she said.

'Why not?'

She wanted to ask him if he was insane. Didn't he have any idea of how painful it was to be apart from him—despite the fact that she kept telling herself over and over again that he was an egotistical tyrant? No, of course he didn't. Acknowledging that would require a little insight and tenderness and genuine emotion—and Salvatore didn't do any of *those* things.

'Because it's not appropriate,' she said slowly. 'Since we are no longer a couple.'

For a moment he thought that she must be playing games, teasing him by putting on a show of reluctance before agreeing to go with him—since they both knew that was what she wanted. But nothing but silence followed her remark.

'You *are* joking?'

'No, Salvatore, I'm not.'

He found himself in the unheard of position of trying to *persuade* a woman to go out with him! 'But it's a world-famous production of one of the most moving operas of all time.'

'Nobody's denying that.'

'And you were desperate to see it.'

Not *that* desperate. 'I'm sure you can find someone else to go with you,' she said.

'And you'd be happy with that?' he demanded. 'Me taking another woman?'

'My feelings on your choice of date are irrelevant.'

'Well, I suggest you think about it,' he said silkily. 'And then let me know.'

But to Salvatore's astonishment—she didn't! There was no phone-call or text. No email or unannounced visit—telling him that she had been a little too hasty and that of course she would love to accompany him to the opera.

Undaunted—indeed, a little fired up by the unexpected chase—Salvatore ordered a gown to be sent to her home, along with a diamond necklace, which was bound to tempt her. Then he sat back and waited for her phone-call.

It wasn't what he had been expecting. Why, she sounded almost *angry*.

'Salvatore—why have you sent these gifts?'

'You don't like them?'

Jessica stared down at the scarlet dress. It was the colour of a poppy, made from the softest silk imaginable and so utterly exquisite that she did not dare try it. The diamond necklace was even more dazzling—pear-shaped drops of rainbow ice dangled in a brilliant loop, falling through her fingers in a glittering stream of light. She swallowed. Did he think she could be bought by such ostentatious presents? 'Why?' she repeated.

Oh, but she was playing with fire. She knew *exactly* why he had sent them. 'They are a sweetener, *cara*,' he purred. 'Wear them to the opera. You'll look wonderful wearing them.'

Of course she wanted to wear them—but she liked them because *he* had sent them and not because of what they were worth. Just as she longed to see *him* and not the wretched opera. But she did not dare—how could she risk her emotional security by putting herself back in a vulnerable situation with a man who didn't love her?

Praying for courage, Jessica closed her fingers over the gems, blocking out their brilliance. 'Let me say it again, Salvatore—I'm not coming to the opera with you.'

Furiously, Salvatore drummed his fingers against one tensed thigh. 'What does it take to persuade you, Jessica?' he demanded. 'You want emeralds? Or a rock the size of Gibraltar?'

He still didn't get it, did he? 'I cannot be *bought*!' she stormed. 'I am *not* for sale!'

It was the first time a woman had ever hung up on

him and Salvatore found himself staring at the disconnected phone with an air of mystification. She had slammed the phone down on him!

He went to his club and swam before having dinner with a wealthy sheikh, but all the time his mind kept drifting back to Jessica and the fiery determination he had heard in her voice.

Did she mean what she said? It seemed that perhaps she did.

Bizarrely, he found time suddenly empty on his hands with nothing but troubled thoughts to fill it. He found himself remembering that weekend in Paris—before he'd discovered that she'd sold the bracelet. It had been about as perfect a weekend as he could have imagined—and yet he remembered, too, the near-joy with which he had leapt on her deception. He had *wanted* to think badly of her.

But she'd sold the jewels to care for her grandmother, hadn't she? He knew that. So did that make her a bad person, or a caring person?

He frowned. And there was something else, too—something which nudged at the edges of his memory.

On the advice of his secretary, he spent the afternoon in Camden market—a busy, hippy sort of place, not his usual kind of destination at all. And he wasn't really sure what he was looking for until he found it.

Later that evening, he knocked on the door of Jessica's house in Shepherd's Bush and the tall girl who was named after the tree opened the door to him, her eyes opening wide in surprise when she saw him, her hand going up immediately to smooth down her tousled blonde hair.

'Oh, hello!'

'I'm looking for Jessica,' he said.

Her face fell. 'I'll go and tell her.'

He could hear the sound of muffled voices and his mouth twisted. If Jessica thought that she was going to get away with not seeing him, then she was wrong. He would kick the damned door down first. And then suddenly she was standing in front of him, looking small—almost frail—in a pair of old, faded jeans and an equally faded sweater.

'Hello, Salvatore,' she said quietly. 'What…what do you want?'

Her face was pale, her grey eyes huge and she was staring up at him with a solemn expression on her face. It was the least welcoming look he could have imagined and Salvatore's eyes narrowed.

'May I come in?'

She wanted to say no, to slam the door in his face. And yet she wanted to gather him in and pull him close against the body which had yearned for him since the last time she had held him.

But her face registered none of this. 'Of course,' she said politely.

He was ushered into the same rather drab sitting room he remembered from a previous visit and Jessica stood looking at him expectantly.

'What can I do for you, Salvatore?'

He recognised that there was to be no warm and

unquestioning welcome and that too surprised him. And apologies didn't come easy to a man who had rarely had to make them. 'I realise that I have offended you,' he began.

She wondered which particular incident he had in mind, but she said nothing.

'That sending you the diamonds and the dress was a rather inelegant gesture.' He gave a short laugh. 'Even though you are probably the only woman in the world who would think so.' Awkwardly, he pulled a slim box from his pocket and handed it to her. 'So I want you to have this instead.'

She stood there, just staring at it. *Still* he didn't get it, did he? 'I don't want it.'

'Take it. Please.'

Something in the way he asked her made it impossible for her to refuse. Reluctantly, Jessica took the box from him and snapped open the lid. Yet it was not the glitter of priceless jewels which greeted her—but an oval moonstone which lay at the centre of a simple silver chain. It was milky-grey—with a kind of inner radiance—the colour of a river. It stirred a memory, but more than that—it stirred her heart.

Stupidly, she felt a lump rise to her throat, the salty flicker of tears at the backs of her eyes, but she blinked them away because it didn't *mean* anything. It was just another offering—another object—a currency with which Salvatore was attempting to buy her.

'I remember you said you liked moonstones,' said Salvatore, and in that moment he felt like the insecure teenager he had never had to be. 'That they reminded you of the Seine.'

For a moment she couldn't speak as she stared down at them. Just nodded. 'Yes. They…they do.' She looked up at him. 'But why have you bought it?'

Salvatore's features hardened. Surely she knew that! 'Because I want to end this stand-off,' he growled. 'I want you back in my life.'

Jessica studied the face which she loved in spite of everything. The beginning of a smile had begun to curve his beautiful lips—because Salvatore would not have considered for a moment that her answer might be anything other than the one he wanted to hear.

And, oh, how easy it would be to have just said yes. To have fallen into his arms with the foolish hopes which her stupid heart couldn't quite keep at bay. But what was the point? She would only be opening up the floodgates to more pain and more heartache. Let their affair stay exactly how it was—slowly dying and fading away to become nothing more than a bittersweet memory.

She shook her head. 'I can't,' she whispered. 'I just can't.'

He seized on the word, ready to do battle with it. 'Can't?'

'I'm not prepared to carry on being your mistress, Salvatore. I just can't do it any more.'

He stared at her. 'Why not?'

Did he want her to spell it out in order to try to win her round with words, or kisses? Or because he simply didn't understand? And maybe he didn't. Maybe

Salvatore had spent his whole life with women giving him exactly what *he* wanted—so that it simply might not have occurred to him that women had needs, too.

'Because the affair has run its course,' she managed. 'It's past its sell-by date. It no longer feels like fun. It feels grubby. Temporary. And I'm not prepared to carry on being your mistress any more.' Painfully, she shrugged her shoulders. 'I've outgrown my role in your life, Salvatore—and you need to find a replacement.'

But as he looked at her bright eyes and trembling lips, something was happening to him—a sudden over-whelming feeling which crystallised into a bone-sure certainty that he didn't *want* a replacement. And that here was a woman who made his heart and his blood sing. Who was making him fight for her. A woman worth fighting for. So fight, Cardini. *Fight!*

'But nobody can replace you, Jessica,' he said urgently. 'No other woman makes me feel the way you do. You feel so right in my life—you always did—and nothing seems the same without you.' He could see her petalled lips begin to open—maybe to mouth her objec-tions—and he shook his head. 'I know you don't want to be my mistress any more—but I don't want you to be. I realise that you do not care for the things my money can buy—that I have gone about this like a fool. A novice.' Now he shrugged, holding the palms of his hands open in a gesture which was almost helpless. 'But then I *am* a novice,' he breathed. 'You see, I have never been in love before, Jessica. My heart is full of love, *cara mia*—and I want you to marry me. That is—'

and his blue eyes glittered with a touch of his familiar arrogance '—if you love me, too.'

There was a breathless pause. 'You know I do,' she whispered.

Their eyes met in a long moment as he held his arms out. 'Ah, Jessica,' he said tenderly. 'Come to me.'

Jessica thought she must be crying, but things were such a blur because she seemed to be laughing, too—with disbelief and joy and wonder—as she went to him like a homing pigeon.

And he gathered her close against his body, stroking the silk of her hair. 'Believe that I love you,' he whispered, just before he kissed her. 'And now let me show you just how much.'

EPILOGUE

'AND your grandmother is happy, I think?'

Beneath the warmth of the Sicilian sun, Jessica smiled at Salvatore as they stood watching the family party, which showed no signs of finishing. It was his nephew Gino's third birthday and the noise levels had been steadily increasing all afternoon, but soon the cake would be cut and then things might start to calm down!

All the different generations of Cardinis were playing some complicated Sicilian version of the game 'catch' and her grandmother seemed to have a natural aptitude for the game, which was making her opponents crow with disbelief.

Jessica wrapped her arms around Salvatore's waist, her heart so full of happiness that she felt it might burst. 'Oh, *caro*—she just loves it. Yet I never thought she'd leave England!'

Salvatore's mouth curved. 'For Sicily? And who in their right mind would turn down an opportunity to live in a place such as this?'

Who indeed? How perfect life had become—so

perfect that sometimes Jessica felt as if she would soon wake up. But this was no dream; this was her reality.

Salvatore had made her his wife in a simple service in a beautiful church in Trapani. The choir's voices had soared in that cool and sacred place, filled with the fragrance of the same white flowers which had been wreathed in abundance around her veil.

When he'd first asked her to marry him and move to his homeland, Jessica had told him that she felt bad about leaving her grandmother in England. 'I mean, I know Sicily's only a plane journey away, but even so I'm the only family she's got, and—'

'But your grandmother will come with us,' he had said, as if no other possibility would ever be entertained. 'In Sicily, family is everything—and every member has their valued place in it.'

Especially wives, it seemed, thought Jessica—still glowing from the passion and the tenderness with which he had woken her this morning. For a man who had fought shy of expressing love, Salvatore certainly seemed to be making up for it!

The Cardini complex was enormous—and the family owned properties on all sides of the island. There was room enough for everyone to mingle without overlapping too much. Because space was important, too. And her grandmother had already formed a deep and close bond with young Gino, which was probably a good thing, as his English mother Emma had confided to Jessica—since she was expecting a second baby.

Salvatore had dissuaded his hot-headed cousin

Giacomo from buying the Phuket hotel and had instead offered him the job of replacing him as chairman in London, since he had decided to relocate to Sicily with his new bride.

And Jessica was learning Italian—or rather, she was learning to speak Sicilian since, as everyone told her rather sternly, the two were really very different.

In fact, on this earthly paradise with Salvatore by her side, she was learning so much about everything that was important. But mostly about love.

BOUGHT:
THE GREEK'S BABY

JENNIE LUCAS

Jennie Lucas grew up dreaming about faraway lands. At fifteen, hungry for experience beyond the borders of her small Idaho city, she went to a Connecticut boarding school on scholarship. She took her first solo trip to Europe at sixteen, then put off college and travelled around the USA, supporting herself with jobs as diverse as petrol station cashier and newspaper advertising assistant.

At twenty-two, she met the man who would be her husband. After their marriage, she graduated from Kent State with a degree in English. Seven years after she started writing, she got the magical call from London that turned her into a published author.

Since then life has been hectic, with a new writing career, a sexy husband and two babies under two, but she's having a wonderful (albeit sleepless) time. She loves immersing herself in dramatic, glamorous, passionate stories. Maybe she can't physically travel to Morocco or Spain right now, but for a few hours a day, while her children are sleeping, she can be there in her books.

Jennie loves to hear from her readers. You can visit her website at www.jennielucas.com, or drop her a note at jennie@jennielucas.com.

To Patty Sowell,
the miracle of our house, with gratitude.

CHAPTER ONE

TALOS XENAKIS had heard a lot of lies in his life, particularly in relation to his beautiful, ruthless ex-mistress. But this one topped them all.

"It can't be true," he said in shock, staring at the doctor. "She's lying."

"I assure you, Mr. Xenakis, it's true," Dr. Bartlett replied gravely. "She has no memory. Not of you, not of me, not even of her accident yesterday. And yet there's no physical injury."

"Because she's lying!"

"She was wearing a seat belt when her head hit the air bag," Dr. Bartlett continued. "There was no concussion."

Talos stared at him with a scowl. He had a reputation as a doctor of immense skill and integrity. He was rich from a lifetime of serving wealthy, aristocratic patients—so he couldn't be bought. He was known as a family man, still completely in love with his wife of fifty years, an adored father of three and grandfather of eight—so he couldn't be seduced. So he honestly must believe Eve Craig had amnesia.

Amnesia.

Talos's lip curled. After all of her devilish cleverness, he would have expected more of her.

Eleven weeks ago, after stabbing him in the back, Eve Craig had vanished from Athens like a ghost. His men had searched for her all over the world without success until two days ago, when she'd suddenly resurfaced in London for her stepfather's funeral.

Talos had dropped a billion-dollar deal in Sydney, ordering his men to trail her until he could reach London on his private jet. Kefalas and Leonidas had been right behind Eve yesterday afternoon when she'd left the private hospital in Harley Street. They'd watched her tuck her long, glossy dark hair beneath a silk scarf, put on big black sunglasses and white driving gloves and drive away in her silver Aston Martin convertible.

Right into a red postbox on the sidewalk.

"It was so strange, boss," Kefalas had told him that morning when he'd arrived from Sydney. "She seemed fine at the funeral. But leaving the doctor's office she drove like a drunk. She didn't even recognize us when we helped her back into the hospital after the accident."

Now, Dr. Bartlett looked equally puzzled as he scratched the back of his wispy white head. "I held her overnight for observation, but cannot find anything physically wrong with her."

Talos ground his teeth. "Because she doesn't have amnesia. She's playing you for a fool!"

The elderly doctor stiffened. "I do not believe Miss Craig is lying, Mr. Xenakis. I have known her since she was fourteen, when she first came here with her mother from America." He shook his head as he mused, "All the tests came back negative. The only symptom seems to be the amnesia. Leading me to perhaps wonder if the accident was merely the catalyst—the trauma was an emotional one."

"You mean she brought it on herself?"

"I wouldn't say that exactly. But this is outside my field. It's why I've recommended a colleague, Dr. Green."

"A psychiatrist."

"Yes."

Talos latched on to the one valuable bit of information. "So if there's nothing physically wrong with her, she can leave the hospital."

The doctor hesitated. "She's certainly strong enough. But as she has no memory, perhaps it would be better if a member of her family…"

"She has no family," Talos interrupted. "Her stepfather was her only relative, and he died three days ago."

"I did hear about Mr. Craig, and was very sorry. But I hoped perhaps Eve might have an aunt or uncle, or even a cousin in Boston…"

"She does not," Talos said evenly, although he had no idea. He only knew nothing was going to keep him from taking Eve away with him today. "I am her…" *What? Ex-lover bent on revenge?* "Boyfriend," he finished smoothly. "I will take care of her."

"So your men told me yesterday, when they said you were on your way." Dr. Bartlett eyed him as if he did not quite like what he saw. "But it does not sound as if you even believe she needs special care."

"If you say she has amnesia, I have no choice but to believe it."

"You called her a liar."

Talos gave a crooked grin. "Creative untruths are part of her charm."

"So you are close?" The doctor looked up at him with narrowed eyes. "Do you plan to marry her?"

Talos knew the answer the man wanted—the only answer that would release Eve into his power. And so he told the truth. "She is everything to me. Everything."

Scrutinizing Talos's expression, the doctor stroked his beard with something like satisfaction, then nodded in a sudden brisk decision. "Very well. I'll release her into your care, Mr. Xenakis. Take good care of her. Take her home."

Take her to Mithridos? Talos would die before he would pollute his home that way. But Athens…yes. He'd lock her up and make her thoroughly regret betraying him. "You will release her to me today?"

The doctor nodded. "Yes. Make her feel loved," he warned. "Make her feel wanted and secure."

"Loved and secure," he repeated, barely able to keep the sneer from his face.

Dr. Bartlett frowned. "Surely, Mr. Xenakis, you can appreciate what these last twenty-four hours have meant to Eve. She's had nothing to cling to. No memory of family or friends to sustain her. No sense of home or memory of belonging. She didn't even know her name until I told her."

"Don't worry," Talos said grimly. "I'll take good care of her."

But as he started to turn away, the doctor stopped him. "There is something else you should know."

"What?"

"Normally I would never disclose this information. But in this unique case, I feel the need for informed care far exceeds the concern for privacy...."

With a muttered curse in Greek, Talos tapped his foot impatiently. "What is it?"

"Eve is pregnant."

At that word, Talos's head shot up. His heart literally stopped in his chest.

"Pregnant?" he choked. "When?"

"When I did the ultrasound yesterday, I estimated conception in mid-June."

June.

For nearly all of that month Talos had barely left her side. He'd kept tabs on his business almost unwillingly, begrudging every moment of his life that wasn't spent in bed with her. Their affair had burned him through, blood and bone. He'd thought—God help him—that he could trust her. Because lust had seized his mind and will.

"I feel I'm at fault," Dr. Bartlett continued regretfully. "If I'd had any idea how upset she was at the news of her pregnancy, I would never have let her drive away from the hospital. But don't worry," he added hastily, "your baby is fine."

His baby.

Talos stared at him, hardly able to breathe.

The doctor suddenly gave a hearty, cheerful laugh, patting him on the back. "Congratulations, Mr. Xenakis. You're going to be a father."

Around her, Eve was dimly aware of a whisper of voices and the distant hum of a radiator. She felt someone—the nurse?—sweep a cool cloth against her forehead. The soft sheets against her skin felt heavy. She smelled the fresh scent of rain and cotton. But she stubbornly kept her eyes closed.

She didn't want to wake up. She didn't want to leave the dark peacefulness of sleep, the warmth of barely remembered dreams that still cradled her like an embrace.

She didn't want to return to the nothingness of existence, where she had no memories. No identity. Nothing to cling to. It was an emptiness far worse than any pain.

And then the doctor had told her three hours ago that she was pregnant.

She couldn't remember conceiving the child. Couldn't even remember the face of her baby's father. But she would meet him today. He would be here any minute.

Covering her head with her pillow, she squeezed her eyes shut. She was racked with nervousness and fear at the thought of meeting him for the first time—the father of her unborn baby!

What kind of man would he be?

She heard the door open and close. She held her breath. Then someone sat heavily next to her, causing her body to lean toward him on the mattress. Strong arms suddenly were around her. She felt the warmth of a man's body, breathed in the woodsy musk of his cologne.

"Eve, I'm here." The man's voice was deep and low, with an exotic accent she couldn't place. "I've come for you."

A thrill rushed through her. With an intake of breath, she pushed aside the pillow.

He was so close to her. She saw the sharpness of his cheekbones first. The dark scruff on his hard jaw. The tawny color of his olive skin. Then, as he drew back, she saw his whole face.

He was, quite simply, breathtaking.

How was it possible for a man to be at once so masculine—and so beautiful? His black hair brushed the top of his ears. He had the face of an angel. Of a warrior. His Roman nose had been broken at least once, from the tiny imperfection of the angle. He had a full, sensual mouth, with a twist of his lips that revealed arrogance and perhaps more—cruelty?

His eyes gleamed down at her, dark as night. And beneath their black depths, for a moment she saw a ravaging fire of hatred—as if he wished she were dead, as if she were a ghost he'd long ago consigned to hell.

Then she blinked, and he was smiling down at her with tender concern.

She must have imagined that fiery hatred, she thought in bewilderment. Not surprising considering how screwy her head had been since the accident—an accident she couldn't even remember!

"Eve," he whispered as he stroked her cheek. "I thought I'd never find you."

The touch of his rough fingers against her skin burned her. She felt a sizzle down her neck to her breasts, making her nipples taut and her belly spiral in a strange tightness. With an intake of breath, she searched his face, hardly able to believe the evidence of her own eyes.

This—this man was her lover? He looked nothing like she'd expected.

When Dr. Bartlett had told her that her boyfriend was on his way from Australia, she'd imagined a kind-looking man with a loving heart, a sense of humor. A gentle man who would share his troubles while they washed dishes together at the end of the day. She'd dreamed of a loving partner. An equal.

Never in her wildest dreams had she ever imagined a dark god like this, cruelly beautiful, masculine and so powerful that he could no doubt slice her heart in two with a look.

"Aren't you glad to see me?" he said in a low voice.

She searched his face, holding her breath.

But no memories rushed through her, no recollections of the hard curve of his cheek or the slightly wicked twist to his sensual lips. No memories of a thousand little intimacies between lovers. Nothing!

He helped her sit up. His hands lingered possessively on her back, causing a sudden heat across her body.

Eve licked her lips nervously.

"You are…you must be…Talos Xenakis?" she ventured, waiting for him to deny it. Almost hoping he would, and that her real boyfriend, the kind-faced man with the gentle eyes, would walk through the door.

The Greek tycoon's hands on her back paused.

"So you do recognize me."

She shook her head. "No. Your two employees…the doctor…they told me your name. They said you were on your way."

He looked down at her, searching her face.

"Dr. Bartlett told me you had amnesia. I didn't believe it. But it's true, isn't it? You really don't remember me."

She could only imagine how that must hurt him! "I'm sorry," she said, rubbing her forehead. "I keep trying, but the first thing I can remember is your employee—Kefalas?—pulling me from my car. It was a lucky thing they were in the car behind me!"

His lips seemed to curve imperceptibly. "Yes. Very lucky." He sat up straight. "You will be leaving the hospital today."

She took a deep breath. "Today?"

"Right now."

"But…" She bit her lip then blurted out, "But I still can't remember anything! I hoped when I saw you…"

"You hoped seeing me would bring your memory back?"

She nodded miserably. There was no point in feeling disappointed, she told herself fiercely, or making him feel more badly about it than he must already!

But she couldn't stop the lump in her throat. She'd been counting on the idea that when she saw the face of the man she loved, the man who loved her, her amnesia would end.

Unless they didn't love each other, she thought suddenly. Unless she'd gotten pregnant by a man who was barely more than a one-night stand.

"I'm sure you must feel so hurt," she said, trying to push away her sudden fear. She said haltingly, "I can only imagine how it must feel, to love someone who can't remember you."

Do you love me? she thought desperately, trying to read his face. *Do I love you?*

"Shhh. It's all right." Lowering his head, he kissed her tenderly on the forehead. The warmth of his nearness was like the summer sun on a winter's day. Then he lifted her chin, and his dark eyes whipped through her like a blast of heat. "Don't worry, Eve. In time, you will remember—everything."

Looking into his face gratefully, Eve realized that her first impression of him had been utterly wrong. He wasn't cruel. He was kind. How else to explain the fact that he could be so gentle and patient and loving, pushing aside his own hurt to focus only on her?

She took a deep breath. She would be as brave as he was. Pushing the blankets aside, she said over the lump in her throat, "I'll get dressed to go."

He stopped her. "Wait. There's something else we need to talk about."

She knew instantly what he meant to discuss. And without the barrier of blankets between them, in just her paper-thin hospital gown, she felt painfully bare, vulnerable in every way. She yanked the blankets back over her body, tugging them halfway to her neck.

"He told you, didn't he?" she whispered.

His voice was low, almost grim. "Yes."

"Are you happy?" Her voice trembled. "About the news?"

She held her breath as his darkly handsome face stared down at her. When he finally spoke, his voice was charged with some emotion she didn't recognize.

"I was surprised."

She searched his gaze. "So the baby wasn't something we planned?"

His hands tightened, twisting the blanket in his grip. He glanced down at it, then looked at her.

"I've never seen you like this," he said in a low voice. His black gaze hungrily caressed her face. With his fingertips, he brushed some dark tendrils from her cheek. "No makeup. Bare."

She tried to pull away. "I'm sure I look terrible."

But he drew her closer. His eyes were dark as he looked down at her, making her shiver from deep within.

"Are you happy about the baby?" she said softly.

He put his arms around her. "I'm going to take good care of you."

Why wouldn't he answer? She swallowed, then lifted

her head to give him a weak smile. "Don't worry, I'm not an invalid. I hope the amnesia will disappear in a day or two. Dr. Bartlett said something about a specialist—"

His arms tightened around her, cradling her against his hard chest.

"You don't need another doctor," he said roughly. "You just need to come home with me."

She could feel the beat of his heart against her cheek through his black button-down shirt. She was enveloped in his masculine scent, sandalwood and amber, exotic and woodsy. Against her will, she closed her eyes. She breathed in his smell, heard the beat of his heart, felt his warmth.

Everything else faded. The private hospital room, the nurses and doctor visible through the window of the door, the sound of one of Talos's men speaking urgently into his cell phone in some language she didn't recognize, the antiseptic smell, the beeps of the machines…it all faded.

There was only this.

Only him.

Held securely in his strong arms, for the first time since her accident she felt safe and loved. She felt as if she had a place in the world. With him.

He kissed her hair softly. She felt the warmth of his breath, the hot caress of his lips, and a tremble went over her. Fear? Longing?

Did he love her?

She reached upward, cupping his rough jawline with her hands. Though his clothes were sharply pressed, the dark shadow on his chin suggested he'd changed clothes on the plane without bothering to shave. He'd rushed here from Australia. He'd flown all night.

Did that mean love?

"Why didn't you come to London with me for my stepfather's funeral?" she said slowly.

He paused. When he spoke, he seemed to choose his words with care.

"I was busy in Sydney acquiring a new company. Believe me," he said, "I never wanted to be away from you for this long."

Eve felt there was something he wasn't telling her. Or was that just her own confusion playing tricks on her? She couldn't trust anything in this hazy, empty world, not even her own mind! "But why—"

"You are so beautiful, Eve," he said, cupping her face. He exhaled in a rush. "I almost feared I'd never see your face again."

"When you heard about the accident, you mean? You were worried about me?" she said in a small voice. When he didn't answer, she licked her lips. With a deep breath, she asked the question that had been burning through her. "Because we love each other?"

His jaw clenched as he took a deep breath.

"You were a virgin when I seduced you, Eve," he said in a low voice. "You'd never been with any man before I took you to my bed three months ago."

She'd been a virgin?

A wave of relief washed over her. Learning she was pregnant by a boyfriend she couldn't remember had been a tremendous shock. She'd wondered why they weren't married—wondered all sorts of things. But if Talos had been her one and only lover, if she'd been a virgin at twenty-five, surely that said something about her character?

But did it also mean love?

She looked up into his handsome face, opening her mouth to ask again, *Do I love you? Do you love me?*

Then she stopped.

There was something beneath his darkly penetrating eyes. Something he wasn't saying. Something hidden beneath his words.

But before she could understand what her intuition was telling her, Talos placed his broad hands over hers. The warmth of his fingers burned her, intertwined with her own. Trapping her, but not against her will. Her heart pounded faster.

"Get ready to leave." He lowered his head to kiss her on the temple, running his hands up and down her bare forearms. "I want to take you home."

Her breathing became short and shallow as he touched her skin. Little prickles of sensation sped up her arms, down her back, making her hair stand on end. The tingle swirled across her earlobes, down her neck, making her naked breasts beneath her thin hospital gown suddenly feel tight and full. She tried to remember the question she'd been asking, but it had already swept from her mind.

"All right," she breathed, looking up into his handsome face.

Gallantly, he helped her from the bed, lifting her gently to her feet. She was more aware than ever of how much taller he was, how much more powerful. He was at least six inches taller, with an extra hundred pounds of pure muscle. Looking up at him, she forgot everything but her own longing and fascinated desire for the man towering over her like a dark angel.

"I'm sorry it took so long for me to reach you, Eve," he said in a low voice. "But I'm here now." He kissed her head softly, his arms tightening around her as he pulled her into an embrace. "And I'm never going to let you go."

CHAPTER TWO

BENEATH heavily lidded eyes, Talos watched Eve as he led her to the black Rolls-Royce purring on the street in front of the hospital.

She wasn't faking her amnesia. In spite of his initial incredulity, he now had no doubt. She had no idea of who he was or what she'd done.

And now she was pregnant with his child.

That changed everything.

He gently helped her to the car. She had no luggage. One of his men had taken her smashed Aston-Martin to the garage, while the other had gone to make quiet amends for the smashed postbox. She wore the black silk dress and carried the black clutch purse from her stepfather's funeral yesterday.

The black dress clung to her breasts and hips when she walked, the silk shimmering and sliding against her hips and breasts. Her dark, glossy hair had been brushed into a fresh ponytail.

She wore no makeup. It made her look different. Talos had never known her to go out without lipstick before—although God knew, with her lustrous skin, full pink lips and sparkling blue eyes, she didn't need it to cause every man she met, from the elderly hospital porter to the teenaged boy walking past them on the sidewalk, to stop and catch his breath.

And as she turned back to face him on the sidewalk with a sweetly innocent smile, Talos was grimly aware that he was far from immune to her charm.

"Where are we going?" she asked, crinkling her forehead. "You never said."

"Home," he replied, guiding her into the backseat of the limousine. He closed the door behind her.

His body's reaction to her was irritating—and troubling. He didn't like it. Because he hated her.

When he'd first seen Eve in the hospital, she'd been curled up on the single bed beneath a thick blanket. She'd looked pale and wan, nothing like the vivacious, tempestuous vixen he remembered. Sleeping, she'd looked innocent, far younger than her twenty-five years.

She'd looked small. Fragile.

Talos had come to London specifically to destroy her. For the last three months, he'd been dreaming of it.

But how could he take his revenge if she not only had no memory of her crimes, but she was pregnant with his baby?

Tightening his hands into fists, he stalked to the other side of the car. Though it was only September, summer had abruptly fled London. A steady drizzle was falling from low gray clouds.

He climbed in beside her and she turned to him without missing a beat. "Where is our home?"

"My home—" he closed his door with a bang "—is Athens."

She gaped at him. "Athens?"

"It's where I live, and I must take care of you." He gave her a brief, tight smile. "Doctor's orders."

"So I live there with you?"

"No."

"We don't live together?"

"You like to travel," he said ironically.

"So where are my clothes?" she said in a small voice. "And my passport?"

"Likely at your stepfather's estate. My staff will collect your things and meet us at the airport."

"But…" She looked out the window, then turned back to face him and said in a rush, lifting her chin, "I want to see my home. My childhood home. Where is it?"

He gave her an assessing glance. "Your stepfather's estate is in Buckinghamshire, I believe. But visiting there won't help you. You spent one night there before the funeral. It hasn't been your home for a long time."

"Please, Talos." Her sapphire eyes gleamed. "I want to see my home."

His brow furrowed as he looked down at her pleading face.

Eve really had changed, he thought. His mistress had never begged him for anything. She'd never even said *please*.

Except…

Except for the first night he'd taken her to his bed, when all her defenses had been briefly stripped away and he'd discovered the most desired woman in the world was, against all expectations, a virgin. As he'd pushed himself inside her, she'd looked up at him in a breathless hush with those violet-blue eyes, and he'd thought…he'd almost thought…

He cut off the memory savagely.

He wouldn't think about how it had once been with her. He wouldn't think how she had nearly made him lose everything, including his mind.

Eve Craig was a fatal habit that he'd finally broken— and he intended to keep it that way.

"Very well," he ground out, turning back to face her. "I will take you home—but just to collect your things. We cannot stay."

Her lovely face brightened. She looked so young without makeup, with her hair in the casual ponytail. She looked barely old enough to be in college, far younger than his own thirty-eight years.

"Thank you," she said warmly.

Thank you. Another phrase he'd never heard from her before.

He turned away, leaning back in the beige leather seat as his chauffeur drove smoothly through the city, turning right from Marylebone to the Edgware Road. As the car merged onto the M1 heading north, Talos stared out at the passing rain, then closed his eyes, tense and weary from jet lag and the whiplash of the past two days.

Eve, pregnant.

He was still reeling.

No wonder she'd crashed her car, he thought dully. Just the thought of losing her figure and not fitting into all her designer clothes must have made her crazy. All those months of not being able to drink champagne and dance till dawn with all of her rich, beautiful, shallow friends? Eve must have been more than shocked—she must have been furious.

Eve, pregnant.

He would not trust her to take care of a house plant, much less a child. She was not even slightly maternal. She wouldn't love a baby. She was the least loving person Talos had ever met.

Slowly, he opened his eyes.

He hadn't even known about the baby an hour ago, but now he was absolutely sure of one thing.

He had to protect his child.

"So I don't live in England," he heard her say. Steeling his expression, he turned to face her. Her face looked bewildered, almost sad as she added hesitantly, "I don't have a home?"

Home. Against his will, he had the sudden image of Eve in his bedroom at Mithridos, spread across his large bed, with the curtains twisting from the sea breeze coming off the sparkling Aegean. That had never happened, and it never would!

"You live in hotels," he answered coldly. "I told you. You travel constantly."

"So how do I hold down a job?" she said in disbelief.

"You don't. You spend your days shopping and attending parties around the world. You're an heiress. A famous beauty."

She gaped at him. "You're joking."

"No." He left it at that. He could hardly explain how she and her dissolute friends traveled in packs like parasites, sucking a luxury hotel dry before moving on to the next. If he told her that, she might hear the scorn in his voice and question the true nature of his feelings.

Malakas, how was it possible that he'd been so caught by her? What madness had possessed him to be so enslaved?

How could he make sure that his child never was neglected, hurt or abandoned by her after she regained her memory?

A new thought suddenly occurred to him.

If she could not remember him, if she could not remember who she was or what she'd done, it meant she would have no idea of what was about to hit her. She would have no defenses.

A slow smile curved his lips as he built his new plan. He could take everything from her, including their baby. And she would never see it coming.

"So I was here for my stepfather's funeral," she said softly. "But I'm not British."

"Your mother was, I believe. You both returned to England some years ago."

She brightened. "My mother!"

"Dead," he informed her brutally.

She froze, her face crumpling. Watching the swift movement of scenery on the outskirts of London through the window behind her, he remembered that her mother's death was fresh news to her. And that he was supposed to be in love with her. He had to make her believe that if he wanted his plan to succeed.

"I'm sorry, Eve," he said abruptly. "But as far as I know, you have no family."

"Oh," she said in a small voice.

Pulling her into his arms, he held her close against his chest, kissing the top of her head. Her hair, messy and unwashed, still managed to smell like vanilla and sugar, the scents he associated with her. The scent that immediately made his body go hard and taut with longing, with the immediate temptation of a long-desired vice.

Thee mou. Why couldn't he stop wanting her? After everything she'd done, the way she'd nearly ruined him, how was it possible that his body still longed for her like a dying man thirsting for water? Was he really such a suicidal fool? Did he have no honor, no pride?

He had pride, he thought, clenching his jaw. It was *her.* Even now, acting so sweetly demure, her innocence attracted him like a flame. He remembered the fire of passion inside her. And how he was the only man who'd ever tasted it.

He felt himself tighten.

Stop! he ordered himself. He wouldn't think about

her in bed. He wouldn't want her. He did have some control over his own body, damn it!

She clenched her fingers against his sleeve, her face pressed into his crisply tailored shirt.

"So I have no one." Her voice was small, almost a whisper. "No parents. No brothers or sisters. No one."

He looked down at her, tipping her chin upwards so he could see the tears sparkling in her beautiful violet-blue eyes. "You have me."

She swallowed, searching his face as if trying to read the emotion behind his expression. He schooled his features into concern and admiration and the closest attempt at love he could manage, never having actually felt it.

A sigh came from her lips as she exhaled. A soft smile traced her lips. "And our baby."

He gave a single grim nod. Their baby was the reason he had to make sure his control over Eve was absolute. The reason he had to make her believe he cared about her.

It was no different, he thought sardonically, than she'd once done to him. He would lull her into believing she could trust him. Make her willingly marry him.

Then—oh, then…

The instant their marriage was final, his life's goal would be to make her remember the truth. He would be with her when she finally remembered. He would see her face as it fell.

And he would crush her. The thought of revenge made his heart glad.

Not revenge, he told himself. *Justice.*

Leaning forward, he held her closer in the backseat of the Rolls-Royce.

"Eve." He cupped her face in his large hands. "I want you to marry me."

Marry him?

Yes, Eve thought in a daze, looking up into his handsome face. Feeling his strong, rough hands against the softness of her skin, the warmth of his touch seared her, tracing down her neck to her breasts and lower still.

How could any man be so masculine, so beautiful, so powerful all at once? Talos was everything her tattered, empty, frightened soul had desired. He would protect her. Love her. He would complete her life.

Yes, yes, yes.

But even as the words rose to her lips, something stopped her. Something she couldn't understand made her pull her face away from his touch.

"Marry you?" she whispered. She searched his dark eyes, her heartbeat quickening in her chest. "I don't even know you."

He blinked. She saw that he was surprised. Then his eyebrows lowered into a frown.

"You knew me well enough to conceive my child."

She swallowed. "But I can't remember you," she said. "It wouldn't be fair to take you as my husband. It wouldn't be right."

"I was raised without a father. I do not intend my

child to endure that. I will give our baby a name. Do not deny me," he said urgently.

Deny him? How could any woman deny anything to a man like Talos Xenakis?

But it didn't feel right.

With a deep breath, she turned away, glancing out at the passing scenery. It had changed since they'd left the outskirts of London, become soft and green beyond the rain-splattered windows. Trees had started to turn orange and yellow, rich autumnal colors between the green.

"Eve."

She looked back at Talos. He was so darkly handsome and powerful, and at the moment his sensual mouth was pressed into a hard line. He was clearly determined to have his way.

But something inside her made her resist him.

"Thank you for asking me to marry you," she said awkwardly. "It's very warm and loving. But my baby won't be born for months—"

"*Our* baby," he corrected her.

"And I can't be your wife when I can't even remember you."

"We'll see," he said softly. Silence fell on their drive as she watched the passing scenery. Finally, the car turned off the road to a smaller lane. She saw a redbrick Georgian mansion at the base of tree-covered hills, reflected in a wide gray lake.

"Is that my stepfather's house?" she breathed in shock.

"Yes."

The car drove up the long lane through the park and woodlands then stopped in front of the entrance. As Talos opened the door and helped her from the car, Eve looked up with an intake of breath. She craned her head back to get a good look at the mansion, with its striking Victorian Gothic parapets stabbing upward into the steel-gray sky.

Holding her hand over her eyes to block out the noon sunlight that had finally penetrated the clouds, she looked back at him. "I lived here as a teenager?"

"And now it is yours, along with a vast fortune."

She looked at him sharply. "How do you know?"

"You knew it yourself yesterday, when you attended the reading of the will."

"But how do *you* know?" she persisted.

He shrugged. "I'll make sure you get a copy of the will. Come." Taking her hand, he escorted her past the grand sweep of the front door. Inside the foyer, five servants waited to greet her, headed by the housekeeper.

"Oh, Miss Craig," the plump woman sniffed into her apron. "Your stepfather loved you so much. He would be so glad to see you've finally come home!"

Home? But it wasn't her home. Apparently, she'd barely set foot in this place for years!

But looking at the elderly housekeeper's sad face, Eve felt a sympathetic pang. She put an arm around her.

"He was a good man, wasn't he?" she said softly.

"Yes, that he was, miss. The best. And he loved you as his own natural-born child. Even though you weren't, and American to boot," she added, wiping her eyes. "He'd be so happy you've finally come back after so long."

Eve paused delicately. "Has it been so…?"

"Six, no, seven years. Mr. Craig always invited you back for Christmas, but…"

Her voice trailed off as she wiped tears with her apron.

"But I never came, did I?" Eve said.

The older woman shook her head wistfully.

Eve swallowed. Apparently she'd taken her stepfather's money and let him pay her bills as she shopped and partied her way around the world, but hadn't even had the grace to return for an occasional visit!

And now he was dead.

"I'm sorry," she whispered over the lump in her throat.

"Let me take you to your room. You'll find it's just as you left it last."

Shortly afterwards, the quietly sobbing housekeeper left them in Eve's old bedroom. In the darkness, with Talos behind her in the only light of the double doorway, Eve yanked back the black curtains, filling the room with gray light.

Turning back to get a good look at her room, she choked back a gasp of dismay. Everything was red and black, down to the king-sized black lacquer bed. Dramatic. Modern. Sexy.

Garish.

Talos leaned against the door frame as Eve looked

through the room, desperate for something, anything that would tell her what she needed to know. She opened closet doors, running her hands idly over the new clothes that hung there. The clothes were like the room, sexy and dramatic. Powerful clothes for a woman who desired attention and knew how to wield it.

Eve shivered.

She pulled open the shelves, touching each item lightly with her hands. Black stiletto heels. A Gucci handbag. A Louis Vuitton suitcase. Finding her passport, she thumbed through it, searching for answers that weren't there. Zanzibar? Mumbai? Cape Town?

"You weren't kidding," she said slowly. "I do travel constantly. Especially for the last three months."

When he didn't reply, she turned back to face him. His face seemed carefully expressionless.

"Yes," was all he said. "I know."

She tossed the passport into her suitcase with the sexy clothes and shoes that all seemed foreign, as if they belonged to someone else. Leaning against the modern black four-poster bed, she looked around her with a heavy sigh. "There's nothing here."

"I told you."

Desolately, she went to the bookshelf. It held only faded fashion magazines, years out of date, and a few slender volumes on etiquette and charm. She picked up the book on top, a splashy pop-culture book and read the title out loud in dismay. *"How to Get Your Man?"*

"That's never been your problem." There was a distinct edge to his voice.

Her heart was breaking, and he was making jokes? She made a huffing sound and chucked the book in his general direction. He caught it midair.

"Look, Eve," he said evenly. "It all doesn't matter."

"It does matter—these things tell me who I am!" She jabbed her finger toward the closet. "I've just found out I was the kind of girl who only cared about her looks, who ignored a stepfather who loved me, and who never bothered to come home at Christmas." Tears rushed into her eyes. "And I let him die alone," she whispered. "How could I have been so cruel?"

Desolately, she picked up a dusty photo in a gilded frame. She saw the image of a man giving a cheeky wink, his arm around a beautiful dark-haired woman who was laughing with joy. Between them was a plump little girl with a big beaming smile and two missing front teeth.

She stared at the adults in the photo for a very long time, but no memories came back to her. They had to be her parents, but she couldn't remember them. Was she really that heartless? Did she truly have no soul?

"What did you find?"

"Nothing. It doesn't help." She threw the photograph across the room, where it bounced softly against her bed. She covered her face with her hands. "I can't remember them. I can't!"

Crossing the bedroom in three long strides, he took her by the shoulders. "I barely knew my parents, but it hasn't hurt me."

"It's not just the past," she whispered. "Why would

you want to be with a person like me? Without substance, without heart?"

He didn't answer.

"And now it's all too late," she said over the lump in her throat. "I've lost my only family. I have no home."

"Your home is with me," he said in a low voice.

She looked up at him. The sunlight from the tall windows gently caressed his face, illuminating floating dust motes like tiny stars all around them in the red-and-black bedroom.

"Let me show you." He slowly stroked up her bare arms, his fingers light against her skin. "Marry me."

Electricity spread up her arms and down her body. She fought the urge to step closer to him, to press her body against his chest. Shaking her head, she breathed, "I can't."

"Why?" he growled.

"I don't want you to marry me out of pity!"

His hands suddenly moved around her, caressing her back through her dress, causing the black silk to slide deliciously over her body with his featherlight touch. "Pity is the last thing I feel for you."

She closed her eyes, leaning forward in spite of herself. Wanting more of his touch. Wanting to feel his warmth. His heat.

He pulled her more deeply into his arms. She felt the scent of him, the warmth of his body beneath his clothes.

"Come away with me," he whispered into her hair. "Come to Athens and be my bride."

She felt the hardness of his body against hers, the strength of his arms around her. He was so much taller and more powerful than she was. His hands ran softly along the edges of her hips, up the length of her back as her breasts crushed against his chest.

She swallowed, trembling. She licked her lips, moving her cheek against his shirt as she looked up at him. "I can't just run away," she sighed. No matter how she wished she could. "I need my memory back, Talos. I can't just float through the world not knowing who I am. I can't marry a virtual stranger, even if you're the father of my child—"

"So I'll take you to the place where we first met. To where we began." She felt his dark gaze fall upon her mouth as he said softly, "I'll show you the place where I first kissed you."

Her bones turned to liquid. She looked up at him, her heart pounding as she licked her lips involuntarily. "Where is that?"

His eyes were hot and dark. "In Venice."

"Venice," she repeated, and the word was a wistful sigh. She looked up at him with yearning, knowing she should refuse—knowing she should stay in London and see the specialist Dr. Bartlett had recommended. But her refusal caught in her throat. Caught by her romantic dreams. *Caught by him.*

Talos reached down to stroke her tender bottom lip with his thumb, caressing her face with his powerful hands.

"Come to Venice," he said darkly. "I will show you

everything." He cupped her face with both hands, holding her hard against his body as he looked down at her, commanding her with his gaze. "And then," he whispered, "you will marry me."

CHAPTER THREE

S\ᴜɴʟɪɢʜᴛ reflected off the water as they took the *motoscafo,* a private water taxi, from the Marco Polo Airport. The September weather was bright and warm as they crossed the lagoon, passing by the Piazza San Marco and the Bridge of Sighs on the way to their hotel.

Venice. Talos had never expected to return here again.

But sometimes, he thought grimly, a man had to change the playbook in the middle of the game. He would do whatever it took, be as romantic a fool as any man could be, in order to lure Eve into marriage before her memory returned.

He looked down at her in his arms as they crossed the water of the canal. Her eyes shone with wonder, her full pink lips were slightly parted as she gazed around the city with awe.

The same way every man who saw Eve looked at *her.*

Even right now in this water taxi. The young Italian driver kept glancing back in his mirror. Talos's bodyguard, Kefalas, was sitting in the seat behind them, and even he had looked at Eve a bit longer than strictly necessary.

Eve was freshly showered and had changed her clothes on his private flight from London. Her dark hair now fell in thick, glossy waves past her bare shoulders, brushing the nipples Talos could easily picture beneath that clinging red jersey dress. The dress showed off the top swell of her overflowing breasts beneath the spaghetti straps, and barely reached halfway down her creamy thighs. She'd put on lipstick, a red color that matched her dress. Her legs were slender and perfect, ending in sharp black stiletto heels.

He couldn't blame either of them for staring. Even though he wanted to kill them for it.

Strange, Talos thought, he'd never been jealous before of other men staring at Eve. He'd always accepted it as his due. He'd taken it for granted that other men would always want what he, Talos, possessed.

But for the first time it caused his stomach to curl. Why? Because Eve was carrying his child? Because he intended to make her his wife?

His wife in name only, he reminded himself. To protect his unborn child. Not because he cared for Eve. He felt nothing for her but scorn. And, he was forced to admit, lust.

Giving the driver a hard stare until the young man blushed and returned his focus to the wheel, Talos pulled Eve closer against him on the seat. She leaned back against his chest, reaching her arms over his neck and smiling up at him.

"It's beautiful here." Her blue eyes were as warm as bluebells in a spring meadow. "Thank you for bringing me to Venice. Even though I'm sure it was very inconvenient…"

He smiled down at her. Taking her hand, he brought it to his lips.

"Nothing is inconvenient to me if it gives you pleasure," he said, and softly pressed his mouth against her skin.

He felt her shiver beneath his touch in the warm afternoon sun. The air was salty and fresh. In the distance, he could hear the calls of seagulls, hear the distant chiming of medieval church bells.

"You're so good to me," she whispered, visibly affected by the way he'd kissed her hand. The realization that she was almost like an innocent, easily swayed by sensual desire, lit a dark fire in his heart.

The femme fatale she'd once been had disappeared along with her memories, it seemed. Dressed in the red dress and lipstick she still looked just like the same arrogant, cruel, fascinating creature she'd been three months ago, but she'd changed completely. With her skittish reactions, her youthful naïveté, she was almost like a virgin.

Except she wasn't—she was pregnant with his baby. And while she'd certainly been a virgin before they'd met, she'd never been innocent!

Remembering how they'd conceived that baby, all of his limbs suddenly seemed to burn where he had contact with her. Looking down into her beautiful face, he saw the vulnerability in her blue eyes, saw her pupils dilate. He was reminded of those hot breathless weeks in Athens when her naked body had been beneath his own. When he'd thought that beneath her achingly beautiful, shallow surface something existed that might be truly rare—truly worth possessing.

And he'd kept right on thinking that up until the day he'd seen her having breakfast with his rival, coldly giving him evidence to destroy Talos's company.

Remember that moment, he told himself harshly. *Remember how she betrayed you—and why.*

But as Eve looked up at him dreamily beneath the elegant, decrepit palazzos of Venice, with the sunlight shining off the canals, all he could suddenly think was that he wanted to kiss her. Now. Hard. To brand her permanently as his, to punish those cherry-red lips until she gasped and cried out in his arms.

His hands tightened around her shoulders, his fingers gripping into her slight frame as he remembered their days and nights in June. He'd been addicted to bedding her. He'd been lost in a woman, in a way he'd never experienced before or since.

He considered himself ruthless. He considered himself strong. But she'd bested him and he'd never seen it coming.

Now, he hated her with all his heart.

But he still wanted her. Wanted her with a consuming desire that could destroy him, if he ever let down his guard.

He would never give in to her temptation. Even if his

weeks of bedding her had been the most erotically charged experience of his life, he would never take her again. If he ever even kissed her, he might be lighting a flame that he could not control.

He watched her nervously lick her lips—those full, cherry-red lips that had once made him shudder and scream with desire so intense he'd literally thought it might kill him.

He could tell she was bewildered by the electric connection between them. She didn't understand it. Unlike the Eve he'd known, who'd kept her feelings so carefully hidden, this girl didn't guard her expression. Her thoughts were clearly bare on her angelically beautiful face.

Good, he told himself harshly. The perfect weapon to use against her. He would convince her to marry him. He would romance her. Woo her. Court her. *Lure her.* He would take her as his wife—today. By any means necessary.

Except one.

He would not take her to his bed. *He would not.*

Eve turned her face up toward the bright Italian sun from the windows of the boat, leaning back against Talos's strong, powerful body as the *motoscafo* bounced across the waves. The leather seat hummed beneath her thighs from the vibrations of the engine.

She took a deep breath of the sharp, salty air. Her skin felt warm. Her body felt hot all over as she leaned against Talos's hard chest. Even through his black shirt she could feel the heat off his skin.

Then he smiled down at her. His smile did all kinds of strange things to her, making her heart pound. Her days of darkness and emptiness in rainy London now seemed like a lonely dream. She was in Italy with Talos. And their baby. She placed her hand on her still-flat belly.

The water taxi slowed, pulled near the dock of a fifteenth-century palazzo. She stared at the high pointed windows that embellished the crumbling red stucco facade with awe at its exotic Gothic beauty. "Is that where we're going?"

His black eyes gleamed as he looked down at her. "Our hotel."

Oh. Their hotel.

She swallowed as she climbed from the taxi to the dock, picturing what it would be like to share a room with this man. To share space. *To share a bed.*

Just thinking of it, she stumbled on the dock.

"Careful," Talos said gruffly, grabbing her arm to steady her. "You don't have your sea legs yet."

All the colors of Venice, the twisting, sparkling water, the bright blue sky and tall, red campanile tower of the nearby piazza, seemed to fade into the background with a swirl of color behind him.

"You're right," she said over the lump in her throat. "I don't."

They stood on the dock as his bodyguard-assistant,

Kefalas, paid the young Italian taxi driver and organized the luggage. But all Eve could see was Talos.

He was so handsome and tall and strong, she thought. She felt his arms tighten around her, and she suddenly wondered if he was going to kiss her. The thought scared her. She jerked away from him nervously. "We will, um, get separate rooms, won't we?"

She heard a low, sensual laugh escape him as he shook his head.

She licked her lips. "But—"

"I don't intend to let you out of my sight." He came forward toward her on the dock, and it took every ounce of her courage not to back away. He loosely brushed a tendril back from the blowing salty breeze. Kissing her temple, he whispered, "Or out of my arms."

Enfolding her hand in his own, he drew her toward the palatial hotel, where they were whisked inside by the waiting staff.

As Eve walked through the exquisite lobby, past soaring gilded arches and the sweeping staircase, she became slowly aware of men's heads whipping around to stare at her, almost like spectators following a tennis match.

It would have been funny, if she hadn't felt like the yellow ball.

Why were they staring at her?

What was wrong with her?

The doorman gaped at her, then jumped to open the door.

The male clerk did a double take from the elaborate desk before he looked away, clearing his throat.

The group of Italian businessmen crossing the lobby weren't so discreet. Three young men in pinstriped suits stopped in place on the marble floor, staring at her with open jaws. One man jabbed another in the ribs with a grin. Speaking rapidly in Italian, he started to come toward her. His friend stopped him by grabbing his wrist, gesturing toward Talos with palpable fear. Apparently too cowed by Talos to approach her, all three men continued to stare at her, murmuring soft words of appreciation.

Eve felt vulnerable.

Exposed.

Her cheeks went hot beneath all the scrutiny. She was grateful when Talos took her hand and led her toward the elevator. She could feel all the men in the lobby stare after her, hear their mournful sighs meld with the click of her stiletto heels on the marble floor. They were probably staring at her backside right now.

Her neck broke out into a cold sweat.

Why were they staring at her?

Then in a flash, she knew.

The dress.

The tiny red dress that she'd taken from her bedroom closet in Buckinghamshire. Compared to the rest of the wardrobe, she'd thought it the simplest, easiest choice, comfortable and casual. It had seemed like a nice, though somewhat small, sundress in stretchy fabric. And since she apparently owned no comfortable shoes whatsoever, she'd chosen the black stiletto sandals, which at least wouldn't squeeze her toes. After her shower, she'd brushed out her dark hair and tentatively put on the lipstick in her handbag.

She'd hoped she would get used to her own clothes, feel confident in them.

Boy, had she been wrong.

Though the knit fabric was indeed soft and stretchy, it was no match for her pregnant breasts, which spilled out quite distressingly over the top. The stiletto heels made her legs very long but also caused her hips to thrust forward and sway with every commanding step.

Comfortable? Casual?

Her clothes cried out for male attention, and no matter where they went, men's eyes centered on her. No matter their nationality, no matter their age or profession, men couldn't stop staring!

She didn't just look trashy, she realized with a horrified intake of breath. She looked like a tart who got paid by the hour!

When the penthouse door finally closed, and the teenaged bellhop left them with one last surreptitious, appreciative glance at Eve's breasts, she let out a huge sigh of relief. Thank heaven, she was finally alone with Talos!

Then she realized…

She was alone with Talos.

Nervously, she glanced around the lavish suite. Beneath the frescoed ceiling, a crystal chandelier sparkled over the old paintings, marble fireplace and gilded furniture. Thick, tasseled curtains parted at the wide windows to reveal a veranda that overlooked the canal. Multiple rooms graced the suite, including a living area and elegant bathroom.

But there was only one bed.

The enormous four-poster stood at the center of the suite. Eve couldn't take her eyes off it.

"Shall we go to dinner?" Talos purred from behind her.

Red-faced, she whirled around to face him, praying he wasn't able to read minds.

"Dinner? Out?" Thinking of all those leering masculine eyes, she shook her head desperately. "I don't really feel like going out tonight."

"Perfect," he said with a sensual curve of his lips. "So we'll stay in."

He came another step toward her, larger and more powerful than any man had a right to be. This royal suite was the size of a house, and yet he somehow filled every inch of the space, filled it to a breaking point. And if he did that to a four-thousand-square-foot suite…

She could only imagine what he'd do to a woman.

No! she wouldn't think about that. Her cheeks flushed with heat. Nervously, she turned toward the window, feeling for all the world like a teenage virgin. She looked out the window across the sparkling water toward the Venetian island on the other side of the lagoon. She could see hotels, palazzos, ferries. She could see parked black gondolas rise and fall in the water in the wake of each passing speedboat bringing tourists to St. Mark's Square.

She felt him touch her shoulder.

"Is this the same hotel we stayed at before?" she stammered. "When we first met?"

"I stayed here alone," he said, looking down at her. "You refused to come up to my suite."

She whirled around to face him. "I did?"

"I tried to change your mind." Reaching down, he caressed her cheek. She took a deep breath at the gentleness of his touch, of his woodsy masculine scent that caused such shivers down her body. He said softly, "You resisted me."

"I did?" she blurted out. "How?" Then she blushed.

He gave a low laugh. His featherlight fingertips moved down her cheek toward her lips. He touched her so softly that she had to strain to feel him, almost as if he weren't quite touching her—forcing her to rise to meet him, whether she willed it or no. His fingers ran softly above the length of her tender bottom lip.

He leaned forward to whisper in her ear.

"You made me chase you. Harder and longer than I've ever chased any woman. No woman has ever been—will ever be—your equal."

As he pulled away from her, Eve's heart was pounding, each rise and fall of her breath shallow and quick.

His dark eyes gleamed down at her as if he knew exactly the tumult he'd created inside her. He was only maybe ten years older than her, and yet he somehow made her feel as though he had twice her strength and about a thousand times her experience!

"So. Shall we go out?" He glanced back at the bed. "Or stay in?"

Stay in this penthouse suite, which for all of its square footage suddenly felt tiny? Spend the evening alone with this powerful man, who made her feel such strange things, knocking her world off-kilter?

"I changed my mind. Let's go out!" she blurted, then blushed at her own nervousness. She felt like a shy young girl, a million miles out of her league.

"So you're hungry after all." At his low laugh, she knew she'd betrayed herself again, but she couldn't help it. Casually, he took her white trenchcoat from the closet, slinging it over one arm. He placed his other hand possessively against the small of her back, and his light touch made her sizzle all over.

Eve almost sighed with the relief of leaving the gorgeous suite—with its enormous bed—safely behind them.

As she followed him out of the hotel into the dusky streets of Venice, she didn't know it would be a classic case of out of the frying pan, into the fire.

CHAPTER FOUR

THE sun was starting to set in earnest, giving the twilight a pink-and-orange glow with a rapidly chilling autumn bite in the air. As a light fog blew in from the lagoon, Talos reached for Eve's hand.

His hand wrapped around her smaller one, their naked palms pressing together, and she gave an involuntary shiver that had nothing to do with the cooling night.

He paused on the walkway between the piazzetta and the canal. "Cold?"

She nodded, because how could she tell him the truth? How could she tell him that his every touch exhilarated and frightened her in equal measure?

"That won't do." Behind his head, she could see the Byzantine white domes, arches and sharp spires of St. Mark's Basilica. Sunset caressed his handsome face in warm reddish-pink light. "Here."

He took the trenchcoat he'd carried on his arm and wrapped it around her. He was so handsome, she thought in a daze as she tied the belt of her coat. So starkly powerful, wearing a black wool coat over a black tailored shirt and black pants. For a moment, she just looked at him, catching her breath.

Then a group of young men walked past them and she heard a low whistle. She looked down and blushed, realizing her slim-fitting white trenchcoat covered her red dress completely. With her legs and collarbone bare, she must look as if she were naked beneath it!

She bit her lip. "Maybe we should take a taxi?"

"The restaurant is close," he said tersely. "Just on the other side of the square." He took her arm, placing it over his own. His eyes were dark as he looked down at her. "Come."

It was incredibly romantic, watching the sun lower over the Grand Canal. Romantic, but not comfortable. Her black stiletto heels twisted her ankles as she walked, but that wasn't the worst thing. She was continually aware of men staring at her as they passed by the walkway. And Talos was aware of it, too. She could tell by the way he held her arm tightly, glowering at any other man who came too close or stared too long. He was like a lion ready to fight, to kill, to protect his female.

Eve felt vulnerable. Like a gazelle about to get ripped to shreds for some lion's dinner. What difference did it make which lion?

She looked up at Talos beside her. Something about him scared her in a way she didn't understand. It was because she couldn't remember him, she told herself. If she did, surely she wouldn't be afraid…?

Behind them, she saw a shadowy figure following at a discreet distance. Nervously, she licked her lips, tasting lipstick flavored like wax and roses. "There's someone following us."

Talos glanced back, then relaxed. "Kefalas."

"Your bodyguard?"

"He'll only come if needed."

"But—"

"It's necessary." He looked down at her. The slant of the setting sun cast his brutally handsome features in a roseate glow as he added roughly, "Just to protect you from all your Italian admirers, it seems."

"I don't like the attention," she whispered. "I don't want them to stare at me."

She could tell by the twist to his lips that he didn't completely believe her. Her cheeks burned pink. She wished she were covered from head to toe in a padded snowsuit.

Her clothes had to change, she thought.

Talos escorted her into a small hotel overlooking the Grand Canal, to the restaurant in the back which had a lovely wide terrace with a view of the water. The restaurant was packed, but somehow they were immediately taken to the best table.

Across the simple candlelit table, they shared an amazing meal of seafood risotto and tagliolini with scampi. The food was a sensual experience. As she finished her risotto, licking her fork with satisfaction, she felt his gaze upon her. And even as the cool night breeze drifted across her bare shoulders and legs, she shivered with sudden heat.

Unable to bear the intensity of his gaze, she looked away. Across the black shadows of gondolas in the water, she saw a beautiful white domed church lit up in the night.

"That's Santa Maria della Salute," he said quietly. "You loved it last time, too."

"Last time?"

"Don't you remember this restaurant?"

"Should I?"

His dark eyes flickered at her in the candlelight. "We came here on our first date."

The waiter brought the dessert of tiramisu, but as she took her first bite of the sweet cake, she could hardly taste it. With a deep breath, she set down her fork. And met his eyes.

He reached for her hand over the table.

"I am glad I found you," he said in a low voice that made her tremble from within. "Glad you're here now."

He was still being so kind and loving to her. She could hardly understand it. She covered her face with one hand.

"You must hate me," she said in a low voice.

His fingers seemed to tighten by reflex over her other wrist. "Why do you say that?"

Tears filled her eyes as she looked up at him. "Because I can't remember you! You are my lover, the father of my child, and you're being so kind to me. You're trying so hard to help me remember. But it's useless, all useless, because my brain—won't—*work!*"

Her voice choked as tears spilled down her cheeks. Aware she was making a scene, desperate to escape all the eyes on her—now those of the women, too, as well as the men—Eve pulled away from him. Throwing her linen napkin on the table, she ran outside.

Talos caught up with her a few moments later, her coat in his arms.

"It's all right," he murmured. He kissed her temple and she felt his hands in her long, loose hair. "It's all right."

"It's not all right," she choked out, gulping back tears. She looked up at him. "How can I be with you and not remember?"

"You need to calm down," he said in a low voice. "This can't be good for the baby—being pushed all over Venice."

"You haven't pushed me. You've been gentle and wonderful." She wiped the tears away angrily. "It's my fault. All mine. Dr. Bartlett said there's no physical reason that I shouldn't remember. So what is it? What's wrong with me?"

He clenched his jaw. "I don't know."

"Maybe I should go back to London. See that specialist—"

"No." His dark gaze caught hers, sensual and intense. He cupped her face with his hands. "You don't need any doctors. You just need time. Time and care. And me. I remember enough for both of us. Marry me, Eve. Make me happy."

Her face felt warm where he touched her. His eyes fell to her mouth, and her lips tingled beneath his gaze as if he'd touched her with his hands. And immediately, her whole body felt sparked, consumed by raging fire, like dry tinder sparked by lightning.

Behind him, she saw the famous Piazza San Marco, toward the tall red campanile and the famous domed white basilica that was as exotic as anything in Cairo or Istanbul. The hour was late, the night was magic, the tourists had melted away into the mists, leaving the two of them alone, drenched in moonlight beside the water.

He was going to kiss her.

She wanted him to kiss her. Ached for it.

As he slowly lowered his head to hers, her whole body vibrated, leaning forward, yearning...

But as she closed her eyes and leaned up for his kiss, she suddenly found herself standing five feet away from him.

She could see the rapid, hoarse rise and fall of his breath as he stared at her in the moonlight with eyes so dark they seemed black.

"What is it, Eve?" he said in a low voice. "Why did you jump away?"

"I don't know," she whispered helplessly over the lump in her throat. "I want to kiss you, but for some reason, I'm...afraid."

He gave a sudden low laugh, a sensual, knowing

sound that caused a rumble to echo off the waves of the water. "You're right to be afraid."

"What do you mean?" she asked, unable to look away.

Reaching for her hand, he kissed her palm. "This fire could consume us both." Slowly, he kissed each knuckle of her hand, causing zings of pleasure to curl up and down her body. "Once I start kissing you, I might never stop."

A shudder of pleasure went through her at those words. Pleasure…desire…fear.

But his face was so strangely dark in the moonlight.

She couldn't blame his mood, she told herself. Not when she'd been so weepy a moment before!

"Come," he said in a low voice. "It's late. Time for bed."

For…bed?

Her knees shook beneath her as he led her back to the hotel. She barely noticed the beautiful sights of Venice, the lights on the gondolas or the islands across the water. All she could see in her mind's eye was the penthouse suite waiting for them.

The *bed* waiting for them.

Biting her lip, she glanced at him sideways through her lashes. He was so breathtakingly handsome and strong. But beyond just his incredible sexiness, he was a good man. He'd been nothing but loving and patient. He hadn't been angry or hurt about the fact she couldn't remember him. No, his only focus had been on making her comfortable. On helping her.

No, that wasn't true. He wanted something else.

He wanted to marry her.

The father of her child, a handsome, powerful Greek tycoon, wanted to marry her. So why couldn't she accept? Why couldn't she at least let him kiss her? Why wouldn't her body let her?

You're right to be afraid.

She heard more low whistles and muttered appreciation in Italian as they passed a new group of young men. Clenching his hands, Talos started to turn toward them. His whole body seemed abruptly tight and angry, almost enraged. He meant to fight them all, she realized. He was suddenly bruising for a fight.

Frightened, she stopped him with a gentle touch on his wrist. "Can I have my coat back?" she implored. "I'm so cold."

He instantly turned back to face her. "Of course, *khriso mou.*" Looking down at her, he tenderly wrapped the coat around her. For a moment, she was lost in his dark gaze. He took her hand in his own. "I'll get you back to the hotel."

Eve exhaled, relieved she'd distracted him before he could start a fight with those young Italians. From the look on Talos's face, she'd been afraid. *For them.* He'd been taut with fury that seemed far beyond what their fairly innocent provocation had deserved.

But she wouldn't allow it to happen again. As they walked past the doorman and into the lobby, Eve vowed she would change her wardrobe completely.

Once inside their penthouse suite, Talos immediately

released her hand. When she came out of the bathroom ten minutes later, after brushing her teeth, he didn't even glance up from the sleek desk near the window where he was working on his laptop. Through the window behind him, she could see the twinkling lights of ferries crossing from the Adriatic Sea.

"Thank you for loaning me your pajama top," she said awkwardly. She gave a laugh that sounded nervous and goofy, even to her own ears. "I must have lost mine. There was nothing in my suitcase."

"You always slept in the nude."

She swallowed, staring at his profile, very aware of the bed behind her. "Well, um…"

"You take the bed." Standing up, he closed his laptop and finally looked at her. His dark gaze, which had been so hot when he'd nearly kissed her near St. Mark's Square, had suddenly cooled. "I'll work in the office so I don't disturb you. I'll sleep on the couch when I'm tired."

After the amount of time she'd spent trying to steady her nerves and steel herself to share a hotel room, she'd never expected this—for him to treat her as if she were a distant guest. She glanced from his tall body and wide shoulders to the small, slender couch. "You won't be able to fit on that!"

"I'll manage." He turned away. "You and the baby need rest." Rising from the desk, he left the room. He paused at the door. "Good night."

He turned off her light. Since she had no other choice,

she climbed into bed and pulled the covers up to her neck. Bereft of his warmth. Miserable. Alone.

She sighed as she turned her head back and forth on the thick, luxurious pillow, trying to get comfortable, trying to make herself sleep with anxious thoughts racing circles in her mind.

Why hadn't she let him kiss her?

She'd yearned to know what it would feel like to have his mouth on hers. She sighed now just thinking about it. And yet she'd jumped away from him without thought. As if she'd placed her hand on a burning stove.

She heard the echo of his dark, haunted voice. *You are right to be afraid.*

Afraid? Eve flipped onto her other side with an impatient huff of breath. Afraid of what? Talos was a good man. Her lover. The father of her child. He'd been so loving, so romantic, so patient with her!

And he wanted to *marry* her.

She needed to do whatever it took to regain her memory, for Talos's sake. For their baby's sake. For her own.

Tomorrow, she promised herself firmly. Tomorrow, she would be brave. Tomorrow, she would let him kiss her.

When Talos woke up the next morning, Eve was gone.

He sat up on the couch with an intake of breath. Looking at the bright light from the windows, he knew he'd overslept; the clock over the mantel said eleven. Where was Eve? He looked at the king-sized bed.

It was empty. Empty and *made*.

She'd made the bed?

With a growl deep in his throat, he stood up, dropping his blankets and pillow haphazardly to the floor. Then he saw the little note in her handwriting written on hotel stationary, neatly affixed to the top pillow.

Gone shopping. Back soon.

He exhaled. So she hadn't regained her memory and run away. He'd ordered Kefalas to keep an eye on her in any case. She wouldn't escape him again.

Eve was out shopping. A humorless smile traced his lips. Apparently she hadn't changed as much as he'd thought.

With a yawn, he raised his arms over his head, stretching his half-naked body. His chest was bare, his legs in pajamas. Every muscle ached, and it wasn't just because he'd managed to fit his six-foot-three frame into a couch that was at most five foot ten. It was from being so close to Eve.

Listening to her breathe.

Remembering the last time he'd slept in a room with her.

The last time she'd been in his bed.

He clawed back his hair. Spending the whole day with her yesterday, pretending to be her devoted lover, had been difficult. Spending the whole night in the same hotel room without trying to seduce her had nearly killed him.

He hated that he still wanted her.

She'd been perfect three months ago, her figure slender but curvaceous in all the right places, but now her newly pregnant breasts were so lush, while her waist was still so tiny, that she was the epitome of any man's dream.

Including his.

He'd purposely stayed in the next room until 3:00 a.m., answering e-mails and making long phone calls to Australia about the Sydney deal. He'd purposefully waited until he'd nearly passed out over his keyboard before he allowed himself to stumble back into the dark bedroom and fall on the couch. As the window's light changed to the grayness of dawn, he'd finally collapsed with exhaustion.

But even in sleep, he'd had endless dreams of making love to her. He'd woken up hard for her.

With a loud curse, Talos twisted his head to crack the vertebrae in his neck. He hurt all over.

Stomping into the bathroom, he turned on the shower then stared blankly at the rapidly steaming water.

He'd always known Eve was shallow and selfish. But he'd been intrigued by all her contradictions, his seductive virgin mistress, the gorgeous beauty who never asked him questions or revealed any of her feelings. Unlike any other woman, she'd taken pleasure in bed without emotion.

He'd been captivated by her. When she was naked beneath him in bed, when he brought her to a gasping climax, her blue eyes had shone up at his with sudden searing vulnerability. He'd thought there was something more inside her soul. Some mystery that only he could solve.

And he'd kept on believing that, right up till the day she'd sneaked from their bed, rifled through his private safe and stolen damaging financial information to give to Jake Skinner over a romantic breakfast.

Overnight, the Xenakis Group's stock had crashed nearly in half, causing him to lose nearly the whole company with margin calls. If Talos hadn't had the resources of his personal fortune to back him up, he would have lost his company. He would have lost everything.

Instead of buying distressed companies at pennies on the dollar, he would have been one of the poor fools forced to sell.

He cursed softly in Greek.

And in spite of all that, he'd nearly kissed her tonight. He'd wanted to take her against the wall of an alley in view of the Bridge of Sighs and possess her utterly. Over and over. Until he had his fill.

He was so tense with fighting his desire for her, that when those Italians had dared to whistle at Eve, he'd almost thrown himself at them. He'd suddenly relished the thought of the relief of pain, of punching them all bloody in an honest fight.

How simple a straightforward street fight had seemed, compared to trying to lure the woman he hated—the woman he wanted—into marriage!

Clenching his fists, Talos stepped into the shower. He leaned back as the hot water coursed over his naked body. He washed his hair, rubbed soap over his chest.

Would it be so bad to give in to temptation?

The insidious thought made his eyes fly open.

Would it be so bad to take what he wanted? To gorge himself until he was sick of her?

Like Scotch.

The first time he'd tasted an expensive single malt Scotch, he'd been only nineteen, newly arrived in New York. He'd done well for his American boss in Athens, but this was a new country—a new world. Waiting for half an hour in Dalton Hunter's office, he'd grown steadily more nervous. He'd finally poured himself a shot of the rich amber-colored liquor from a crystal decanter on a silver tray. He'd had one delicious taste before he'd looked up to see Dalton watching him from the door.

Wondering if he was about to get sacked on his first day, Talos lifted his chin and observed defiantly, "I thought you'd want me to learn how to hold my liquor. As an asset to the company."

"Quite so," Dalton said, sounding amused. Then his eyes narrowed. "So drink it all."

Talos had looked at the nearly full decanter in shock. "All?"

"Right now. Or get out."

So Talos had drunk the entire decanter, gulping down the smooth, smoky Scotch as if it were water. However, his bravado had been lessened when he'd spent the whole afternoon puking in the office bathroom, aware of the other employees laughing at him in the hallway.

When he'd finally gone back to his boss, he'd been red-faced, sweaty, humiliated.

"Now you know not to steal from me," Dalton had said before he coldly turned away. "Get to work."

Talos still grimaced as he remembered that day. He'd never been able to touch Scotch again. Almost twenty years later, just the smell of it still made him sick.

And that was how he wished he could feel about Eve.

He wished he could get her out of his system once and for all. Until he never wanted her again. Until the thought of bedding her was as disgusting as a flawless Baccarat crystal decanter of imported single malt Scotch.

Turning off the water, he toweled himself dry. He pulled his clothes from the closet where someone in his staff had neatly put them away. He stepped into his boxers and black pants, then stared at himself in the half-fogged mirror. He took a deep breath.

No.

He wouldn't give in to lust.

He wouldn't be seduced by her again.

Fiercely, he pushed aside the thought of Eve in his bed, her skin glowing with rough lovemaking and her eyes full of desire.

He'd once planned to take her new fortune from her under threat of prosecuting her for theft and corporate espionage.

But now…

All he wanted was their child, safe and healthy in his

arms. And Eve to disappear from their lives forever after the baby was born.

As he buttoned his sharply tailored white shirt, he glared at himself in the mirror. Every time he thought of the lustful fool he'd been a few months ago, neglecting his business, spending every hour in bed with her, making love to her day and night, it made him grind his teeth with rage.

He would never let it happen again.

He would never lower his guard. Never give up control again.

Talos had to convince her to marry him as soon as possible. Today, he thought, leaning in toward the mirror as he shaved his jaw. He couldn't risk her regaining her memory before he'd tied her down as his bride, giving his child a name. Then he would help her remember. And after the baby was born, he would blackmail Eve with the choice of her child or her money.

He had no doubt which she'd choose.

So today, he would act the part of a besotted lover. He would tempt her. Lure her. He would whisper sweet words. Poetry. Flowers. Jewelry. Whatever it took. His lip curled. How hard could it be?

He dropped the razor to the counter, wiping the last vestiges of shaving cream off his face with a towel.

He would not, repeat, would not—he glared at himself—take her to his bed.

Damn it, he wouldn't!

He heard a door slam and suddenly Eve was standing

behind him. His jaw dropped as he looked at her in the mirror. She smiled back serenely.

"Good morning."

"Eve." He whirled around with a gasp. "What have you done?"

CHAPTER FIVE

EVE had been beaming at him, but now she felt suddenly shy. She put her hand to her hair, which yesterday had hung past her breasts but now barely touched her collarbone. "I had my hair cut."

"I can see that."

"So why did you ask?" she retorted pertly, squaring her shoulders. "Honestly!"

He ignored that, walking around her in a circle in the wide marble bathroom, looking her up and down.

She lifted her chin defiantly, daring him to criticize her.

The sleekly modern, rather than sexy, blunt-cut pageboy hairstyle wasn't her only change. Instead of the tight red dress and overflowing cleavage she'd had last night, she was now dressed in a cotton jersey cardigan and long knit skirt in pale rose. The simple garments were still pretty, she hoped, but natural—not to mention stretchy against her expanding pregnancy. And the pink flat sandals were certainly easier to wear than the stiletto heels.

She now felt comfortable in her own skin rather than like someone trying to gain attention through her clothing.

But he only frowned at her.

"I don't understand," he muttered, lifting his hand as if to touch her, then dropping it again. "Where did you buy this?"

"At a boutique in the Mercerie recommended by the concierge."

"Did you take Kefalas with you?"

"Yes," she sighed. "I didn't want to, but he insisted on it. He wouldn't even let me use the credit cards in my purse, but insisted I charge everything to your accounts."

"Good." He peered down at her. "You look different," he mumbled.

Different as in bad? She shuffled her feet, feeling awkward under his scrutiny.

"Why the makeover?" he asked, tilting his head.

She took a deep breath. How could she explain how horrifying it had been to have men constantly gawking at her? How to explain how wretched she'd felt when Talos had nearly started a brawl against five men just because of some strangers' low whistles and murmured appreciation of her charms that were too flagrantly on display? She licked her bare lips.

"Um," she managed, "the clothes in my suitcase just, er, didn't fit right."

He lifted a dark eyebrow. "That's not what you said when I bought them for you in Athens."

"You bought the clothes?" she blurted out. "Even the red dress?"

"Yes."

She swallowed. Now she'd sounded ungrateful. "They were all lovely. Really. But…"

"But?"

"But they're not comfortable. They, um, made people look at me."

He stared at her. "I thought you liked that."

"It was still a lovely gift," she stammered. "And I'm so grateful. That you picked them out for me is terribly sweet."

"Lovely?" he repeated in a surly voice. *"Sweet?"*

"And I don't mean to be critical of your taste, but—"

"I didn't pick them out for you," he ground out. "I just paid for them. You chose."

She had? What had she been thinking? "Oh. Um. Don't worry, I'm sure the charity shops will sell them quickly," she said apologetically. "They're so glamorous—so well-made!"

He glanced at her empty suitcase with surprise. Glanced at the many bags that Kefalas had just left inside the doorway before discreetly disappearing.

"You gave away all your designer clothes?" he said incredulously. "The Gucci? The Versace?"

"Are they your favorite designers?" she said, chagrined to be so rude.

"No!" he nearly shouted. "They're yours!"

"Oh," she said. She bit her lip. "Well, those clothes are just a little too tight for me now. Not to mention too sexy." She brightened as a sudden explanation occurred to her. "Maybe my tastes have changed because I'm about to be a mother," she said happily, relieved to have an explanation. "That's probably it, don't you think?"

He stared at her. He started to speak, then visibly bit back the words. Finally, he silently held out his arm. She took it in her own.

"You look beautiful," he said quietly.

She peeked up at him, hoping he really meant it. "Really?"

"Yes." He gave her a slow-rising smile. It lit up his face, making him so handsome that he took her breath away. Reaching down, he stroked her bare cheek. "I've never seen you look more radiant."

She exhaled. She hadn't realized until that moment that she'd been tense, wondering what his reaction would be. She'd cut her hair. She'd gotten rid of the low-cut, tight dress and the stiletto heels. Would he still approve of her? Would he still want her in his life?

His hot, smoldering glance told her that yes, he approved, and yes, he wanted her.

The *real* her. Without all the tarty trimmings.

"Now," he said as his smile sharpened, "let's go get what we came here for."

For the rest of the day, they explored the charms of Venice, from walking beneath the medieval overhangs of the Calle del Paradiso to sharing lunch on the wide outdoor terrace of the Hotel Cipriani.

The fog thickened throughout the afternoon as the capricious autumn weather turned melancholy. But Eve barely noticed that the Italian sunshine had disappeared. As they strolled along canals as gray as the lowering sky, she felt warm and contented. Talos smiled down at her, his dark eyes warming her with the heat of burning coal as they laughed and talked, walking down the tree-lined paths through the grassy Giardini.

He bought her a fiery orange rose from a stall in an outdoor market. When he told her in a low voice how beautiful she was to him, how much he wanted her to be his wife, she glowed from within. She barely heard the sad, plaintive cries of the gulls soaring through the heavy clouds overhead.

As the afternoon drew on, rain finally started to drizzle. The fair-weather tourists had scattered beneath the cold-blowing winds, but Eve had never felt more gloriously lit up inside.

In her new clothes, she got occasional second glances from men, but only from up close—not from across the street. She wasn't forced to endure the endless hot stares of strange men, while knowing that only the presence of powerful, darkly dangerous Talos kept the other males at bay.

Now, she felt safe.

She felt…free.

She never wanted the day to end. She glanced down at his hand in hers as they walked. He was so possessive, so attentive. So romantic and loving.

She felt his eyes on her constantly. Any time she turned her head, she caught his gaze. Even when he didn't touch her, she felt his presence like electricity. Like fire.

As the rain started to fall more heavily, he drew her back inside an elaborate Gothic doorway. Then, to her surprise, he turned around to knock on the door of the palazzo.

"What are we doing here?" she asked, confused.

"You'll see."

They were admitted by a housekeeper. She told them in heavily accented English that, sadly, his friends the marchese and marchesa were away on vacation. But when Talos, with his most charming smile, asked to see the ballroom, she could not resist.

Who could? Eve thought.

Once the housekeeper left them alone in the enormous gilded ballroom, beneath the medieval fifteenth-century timbers and decorated stucco rosework, Eve could not believe the ballroom's size or beauty. To get a better view, she walked halfway up the sweeping stairs.

"And that is where I first saw you," Talos said in a low voice behind her.

She whirled around. "Here?"

"At the charity ball the first weekend in June."

The sun shone weakly through the tall windows of the palazzo, leaving a tracery of the Gothic rose pattern of the facade on the marble floor. She could almost imagine long-ago pirates coming to plunder the wealth of La Serenissima.

"Before that day," he said, staring at the sunlight through the multicolored glass of the windows, "I'd scoffed at the rumors about you. No woman could be that beautiful, I said. No woman could be that mesmerizing." Slowly, he turned to look at her. His dark eyes sizzled through her as he said in a low voice, "Then we met."

Talos looked just like the dark corsair she'd imagined, the Barbary pirate who'd come to plunder the medieval city—to take what he wanted and burn the rest.

She blinked. How had she come up with such a brutal, cruel image? Where had that come from?

"I saw you coming down those stairs in a long red dress," he said softly. "You were on the arm of my greatest business rival, but I knew at once that I would take you from him." Slowly, he walked up the stairs toward her. "I would have taken you from the devil himself."

As he came up the stairs toward her, she was unable to move. *Unable to breathe.*

"You made me pursue you across Venice for a week before you finally surrendered and agreed to accompany me to Athens. Where I finally discovered to my surprise that you were a virgin." He fixed his dark eyes on her and a flash of heat coursed through her body. "For the first time in my life, I found myself wanting a woman *more* after I had bedded her, instead of less."

He bent his head toward her. She couldn't move, couldn't breathe.

"The more I had of you," he whispered, "the more I wanted."

But as he lowered his head to kiss her, he suddenly stopped, then stiffened. Without touching her, he wrenched away, his eyes cold. "Come. We're done here."

After thanking the housekeeper, he led her from the palazzo. Outside, as the storm clouds brewed above them, she could feel a storm building between them as well, a tension that had nothing to do with tenderness.

He led her across an elaborate covered bridge that crossed the Grand Canal. It was momentarily empty of tourists, and as the cold, wet wind howled around them, he finally turned to face her.

His eyes were dark and hot.

A little thrill of jumbled fear and desire went through her as he took her in his arms. She felt his fingers brush her skin, felt his muscular body hard against hers. The tension increased inside her, tightening into a coil low in her belly.

"This," he said hoarsely, "is where I first kissed you."

He leaned forward, stroking the back of her head. Brushing stray tendrils from her cheek, he cupped her face with his hands. Staring up at his handsome face, she was aware of tiny details. The dark scruff on his chin, though he had shaved just hours before. She'd thought his eyes were black, but now she saw they were a deep brown, with slivers of honey-gold.

"And," he said in a low voice, lowering his head toward her, "this is where I'm going to kiss you now."

She trembled all over, her heart pounding like a frantic hummingbird's wing. She wanted him to kiss her—but at the same time something pushed her to flee!

But she couldn't. This time, he held her fast. He wouldn't let her back away.

It was as if she'd never been kissed before. His lips were gentle at first on her mouth. Then he spread her lips wide. He teased her with his tongue, licking her lips, entwining her tongue with his.

Desire and need swept through her like a fire. And she forgot about running away. She couldn't resist. *She didn't want to.*

His kiss hardened, deepened. Instead of tempting and luring, he suddenly demanded and took. His body pressed against hers so tightly she was no longer sure where he ended and she began.

The kiss was like nothing she'd felt before.

Just like a kiss should be.

She was dazed, lost in him. As he pulled away, a small whimper of protest escaped her. He looked down at her. There was a fire in his dark eyes.

"Now, *glyka mou*," he whispered. "You belong to me."

Above their heads, she could hear the caw of seagulls soaring high above, hear the ringing of the distant church bells. She could hear the lap of the water beneath them, the sound of a speedboat, hear the cries of vendors from the nearby Rialto market.

You belong to me. She closed her eyes as the echo of

those words went through her. He'd spoken those words to her before. He'd kissed her here before.

You belong to me.

That hot, humid summer night, the moon had been full, washing both of them in veils of silver. She remembered the press of his hands against her bare shoulders, over her dress. She remembered desperately wanting him to kiss her. Remembered a sense of relief and triumph as he took her in a hard, savage kiss. Remembering sinking into his arms, so tight, so tight, at last…

Eve's eyes flew open as she drew back from him with an intake of breath. "I remembered something!"

Talos's eyes widened. Then his jaw tightened.

"What exactly did you remember?" he said, his voice low and strained, but in her excitement, she didn't pause to wonder why. She gave him a joyful smile as tears rose to her eyes.

"Our first kiss. It was here on this bridge, just like you said! Oh, Talos, I'm getting my memory back. It's coming back! Everything is going to be all right!"

She threw her arms around him, holding him tightly, overwhelmed by gratitude and relief. She pressed her face to his chest, squeezing her eyes shut to hold back the tears.

Her mind might not remember much about him, but her body instinctively did. She'd been so afraid, but now…

But now…

As she held him, her heart quickened, galloping

faster and faster. The mood between them suddenly changed, electrified. A moment before, she'd just been joyful to have a memory to cling to, some sense of who she was and her past. But as he held her body close, as she breathed in the scent of his skin and pressed her cheek against his soft black shirt, she suddenly felt quite different.

Her cheeks grew hot as she looked up into his eyes.

"Eve, my beautiful Eve," he whispered, touching her face. "Marry me. Be my wife."

Yes, she opened her mouth to say.

But she forced herself to shake her head. "You deserve so much more," she said softly. "You deserve a wife who can remember everything about loving you."

His lips curled with a faint hint of mockery. "Don't worry. I'll get what I deserve." He paused, then his eyes glowed down at her. "After you are my wife, I will devote myself night and day to helping you remember your past. I swear it."

She swallowed, picturing how wonderful it would be to be his wife. How right it would be, to be married as they awaited the birth of their child. Perhaps then her body wouldn't be so afraid for him to kiss her.

Perhaps her sense of honor would accept far more than a kiss.

"It would be selfish of me to accept," she gasped, clinging to her decision by her fingernails.

He traced her tender, bruised lower lip with his fingertip. "It would be selfish of you to refuse. Marry me. For the baby's sake." He paused. "For mine."

She shuddered as his stroke against her lip sent sparks down her body, making her nipples tighten, causing her to shiver all over.

He thought she was being selfish when she was only refusing him for his own sake?

She exhaled. She couldn't fight it anymore. Not when all she wanted to do was be loved and protected and make sure her baby was, too.

"Marry me," he murmured between kisses to her eyelids, her forehead, her throat. She could hardly think straight. He held her so gently, so tenderly. With such love. "Marry me now."

Her eyes were blurry with tears as she stared up at his darkly handsome face. There was a halo of light behind his head, and in the distance she could see birds flying up through the darkly shifting gray sky.

Then he lowered his lips to hers.

Her last thought before he kissed her was that she couldn't remember loving him, but perhaps she didn't need to remember.

Perhaps…she could just fall in love with him all over again.

CHAPTER SIX

KISSING Eve was like falling into hell.

It was fire. Sheer fire running through him. Talos placed his hand on the back of her head, his fingers twining in her beautiful hair, as he deepened the kiss.

For months, he'd hated her. *Hungered for her.*

Was that why finally kissing her now overwhelmed his senses more than ever before?

It wasn't just desire that had changed the kiss, he realized. It was Eve. The kiss was different because *she* was different.

Wrenching away, he looked down at her. Her eyes remained closed. A blissful smile traced her full, bare lips. In her new clothes and hairstyle, she appeared sweet, natural and true.

The Eve he remembered had been none of those things.

Her eyes were still closed as she leaned forward, licking her lips with a tiny dart of her pink tongue. He nearly groaned. He wanted to take her to bed. Now.

He'd already started to pick her up to take her back to the hotel when he caught himself.

No!

He took a deep breath. He couldn't forget who he was really dealing with. The kind, innocent girl in front of him was an illusion. The real Eve Craig was a shallow vixen, a selfish liar. She'd given him her virginity just so she could betray him for another man. He couldn't let her win.

This time, the victory would be his.

"Marry me," he demanded, barely holding himself back from kissing her again. "Marry me now."

"All right," she whispered. "All right."

He exhaled in a rush. Pulling away, he looked down at her fiercely. "Today."

"I'll marry you today," she murmured, looking up at him with a happy, almost tearful smile.

"Talos? Getting married?" a man said behind them. "I can't believe I just heard that!"

Talos whirled around in consternation to see an old friend grinning at him. The man split his time between New York and Tuscany—what the hell was he doing in Venice?

"Roark," he said faintly. "What are you doing here?"

"I never thought I'd see this day," Roark Navarre replied with a snicker. "You always said you'd never get married. You gave me a hell of a time when I married Lia. How the mighty have fallen!" Laughing, he took a step forward. "I can't wait to meet the woman who—"

Then Eve shyly turned to face him, and the grin dropped from Roark's face.

He stopped, his eyes widening.

Eve snuggled back in Talos's arms. A pink blush suffused her cheeks as she looked at Roark with quiet happiness.

His old friend gave Talos a sharply questioning glance. "Is this some kind of joke?"

Eve blinked, furrowing her brow. She glanced between the two men. "What do you mean? A joke?"

"He just can't believe a woman like you would settle for a man like me," Talos told her lightly, then over Eve's head, he stared hard at Roark. "Isn't that right?"

His friend got the message. "Yes. Exactly right."

"I wouldn't say I'm settling exactly," Eve teased him, then looked back at Roark. "Have we met?"

Roark frowned, blinking as if he were in some kind of weird upside-down world. "Several times. At parties, mostly. You were once on a charity committee with my wife."

"Oh." Eve held out her hand with a friendly, apologetic smile. "I'm so sorry. I've had some memory problems lately. What's your name?"

"Roark Navarre. My wife is Lia."

"Lovely to meet you. Is she here?"

"No. She's at home with our kids in Tuscany." Roark shook her hand, then shot Talos a questioning look. "I came to Venice to buy her a gift. Today's our third wedding anniversary."

"How romantic!"

Roark cleared his throat. "Not as romantic as the two of you, it seems. You're really getting married today?"

"Yes," she said shyly, glancing back at Talos. She radiated contentment and quiet joy.

Roark had reason to look shocked, Talos thought. He was one of the few people who knew the whole story of how Eve had stolen the documents from his safe and given them to his American rival, who'd promptly released them to the press with all sorts of nasty insinuations. Roark was undoubtedly wondering why, instead of ripping her head off for nearly ruining his billion-dollar company, Talos had proposed that she become his wife.

Roark wasn't much of a talker—the two men had become friends over mutually beneficial business deals in New York and the occasional Knicks basketball game—but any moment he might say something to give it away.

Once Eve realized their past wasn't as rosy as he'd implied, she would never agree to marry him today. And she'd already had her first memory. The clock was ticking. The rest might come tumbling down at any moment. She could get her memory back, then all would be lost. His revenge. His child's name. He had to marry her as soon as possible. Now, before she remembered everything and ran away again, this time taking his baby with her.

"Yes, we're getting married today," Talos confirmed. "And we have additional good news," he said evenly. "We're having a baby."

"Oh," Roark said, then, *"Oh."* He cleared his throat, then suddenly smiled, as if it all made sense now.

A great time to leave. "So if you'll excuse us, we'll be on our way…."

"On your way!" Roark shook his head, clapping Talos heartily on the shoulder. "I wouldn't hear of it. Come down to Tuscany, man. Just three hours' drive from here. I was just headed back home."

"But it's your anniversary," Eve blurted out. "We couldn't possibly intrude."

"Nonsense." He grinned. "I'll call Lia. She hasn't planned an event for ages, since she's been home with the babies. She'll love the excuse for an impromptu party. And she's been wanting a chance to show off the new place since we finished rebuilding the castle…"

"A castle?" Eve breathed. "In Tuscany?"

"Yes. The oldest part is the medieval walls around the rose garden. Particularly beautiful in September. 'Season of mists and mellow fruitfulness,' and all that," he added, looking a bit embarrassed as he glanced down at the package in his arms.

"Keats," she said in surprise.

"Lia loves poetry," he sighed. He held up the wrapped package. "It's a first edition."

Eve shot Talos an imploring look. "It all sounds lovely."

A romantic wedding? With his friends in attendance?

"Absolutely not," Talos said firmly. "We're fine with a quick visit to fill out the paperwork here."

Leaning against his chest, Eve reached her arms up

over his neck and looked back at him pleadingly. "Oh please, Talos. I would far rather have a real wedding with some of your friends then just with strangers." She paused and suddenly looked wistful. "With no friends and no wedding party, it wouldn't seem quite real."

No, it wouldn't, Talos thought crossly. And that was just the point. This marriage *wasn't* real. It was a means to an end.

"But I understand," she said with a sigh. "You don't want to bother your friends on their anniversary." She brightened. "Perhaps we could wait a few days, plan something here in Venice and invite them."

"All right," Talos said through clenched teeth. He would lose this battle to win the war.

"All right?" she repeated.

"We'll wed in Tuscany."

"Oh, thank you!" she cried, whirling around in his arms to embrace him. "You're so good to me!"

"I'll get my car," Roark said.

"No." Holding her in his arms, Talos looked over her head at Roark. "My men will sort out your car. We'll take my plane. There must be no delay."

"I understand." Glancing between the two of them with an amused grin, his friend gave a snort. "I've felt that way myself, too." He pulled out his cell phone. "I'll tell Lia we're on our way."

Eve had never expected when she woke up that morning that today would be her wedding day. Or that she would get married in a castle in Tuscany.

The beautiful Lia Navarre, called *Contessa* by her housekeeper, had immediately taken Eve under her wing. She'd treated her like a dear friend, even though they'd apparently met only once or twice before. When Eve had nervously told her about her amnesia, Lia had only laughed and said she thought amnesia would be an asset in any marriage.

"Believe me," she'd added dryly, "there are a few things about my own marriage I wouldn't mind forgetting."

Eve had watched in awe as Lia simultaneously arranged for a designer to bring six wedding dresses into the bright morning room and organized flower arrangements over the phone, all as she chattered in Italian with her three-year-old daughter and nursed her new baby son to sleep in her arms.

"I hope to be a mother with half your skill," Eve said wistfully as the wedding designer helped her try on yet another dress. She watched Lia tuck her sleeping baby into a nearby bassinet. "You do everything so well, and all at the same time."

Lia looked up with a snicker. "It might look that way, but believe me, I always wonder if I'm doing enough, or if I'm even doing it right. I'm sure you'll do much better." She tilted her head at Eve. "You know, I never knew you very well, but something about you always confused me."

"What?"

"You've cultivated this image as a party girl, but the time I worked with you on a charity fundraiser, I was shocked at your hard work and drive. You are the most determined person I've ever met, but you just don't let on. You hide it. Why?"

Eve blinked at her, then frowned, turning away with a sigh. "I don't know what to think. Talos described me differently. And now according to you, I'm hardworking and driven? It's like I'm two different people!"

Lia looked at her thoughtfully. "Sometimes we show different sides of ourselves to people for a reason."

"Like what?"

"Oh, I don't know. From a desire to please. From something to hide or something to gain. Oh, this one is lovely." Zipping up Eve's dress, Lia stepped back with a critical eye, then nodded with satisfaction. "Perfect." She looked down at her three-year-old daughter. "Do you like it, Ruby?"

The little girl nodded, her eyes big.

"What do you think?" Lia asked Eve.

Eve looked into the large gilded mirror across the room. The dress was in simple cream-colored silk, cut to accentuate the swell of her breasts and her lush body, falling softly over her belly. Her hair looked glossy and dark, brushing the edges of her pale, bare shoulders. Her blue eyes shone back at her.

Her throat suddenly hurt too much to speak, so she just nodded.

"This is the one," Lia told the designer, who happily started pinning the hem.

"I'm the flower girl," Ruby intoned solemnly to Eve.

"Thank you so much," Eve told her with a big smile.

But as Lia positioned a veil over her chignon, Eve saw herself in the mirror and her heart pounded in her chest.

In one hour, she would be married to a man she still barely knew. A man she'd only really known for the last few days.

But I'm carrying his child, she argued with herself. And when he kissed her, he'd managed to brush aside all her nervousness, all her fears. Something about his kiss was magic. And tonight, he would be kissing her again.

More than just kissing her.

Tonight, their wedding night, he would take her to bed and make love to her.

A hot shiver went over her body, and suddenly, she could think of nothing else. All her questions went out the window. All she could think about was the bed that waited for them at the end of the aisle.

What would it feel like when Talos made love to her?

If it was half as wonderful as the kiss had been, she feared she might die of ecstatic joy.

"I hope you'll be very happy, Eve," Lia said to her softly, and there were suddenly tears in her eyes. "Marriage turns romance into love that lasts forever. It creates a family."

A family. Just what Eve wanted more than anything in the world. She nodded, her heart in her throat.

It seemed scant minutes later when, holding freshly cut orange-red roses that matched the blush on her cheeks, she stepped out of the Italian castle into a Tuscan fairyland.

Sunset was falling over the vineyard and green rolling hills. Outside on the covered terrace a million lights drifted from the ceiling, tangled in wisteria. Next to the terrace she saw an old medieval stone wall, overgrown with roses.

The fairy lights sparkled over her head as she stepped onto the stone floor in her simple white sandals. A musician sitting in the back played the first notes on a guitar, accompanied by a flute. All so simple and so magical.

Then she saw Talos.

He was waiting for her at the other end of the terrace. On one side of him stood a friend of Lia's, the mayor of a nearby town who'd agreed to conduct the hastily arranged civil ceremony. On his other side stood his friend Roark. Eve saw the man's face light up at the sight of Lia and their little girl walking ahead in a sweet, frothy cotton dress. At her mother's urging, little Ruby tossed rose petals haphazardly in Eve's path.

Roark picked up his daughter with delighted praise when she reached the end of the aisle. His smile widened as he met his wife's eyes. Seeing their love for each other, as Lia held their plump baby son who looked so dapper in his little suit, Eve's heart stopped in her chest. *This was just what she wanted.*

A life like this.

A love like this.

But when she looked back at her bridegroom with a joyful smile, his expression stopped her cold.

His gaze was dark. Full of heat and fire. But there was something else. Something she didn't understand that frightened her.

The guitar music suddenly trailed off, and she realized that she'd stopped walking halfway down the aisle. With a deep breath, telling herself she was being silly, she started walking again.

Stop acting like a scared virgin! she chided herself.

When she reached the waiting men, Talos pulled her veil up over her head. She looked up at him with a shy smile.

He didn't return it. Instead, his gaze burned through her, incinerating every drop of blood and bone inside her body. As if they were already in bed.

The mayor began to speak, but his accented words faded into the background. The Navarres disappeared. So did Tuscany, along with the fairy lights and poetry of the mists.

There was only Talos.

His heat.

His fire.

She was dimly aware of repeating the mayor's words, of hearing Talos's deep voice beside her. He slipped a big diamond ring over her finger, then kissed her softly, brushing his mouth against hers.

And just like that—they were man and wife.

CHAPTER SEVEN

FROM the moment Talos saw her in the wedding dress, so lovely and sweet with her shy, happy smile, an earthquake went through his soul.

Eve wore a simple, modest cream-colored wedding dress, with her dark hair beneath a light veil, and she held flame-colored roses in her unmanicured hands. There was no artifice about her. Just beauty. And innocence.

In the brief kiss he gave her after they were wed, his soul trembled within his body. He knew he was on a razor's edge of seducing this beautiful woman, whose fire had once burned him so badly, but who now seemed to shine like the first spring sun after a long, gray winter.

His throat choked as he pulled away from the brief kiss.

Eve, his lying ex-mistress, his hated enemy, was now his wife.

Her big blue eyes shone up at him with such hope and joy, the color of bluebells and violets. He could almost feel the sunlight when he touched her. His longing for her was no longer just about lust, but something more. He longed for her warmth. He could almost hear the laughter of children—his children—bounding through a brightly lit meadow amid cascading sunlight in her innocent promise of happiness.

Lies, he told himself harshly. The woman in front of him, the woman he'd just married, did not really exist.

His hands clenched into fists. She made him want something more. She made him want things he'd never had.

A family.

A home.

This was even more insidious than her earlier betrayal. This kind, loving version of Eve was just an illusion. If he ever allowed himself to care for her, if he ever allowed himself to trust, he would be the biggest fool to walk the earth.

Because as soon as she regained her memory, this woman would disappear. And any day now, she would become the treacherous, selfish woman he remembered.

During the wedding dinner after the ceremony, he watched Eve as she held the baby and entertained three-year-old Ruby. Talos couldn't take his eyes off his bride's radiant beauty—or stop wondering at her generous spirit. The dinner was deliberately simple, homemade pasta and wine from the Navarres' own vintage.

Toward the end of the dinner, Roark and Lia toasted their anniversary with champagne in a private moment, while Eve, still dressed in her simple wedding gown,

cuddled their sleeping baby and kept the little girl entertained with charming fairy tales made up out of the air.

What a mother she would make, Talos found himself
thinking as he watched her. *What a wife she would
make.*

Against his will, his gaze fell upon the neckline and
bodice of her gown. His eyes traced her creamy skin,
the lush breasts plumped forward as she leaned over to
pick a toy from the stone floor.

He wanted Eve so much it hurt. He ached to caress
her. His body tightened painfully, his hand gripping the
crystal goblet of red wine.

"Talos?" With a questioning look, Eve placed her
small, slender hand over his. Her caress and the tender
expression of her impossibly beautiful shining face
caused a shock wave to go through him.

And he suddenly realized that this sweetly loving
woman was more dangerous than the seductive, sexy
mistress had ever been.

He wanted her. All of her.

In his bed.

In his life.

He hungered for the dream she offered him. Hungered for her illusion to be true. Most of all, he hungered
for the bedroom he knew awaited them in the guest
wing of the castle, festooned with rose petals, candles
and soft sheets.

No, he told himself furiously. He couldn't give in!

Ripping his hand away from Eve's, he crashed the

crystal goblet down so hard on the table that it cracked, exploding red wine all over the wood like blood.

Three-year-old Ruby cried out in shock.

Roark and Lia, who'd been cuddled at the other end of the table with intimate, private laughter, looked up with a gasp.

"Sorry," Talos muttered. He rose to his feet. "Sorry." Staring at their faces, he backed away.

"What is it?" Eve whispered. "What's wrong?"

He had the sudden image of her pale, frightened face.

"We have to go," he ground out. He focused on his friends behind her. Roark and Lia had gone far beyond the call of duty to create a fairytale wedding for them with only a few hours' notice, though they had their own responsibilities with their young children; though they had their own anniversary to celebrate. "Thanks for arranging our wedding."

"Surely you're not leaving?" Lia demanded. "I prepared a guest room for you…"

Yes, he'd seen the honeymoon suite, and he wanted no part of it.

"Sorry," he bit out. "We can't stay."

Lia's eyes widened. Talos knew he was being incredibly callous but he would explain to Roark later. His old friend would understand, and he'd make his amends to his wife. All Talos knew was that he couldn't stay for another hour in this romantic place so filled with happy dreams that for him would always be lies.

Talos broke out in a cold sweat.

He had to get out of here.

He had to end this.

He'd won his objective. Eve was his wife. His war was half won. Now all he had to do was make her regain her memory. Now. Before the temptation was too much.

Before Eve finished what she'd started three months ago, and finally crushed him into ashes and dust.

He abruptly turned on his heel, whirling away from the terrace with its overhanging wisteria and fairy lights gleaming in the night.

"Talos? Talos!" he heard his wife cry after him as he strode into the villa, but he didn't look back. Instead, he opened his cell phone and started to bark out orders.

Eve had started this war three months ago.

Now he would finish it.

"Mrs. Xenakis, the plane will be landing shortly."

Eve woke up blearily to discover a pretty brunette flight attendant standing over her, holding a tray. Sitting up straight in the white leather chair, she rubbed her eyes, feeling sweaty and disoriented. She smoothed her wedding dress with her hands, but it didn't help. The cream-colored silk was wrinkled and wilted.

Just like her wedding day.

Eve's head was still spinning. One moment, she'd been a happy bride, pledging her fealty and her faith to the father of her unborn child.

The next, Talos had been dragging her from the castle, pushing her into a car that took them back to the private airport. They'd left without even properly thanking Lia and Roark for the lovely wedding they'd created.

Talos had forced her to leave the cheerfully decorated table with its flowers and lights, the homemade pasta and bread. They'd fled the celebration as if they were thieves in the night, rudely abandoning their kind hosts without explanation as Talos herded her onto his private plane.

There, he'd utterly ignored her and refused to answer any of her questions. He'd gone to the other side of the large cabin to a desk that was as far away from Eve as possible. He'd barked an order to a flight attendant for a shot of Scotch whisky—then hadn't even drunk it. He'd just taken a deep sniff of the amber-colored Scotch before handing it back, telling the flight attendant to pour it out.

Had he gone mad?

Or had she?

He'd spent the rest of the short flight working on his computer. Bewildered and hurt, Eve had fallen asleep staring out the small window of the plane, watching the lights of the Italian coastline disappear over the black emptiness of the Adriatic.

Now, as she looked out the small round window, she saw small clusters of lights amid the darkness, like scattered stars in the night. "Where are we?"

"Beginning our descent into Athens, madam."

"Athens!" Eve cried. "How long was I sleeping?"

The brunette gave a sympathetic smile. "Almost two hours."

Two hours. She glanced over at her new husband,

who was still sitting at his desk, staring at his laptop screen with hard eyes.

Maybe he has work to do, she tried to tell herself. Urgent, unavoidable work that he was desperate to finish so they could properly enjoy our honeymoon.

But she wasn't completely comforted by her explanation. Not when he'd turned so cold and unresponsive from the moment he'd become her husband.

It was almost as if he were angry at her. But that didn't make sense. Hadn't he come to London, desperate to find her? Hadn't he proposed marriage when he found out she was pregnant with his child? Hadn't he spent days passionately, tenderly convincing her to marry him?

She'd finally agreed to be his wife. They'd had a romantic, perfect wedding. So why was he suddenly acting like a man who despised the thought of her existence?

She rubbed her head wearily, causing more tendrils to tumble from her chignon. It didn't make sense. Was her confusion caused by her amnesia? Why couldn't she understand him?

The flight attendant carefully set down her tray on a nearby table. "Mr. Xenakis thought you might wish to have a snack before we land."

Eve saw a nice selection of cut fruits and bread and cheeses, as well as sparkling water and juices. She glanced at her husband across the cabin. "He didn't want to join me?" she said, trying—and failing—to keep the hurt from her voice.

The flight attendant gave her a sympathetic look. "Sorry, madam."

As the flight attendant departed, Eve tried furiously to think, to understand. Talos couldn't have married her for her money, since her fortune, nice as it was, was just a fraction of his. Then why?

Because she was pregnant with his baby? He'd said he wanted to give their baby a name. Was that the only reason?

No, she told herself desperately. He'd married her because he loved her.

Although he'd never said the words, had he?

She drank the water and ate the fruit, though she had no appetite as the plane landed. Talos, in spite of her hurt glances, continued to ignore her long after the plane had landed on the tarmac. After the plane door opened and they came down the stairs, she took a deep breath.

Athens at midnight.

His assistants and various bodyguards were waiting for him on the tarmac, along with two cars to whisk their entourage into the city. They were swiftly and seamlessly escorted through customs. Within minutes, she was seated next to her husband in the back of a black Bentley as the chauffeur drove them on the six-lane highway into the city.

She stared at him until he finally looked at her.

"Talos, why are you acting like this?" she asked quietly.

"Like what?" he demanded.

"Like a jerk."

Clenching his jaw, he looked out at the darkness of the passing city. "I'm sorry if you are so needy and insecure that you feel you must be the center of my attention at every moment," he said in a low voice. "But unlike you, I am not content just to sponge off an income earned by someone else. Unlike you, I own a business and must run it. The fact that we're married does not mean I intend to spend my every hour worshipping you."

She gaped at him, openmouthed.

He'd ignored her for the hours since their wedding, he'd rudely insulted their friends, he'd dragged her from Italy to Greece without explanation…and now he was trying to make her think *she* was the one with the problem?

Biting back an angry retort, she took a deep breath and tried to see things from his position, tried to see if there was a possibility she was being unreasonable.

Nope.

Clasping her hands together, she took another deep, calming breath. She was his wife now. She wanted to be loving and understanding. They were on their honeymoon. She didn't want to start a fight over something so small as his strangely irritated mood.

On the other hand, she wasn't a doormat, and he'd best learn that right now.

"Of course I understand you must work," she tried in her kindest, most understanding voice. "But that doesn't explain why you've been so cold to me all night. Or why you dragged us away from Tuscany." She swallowed. "After your friends went to such trouble, we could have at least spent the night there…."

His dark eyes stabbed daggers at her. "It didn't interest me."

She flushed, feeling humiliated as she sat unwanted in her wrinkled, sad little wedding dress. All night long she'd felt a thrilling ache, a twitter in her belly as she'd imagined their wedding night, thinking of him kissing her, yearning to experience what it felt like when he made love to her.

Apparently the same thought interested him not at all.

"Why are you pushing me away like this?" she whispered. "You've done it since the moment I became your wife. Do you—do you regret marrying me?"

He stared at her for a moment, then turned away, pulling his laptop from his leather briefcase. "We'll be home soon."

"Why are you acting as if you suddenly hate me?"

He closed the laptop with a loud snap. "I'm not going to discuss this right now, Eve."

"Then when?"

His phone rang. He looked down at it before he gave her a narrowed glance. "You'll know everything soon enough." Turning from her, he opened the phone and barked, "Xenakis."

As he spoke on the phone in Greek, she glanced down at the bright diamond ring on her finger. It sparkled at her, sharp facets without a soul. With a sense of foreboding, she looked up through the window at the darkly sprawling city of ancient white buildings and olive trees surrounded by cragged mountains.

Why would Talos marry her if he intended to treat her like this?

She placed her hand on her belly, where their baby was growing inside her. Her stomach was starting to grow more rounded beneath the swell of her breasts.

I wouldn't have given him my virginity unless he was worthy of my love, she told herself.

How do you know? the gleefully sadistic whisper asked. *How do you know what sort of person you are?*

Shut up, she told the voice sharply. *I know.*

But it was too late. Fear had already crept inside her, a dull poison of fear she could neither dispel nor reason away.

She hadn't wanted to marry him so quickly. She'd tried to resist, to delay. But he'd kept insisting. Courting her. Wooing her.

He'd been so loving. So patient. So *perfect.*

And then he'd kissed her on the bridge in Venice, and all of her objections had been swept away in a storm of fierce, blind desire unlike anything she could possibly withstand. His embrace had stolen her strength away, leaving her abject in his arms, with no choice but to surrender to his will.

Now, it seemed there would be no more kisses.

Had she made a horrible mistake marrying Talos?

You're right to be afraid, he'd said with that strange light in his eyes.

Was it possible he'd married her just because she was pregnant with his child? Or for some other, darker reason of his own?

It couldn't be for love—not when he acted like this!

The Bentley pulled up outside an elegant fin de siècle building, nine stories high, on an imposing square in the center of the city. Talos got out without a backward glance. For the first time, he allowed the chauffeur to assist her from the car.

Stepping out on the sidewalk, Eve looked up at the building and the Acropolis, lit up on the high crag above them. She nearly jumped at Talos's voice behind her.

"Beautiful, isn't it?"

She whirled around to see him looking at her with a cruel amusement.

"Yes," she said over the lump in her throat. Beautiful and haughty and a bit savage, just like him.

As his driver and the bellman dealt with the luggage, Talos stepped closer to her. He was so close she could feel his breath, feel the warmth of his strong body beneath his clothes. Leaning forward, not touching her, he whispered, "You'll love the view from the penthouse."

She shivered as he leaned forward.

"It's where you first gave yourself to me," he whispered in her ear, brushing his lips against her tender flesh. "For weeks, we never left our bed."

He stood away from her, his dark eyes gleaming. And though she tried to hide the reaction he'd caused in her, she knew he could read her tension. Her desire.

It infuriated her. Defiantly, she lifted her chin. "Well, I hope you enjoyed it, because it won't happen again."

His eyes darkened at her challenge. He grabbed her hand, and though she tried to pull it away, he would not release her. As the staff and bodyguards trailed them, they went through the exquisite lobby and up the elevator.

It was only when they were alone in the large penthouse condo that he released her.

She rubbed her wrist, staring at him. "Why were you so determined to marry me right away, Talos?" she demanded. "Why? I want the truth right now!"

"The truth?" he said tersely. "What a novel idea where you're concerned."

She pushed aside the little pain at his jab. "Was it because I'm pregnant?"

He looked away. "I will always protect my child."

Pain went through her. Not love, then. Nothing to do with love. "If it was only for the baby's sake, why did you lie?" she said hoarsely. "Why did you say you loved me?"

"I never lied to you." His mouth pressed into a hard line as he stared down at her. "I said I wished to marry you and give the baby a name. Both of which are true."

She shook her head, fighting unbidden tears. "You made me believe you loved me," she whispered. "You tricked me into marriage. Don't you have any sense of honor—any honor at all?"

"Honor!" Their faces were an inch apart as he looked at her with a sneer. "You accuse *me* of dishonor!"

She felt suddenly afraid, trapped, his hard body over hers, his strong hands like shackles on her wrists.

Then she felt his breath on her skin. Heard his breathing change as the mood between them electrified, changing from anger to something else. His grip on her wrists tightened, his gaze dropping to her mouth. Her heart stopped in her chest, then began to flutter wildly. *Thum-thumm. Thumm-thum.* She tingled from her lips to her breasts down to her deepest core.

With a savage intake of breath, he dropped her wrists.

Turning away from her, he walked down the hall. His footsteps echoed heavily against the marble floor. A moment later, he returned with something flimsy and silver that sparkled in his hands.

"Get dressed," he said, his lip curling with scorn. He tossed the silvery fabric at her. "Wear that."

For a moment, she just stared at him, holding the sequined fabric close to her chest. Behind him, the floor-to-ceiling windows revealed the majestic Acropolis, lit up with brilliant lights on the cragged mountain like a torch above the city. She could see the white stone buildings below them, interspersed with palm and olive trees. Her heart was still pounding, her brain in a fog from his closeness a moment ago.

Then she held up the tiny cocktail dress, metallic and shiny and silver. It was dead sexy—and hard. Just like all the clothes she'd given away in Venice.

"No." She lifted her chin. "I told you. I don't want to dress like that anymore."

"You'll do what I tell you."

"I'm your wife, not your slave."

Crossing the room in three strides of his powerful legs, he grabbed her by the shoulders. "You'll obey me, or—"

She tossed her hair back, revealing her neck as she glared at him. "Or what?"

Their eyes locked, held. She heard the quickening of his breath, the gasp of her own.

He wanted to kiss her. She knew it. She could feel it.

But abruptly, he released her. His expression became a mask and he looked almost bored as he glanced at his expensive platinum watch.

"You'd best hurry. We leave in ten minutes." He paused at the door. "Look your best, won't you?" he said coolly. "A special friend of yours will be at the party."

"Party? What party? What special friend?"

But he left her without answer, leaving her to change her clothes alone.

Alone, she thought bitterly.

She hadn't even known what that word really meant until she became a wife.

CHAPTER EIGHT

HE'D been too gentle with her, Talos thought grimly.

As he sat next to Eve on the short drive west toward the nearby neighborhood of Monastiráki, he ignored her angry, shallow huffs of breath beside him. He'd been tempted to tell her everything in the penthouse, but he'd held back for the sake of his child in her belly. For fear the shock would cause miscarriage.

Ridiculous, he thought now, grinding his teeth. Eve was too strong for that. His ex-mistress—his *wife,* he corrected himself—was as hard as steel. A force of nature. Ridiculous to worry about an emotional shock causing injury to their unborn child, when the Eve he'd known had no feelings whatsoever!

But in mere moments, she would finally remember everything—and be forced to admit everything—when she saw her lover.

Clenching his jaw, he stared out the window. The Bentley drove past the dark alley, not too far from Constitution Square where he'd committed his one and only criminal act. At fifteen, two months after his mother had died, he'd smashed the window of an expensive car. It had not gone as planned. The owner of the car had stumbled upon Talos on the sidewalk, holding the ripped-out car stereo in his hands.

Talos hadn't tried to deny his crime. He'd openly confessed and, with as much charm as his self-taught English could muster, suggested he'd done the man a favor. "I think a different brand of stereo might suit you better." Then, with a bowed head, he'd waited for him to call the police.

Instead, Dalton Hunter had hired him on the spot. "Our Athens office could use a kid like you," he'd said with a laugh. And Talos had soon found himself the new messenger and office boy for the American CEO's worldwide shipping corporation.

From that day, remembering his crime with shame, Talos had been obsessed with justice.

After climbing the corporate ladder and making some lucky investments, he'd made his first million by the age of twenty-four. The father who'd abandoned his mother when she was pregnant with Talos had read about him in the newspaper and had contacted him.

Not to ask for money, he'd said. Just for a visit.

Talos had refused even to speak with him.

A man earned the circumstances of his life. He got what he deserved.

And Yiorgos had caused Talos's mother financial and emotional distress which had ultimately led to her early death. The man might share Talos's DNA, but that was all. Dalton Hunter had been far more of a father to him than that man had ever been.

At least so Talos had thought until eleven years ago, when Dalton had turned out to be utterly corrupt.

But when it came to corruption, one woman had beaten them all.

He glanced at Eve. She looked coldly beautiful in the tiny silver cocktail dress and stiletto heels. Her lips were scarlet as blood, her eyelashes black as night against her white skin. Just like the ruthless mistress he remembered. As if nothing had changed.

Wasn't that what he'd wanted?

The car stopped in front of an old white building, once part of a thirteenth-century monastery, now an art gallery nightclub started by a friend. Talos climbed out of the car, straightening the cuff links on the white shirt beneath his black blazer as he waited. The chauffeur opened Eve's door, and she walked up to him on stiletto heels with a graceful swing of her hips.

"What is it?" she said acidly, tossing her head. Her lip curled. "Aren't you happy with how I look?"

Was he happy? He looked down at her. Eve's glossy dark hair had been pulled back into a severe ponytail that revealed the perfection of her bone structure and her creamy skin. Silver earrings dangled against her long neck. A tight silver cuff coiled up her bare arm in the shape of a snake.

She was a cold goddess.

Breathtaking.

Powerful.

"You'll do," he said evenly. He yanked her toward the door.

The asymmetrical straps of her silver dress hung askew on her shoulders, apparently threatening to fall at any moment to reveal her amazing breasts. He knew it was only a cunning artifice of design, but as they walked into the crumbling white building, and he heard the tap-tap-tap of her six-inch-high silver stiletto heels beside him, he watched men get whiplash from turning their heads to gawk at her.

Eve lifted her chin stonily, pretending not to notice. She was graceful, full of dignity. But he could feel her simmering fury rising from her beautiful body in waves.

Talos glared at them with a snarl curling his lip.

In the past, he'd been arrogantly proud to have the woman that every other man wanted. He'd taken it as his due—other, lesser men always envied what Talos possessed.

That had changed in Venice. And now, when he saw men craning their heads to look at her, pure rage washed over him.

Why? Why was he so angry and possessive? Because she was his wife?

Wife in name only, he told himself fiercely. And tonight, he would finally get his revenge. Once she saw her old love, she would remember everything. He would see her face crumple when she realized how she'd been caught.

"Talos!" The hostess, a thirtysomething socialite married to a Greek tycoon three times her age, came forward to greet him with a big smile. "What a wonderful surprise, darling! Your assistant sent your regrets. And—" She looked at Eve and her eyes went wide. "Oh my goodness. Eve Craig. I didn't expect—I never thought you might—"

"Is Skinner here?" Talos interrupted.

The woman had been staring at Eve in consternation, but now she whirled to face Talos, biting her lip. "I heard you were in Australia. I never would have invited him otherwise," she implored. "Please, darling, I don't want trouble!"

"Don't worry, Agata," he replied, gritting his teeth into a smile. "We're just going to have a bit of a chat."

She exhaled. "I'll hold you to that." She eyed Eve, then as photographers came close to take their picture, put her arm around her and smiled before giving her an air kiss. "I didn't realize you and Talos were still an item, Eve darling."

"We are," Eve replied coldly, then folded her arms as she waited for Talos.

Clenching his jaw, he looked downstairs over the railing. The cavernous white stone building was decorated with candles and modern-day icons looking up mournfully from gilded frames. All of the international party set was here to celebrate Agata's twenty-ninth birthday—her third such party, if he recalled correctly. Suddenly, across the room, past the dance floor and the colorfully painted wooden bar with Agata's hand-selected shirtless bartenders, Talos saw his rival—Jake Skinner.

Talos glanced quickly at Eve, waiting for her to see the tall American tycoon. Instead, she was staring up at him with an angry frown, searing him with her violet-blue eyes.

"Enjoying yourself?" she said acidly. "Is this why you married me? So you could parade me at parties like your little doll?"

"I can do whatever I want with you," he said coldly.

Cupping her bare arm, he steered her down the stairs and straight across the room to Jake Skinner. With a flicker of his eyes, Talos looked between them, waiting for recognition to cross Eve's beautiful face at the sight of the man she'd dated before Talos. The man who held her loyalty. *The man she loved.*

Whirling around, the rugged American playboy nearly gasped at the sight of Talos. He looked around nervously for the exits. "Xenakis, it's a public place. Don't even think about—"

"Relax. I'm here to enjoy myself."

Skinner visibly exhaled.

"No hard feelings, right?" he said in a jocular voice. "I only gave that document to the press because it seemed as if you were breaking the law."

That, plus he'd hoped to gain massive profit for his own shareholders, Talos thought. He bared his teeth into a smile. "Of course, I understand. For all you knew, I might have been guilty. And no one—" he looked down at Eve "—should remain unpunished for their crimes."

Eve's brow furrowed as she stared up at him, as if

trying to understand the meaning beneath his words. She didn't seem to have any interest in Jake Skinner whatsoever.

Why wasn't this working? Skinner was the love of her life. He had to be. There could be no other reason for her cold-blooded betrayal of him in June. So why wasn't she reacting at the sight of him? Why wasn't she crying out his name, gasping out her sudden memory, turning to Talos in horror and realizing she'd been irrevocably caught?

Clenching his jaw, Talos turned to give his rival a hard smile. "And just to show you there's no hard feelings, Skinner, here's a little peace offering."

He shoved Eve toward him. She stumbled in surprise, nearly tripping on her six-inch stiletto heels.

The American's jaw dropped, and his voice hit a high octave as he gasped, "Your peace offering is—Eve?"

"Forget it, you bastard," Eve said furiously, whirling back to face Talos. "I won't do it. I won't even dance with him—"

"You will."

She sucked in her breath, and for a moment he thought she meant to slap his face.

Then she straightened her spine with graceful dignity.

"What a lovely idea," she said coldly, turning to Skinner with a smile on her scarlet lips. "Shall we dance?"

"Yes," the man breathed. "Oh, yes."

His eyes held such flagrant desire that Talos's hands clenched into fists at his sides. He watched as his business rival collected his wife, taking her hand in his own, and escorted her to the dance floor.

And as the music started, Talos was unable to look away.

Eve was a beautiful dancer. She always had been. Every step she took caused the silvery sequined dress to move in waves over her luscious body. Without touching the other man, she moved slowly, sensually, in front of him, holding her arms over her head. The bottom of the dress barely brushed her thighs as she swayed her hips, closing her eyes.

Jake Skinner, along with nearly every other man on the dance floor, had stopped to gape at her, slack-jawed. The other women on the floor, many of whom were also very beautiful, noticed their men had frozen in place and they, too, turned to glare.

With her eyes still closed, Eve swayed to the music.

She moved like the seductive siren of every man's hungry dreams.

Talos suddenly felt as though he was choking for air—or dying of thirst. Grabbing a martini from a waiter who'd stopped in front of him to stare at his wife, Talos gulped it all down at once.

Then he looked back at Eve. Every man in the room was staring at her. He felt a sudden stabbing pain against his palm and looked down, realizing he'd just shattered the martini glass in his hand.

"Me singkorite!" With a gasp, a nearby waiter turned and scurried to grab a broom.

"Oriste." Agata was suddenly standing next to him. She held out a small towel.

Talos took it. *"Efkharisto."*

"You're wasting your time with her," she said quietly, nodding toward Eve. "You're going to get hurt."

"You're wrong." Talos wiped the blood off his hand with the towel. The cuts weren't deep. "She can't hurt me."

But he knew he was lying. Eve had cut him to the bone long ago.

He watched her across the room, dancing with her eyes closed, her arms swaying over her head. His lust for Eve cut far deeper than any blade. Like every other man in the room, he wanted her so badly that every nerve in his body vibrated with her music. And after three months of constant longing, an increasingly frustrated desire had left him frayed like fabric, falling apart at the edges.

After being so close to her, courting her, of having her in his bed but not being able to touch her, he was going mad. *Lust for her was killing him.*

He'd been so certain that coming to the party tonight would cause Eve to regain her memory and return to the cruel, grasping seductress he remembered. And she had—but in a way he'd never expected.

She was taunting him.

Watching her move and sway, he swallowed his lust, his whole body in a hot sweat. As the song ended, Talos felt, rather than heard, the low deep growl of every man in the place wanting Eve. Felt the press of male footsteps and bodies leaning toward her.

As if coming out of a trance, Eve slowly opened her eyes.

Talos saw Jake Skinner reach for her as the dance ended. Reaching with his hands, with his hungry eyes, with his mouth—

Suddenly, Talos found himself across the room and in the middle of the dance floor.

He pushed his rival aside.

"Stay—away—from—my—wife!"

He drew back in shock. "Your wife?" Skinner gasped. He backed away, his face turning white. "You're married?"

Eve just tilted her head quizzically. "As a matter of fact, we are." She tossed Talos a look through narrowed eyes. "I didn't know you cared."

"I care," he ground out. Tightening his jaw, Talos looked at his American rival. Every muscle was taut with the control it took not to attack the other man. "Stay away from my wife," he said again in a low voice.

Skinner looked between them quickly. What he saw in Talos's face must have convinced him, because he turned and ran, pushing his way past the party guests, nearly knocking over their hostess in his haste.

Talos felt the eyes of the whole room upon them. So much for telling Agata that he wouldn't make a scene.

"Happy birthday," he told Agata abruptly. "Thanks for the party."

Lacing his fingers through Eve's, he escorted her out of the building. Only when they were on the sidewalk and the cooling night air hit their skin, did he turn to her.

"You little fool," he bit out. "What were you thinking with that little show?"

But she clearly wasn't going to let him railroad her.

"Isn't that what you wanted?" she retorted furiously, tossing her head. "Isn't this who you want me to be?" She blinked back sudden tears. "And you think just because you don't want me, you can pass me off to your friends—"

He pushed toward her, backing her into the darkness of the rough, rubbish-strewn alley.

"You think I don't want you?" he said dangerously.

When her heels hit the stone wall, she stopped, lifting her chin. Her eyes shimmered in the moonlight as she matched him toe-to-toe, holding her ground.

"I think you're a liar," she said hoarsely. "You lured me into marrying you under false pretenses, and now you want to punish me for some reason. I don't know why, but I was a fool to trust your words, your lying kisses. I can't believe I ever let you touch me. I never will again—"

He cut her off with a kiss, pushing her back against the rough stone, holding her wrists like shackles against the wall. He spread her lips wide, thrusting his tongue inside her mouth, deepening the kiss until she sagged in his arms. *Until she started to kiss him back.*

The moment he felt her lips move against his, as she

matched his fire with her own, a surge of reckless joy went through him that he could not control.

He was going to take her right here in the alley. Against the wall. Damn the consequences.

He would possess her now, even if he died for it.

Eve's breath came in little gasps as he slowly kissed up her neck, his arms tracing up and down her naked skin.

"Why are you doing this?" she whispered. Feeling his mouth on her sent sparks down her body until she thought she might forget to breathe. "I did what you wanted. Why are you so angry? Why do you feel possessive because I danced with your friend—exactly as you wanted?"

"Seeing all those other men lusting for you was never what I wanted," he ground out.

"Then why?" she managed as his hands stroked her roughly over the sequins of her dress. "Why are you killing me like this—kissing me one moment then pushing me away the next? As if you hate me? Why are you torturing me?"

His hands stilled. He looked down at her, and the fire in his eyes of a moment before had changed to longing. To confusion. *To pain.*

Staring down at her, he suddenly yanked off his black blazer. Without a word, he wrapped it around her tiny silver dress. The jacket hung long on her, covering her modestly to mid-thigh.

Grabbing the jacket's lapels, he pulled her close.

He leaned his head forward, pressing his forehead against hers.

When he spoke, his voice was so low she barely heard his words. "I'm sorry."

And just like that, she exhaled.

He pulled her gently from the alley to the Bentley waiting for them on the street. Without explanation, Talos opened Eve's door and helped her inside. He didn't speak to her in the car—he didn't even look at her.

But he held her hand tightly all the way to his penthouse.

When they arrived at his apartment a few moments later, he helped her out of the car. Still, he held her hand and didn't let go.

She stared up at him in a daze, unable to look away from his darkly handsome face as they crossed the lobby of the elegant nineteenth-century building and went into the elevator. At the door of the penthouse, Talos unlocked it and turned to her, his face dark with need.

"I should have done this a long time ago."

He lifted her in his arms. His body glowed with warmth and heat she could almost see, burning off his body in waves. Holding her closely, Talos kicked the door open, then kicked it closed behind them.

Crossing the penthouse, with the view of the lit-up Acropolis on the mountain floating high above the night, he gently set her on her feet on the marble floor. Never taking his eyes from hers, he peeled his large black jacket off her shoulders, dropping it to the floor.

She closed her eyes, her breath shortening as she felt

him reach behind her head and undo her ponytail. Her hair fell softly against her shoulders in one shake.

She felt his hands run over her body, stroking her over her silvery cocktail dress.

"You're mine, Eve," he whispered. He traced his large hands over her hips, over her slender waist.

He ran his hands back over her whisper-thin silver dress, causing it to slink and move over her body like a caress. She felt his thumbs brush against her breasts, making her nipples harden to agonizing intensity beneath the fabric. Her breasts felt heavy and swollen, swaying as he cupped them reverently in his hands. Her whole body felt tight and hot. She felt dizzy all over, her knees weak.

Her eyes flew open as he knelt at her feet. The room seemed to spin around her as she watched him stroke slowly down her bare legs, from her thighs to the backs of her knees. Massaging her calves, he slowly removed one stiletto heel, then the other, dragging them gently against the tender hollow of her foot. He sent the shoes skidding across the floor.

His gaze locked on hers, hot and dark.

Slowly, he rose back to his feet. Never taking his eyes from hers, he removed his tuxedo tie. He unbuttoned his white shirt, dropping it carelessly to the floor. She had the sudden vision of his bare chest, powerfully muscled and laced with dark hair.

Then he stood naked and powerful in front of her. His olive skin gleamed in the sharp moonlight, which cascaded over the hard planes of his body. Every inch of his muscular body exuded masculine power. Looking down, she saw how much he wanted her, and she swallowed, afraid of his strength, his size. She was pregnant with his child, and yet with no memory she felt as shy as a virgin.

Murmuring endearments in Greek, he picked Eve up in his arms. Carrying her across the room, he gently set her down on the enormous bed. Stretching her arms above her, he pulled off her little sliver of a gown. Pushing her back against the pillows, he pulled off her panties. And suddenly she was naked in front of him, naked on their bed.

The thought terrified her, but before she could move away, he was on top of her. She felt his hardness against her belly as he slowly kissed her neck, sucking on her earlobes, softly brushing back her hair as he whispered in her ear, "*Ekho sizigho.* My sweet one."

He cupped her breasts together, nuzzling between them, thumbing the nipples until they tightened to agonizing points. He suckled first one, then the other, before moving down her body to kiss her belly. His hands stroked her hips, brushing her thighs before he moved up to kiss her mouth. His kiss was hard, hungry. He wrapped his arms beneath her shoulders, holding her tightly to his body. She gasped as she felt him between her legs, pushing her thighs apart.

A satisfied masculine growl escaped him as he moved his hardness against her slick, wet heat. She twisted beneath him as the low tension built deeper and deeper inside her, making her breath come out in quick little pants, making her body sizzle from her taut nipples to her hot molten core. She was melting for him, melting to nothing, and if he didn't…

He slid inside her with a single deep stroke.

Her back arched. She cried out as he filled her to the hilt, releasing pleasure so deep inside it was almost pain.

He choked out a gasp, closing his eyes as he thrust inside her again, pulling back, riding her hard and slow. Each stab was deeper, spiraling a sweet ecstasy so far inside her that she thought she might be devoured by it.

He spread her wide, splitting her apart. Harder, faster, pain, pleasure. Just four times. Four thrusts, each one deeper and harder than the last.

And she exploded.

CHAPTER NINE

As Talos felt her body tighten, he knew he could not last.

Touching her was heaven. Her skin was even softer than he remembered. She tasted sweet, so sweet. The very first time he slid inside her, he nearly lost control. With every thick thrust he watched her full breasts sway from the force of his possession, and he gasped out each breath. How long had he wanted her?

How had he denied himself for so long?

With each slow thrust inside her, he shattered a little more, until he was coming apart like Venetian stucco falling into the water. His whole body shook with the agony of holding himself back when all he wanted to do was bury himself in her completely, to lose himself in the ecstasy of making love to her. Every nerve was on fire. It had never felt like this before—not even with her.

Three thrusts, and he was shaking with the desperate effort to stay in control. He grunted as he shoved into her roughly, pushing all the way to the hilt in pleasure so great he nearly lost his mind. He heard her soft gasp spread to a scream and felt her shudder as her body convulsed around him. And he could hold back no longer. With a shout, he shoved inside her one last time with a guttural cry, pulsing and spurting inside her.

Spent, he collapsed next to her, pulling her into his arms, holding her tightly.

Now, as he looked at the gray light coming from the windows, he realized it was already morning. They'd slept in each other's arms for at least two hours.

Something he'd never done before.

Oh, they'd slept in bed together, of course, between stretches of nearly constant lovemaking. But he'd never just held her like this, cradling her against his chest as they drowsed.

He felt…contented. *Protective*.

He stared down at her naked beauty. The white cotton sheets had fallen past her hips. Her skin was lustrous and creamy. Her breasts were heavy and swelling, the tips that he'd suckled so recently now a shade of pink that was the color of deep pink roses. The slight swell of his child in her belly only made her look more feminine, like a goddess of fertility.

He felt himself instantly go hard. He already wanted her again. And not just her body…

How had she changed so much?

How could losing her memory make her into such a different person?

He'd tried to resist her. He had every reason in the world to punish and hurt her. *But he could not.*

Something inside Talos wouldn't let him do it. Even as his exacting soul cried out for justice, he could not hurt her.

There was only one card left to play. One last chance for justice.

He could tell her the truth.

He could take her to the place where she'd betrayed him.

It was his last chance.

Because this new Eve, the woman now sleeping in his arms, was too beautiful, too real, too vulnerable. Too warm and natural and loving.

He'd counted on her having no defenses. He'd never thought that her innocence would cause him to lose his own defenses.

But sooner or later, Eve would revert to her true self, the cold, cruel, clever siren who'd sold him out for love or money. The woman who would undoubtedly hate their baby because of what the pregnancy did to her perfect figure. The woman who would ignore and neglect her child for her own selfish pursuits.

Who would never want to settle down with any man for long.

His fingers tightened on her as he took a deep breath. He had to end this. *Today*. He had to erase this new woman completely. Before he…before he…

He suddenly heard a strange sound. Frowning, he looked down at the woman in his arms.

For a moment, he heard only the quiet snuffle of her

breathing and the sound of morning birds singing outside in the pale blue of dawn.

Then he heard Eve suck in her breath again. And she started to scream.

Cradled in Talos's strong arms, beneath the soft dawn spilling from the windows, Eve hadn't wanted to wake up. She'd pressed her head against his naked chest, relishing the feel of his warm skin laced with dark hair.

His body was so much larger than her own. Snuggled against him in the enormous bed, she'd felt protected. Safe. *Loved.* There was so much about him she still didn't understand. But still, she was falling in love with him all over again.

Drowsy and content, she'd listened to the beat of his heart against her cheek. The beat grew louder, like the sound of heavy footsteps stomping in unison against a hard stone floor. *Step. Step. Step.*

She felt suddenly cold as she looked at the blurry faces around her. Her mother's sobbing face came into sharp focus. She clung to Eve, wailing as they watched her father's coffin pass out of the church on the shoulders of old men. Eve clutched her mother's hands in her own, suddenly terrified that her father's death would cause her to lose both her parents. In the last week, she'd lost her father, their home, their fortune, their reputation. And it was all that man's fault. He'd destroyed her father with all his lies. He'd heartlessly destroyed them all....

Now outside, standing on the frozen grass of the

cemetery beside the dark-clothed mourners, she saw the cold March wind blow her mother's black veil back like a dark spirit. She saw her mother stretch her arms toward the coffin as her beloved husband was lowered into the earth, as if she intended to bury herself in the same cold grave....

"No!" Eve screamed. "Please!"

"Eve!" She suddenly felt a man's strong, protective arms around her, his voice anxious as he enveloped her with his warmth. "Wake up. Wake up."

With a choked gasp, Eve opened her eyes. And saw Talos's face.

"What—what is it?"

"You were screaming." He held her tightly, stroking her face, stroking her hair. His dark eyes were full of concern. "Did you have a dream?"

A dream?

Pain racked through her, and suddenly her head was pounding as if her skull had been fractured into pieces. She pushed away from him as tears streamed down her face. For some reason, she suddenly couldn't stand his touch.

"I remembered my father's funeral," she whispered.

She pushed away, standing up, then realized she was naked. She froze, remembering their night together. Remembering how happy she'd been sleeping in his arms...

She took a deep, ragged breath, pushing her hair out of her eyes. "I'll go take a shower." Before he could reply, she added quickly, "Alone."

Talos's eyes darkened. He turned away from her, reaching into his closet. "Fine."

She took a quick shower, trying to wash away the sharp pain of her memory. She quickly dressed in clothes for the hot Greek sun—a pale pink tank top, a short knit skirt and white flat sandals. Brushing her hair, she stared at herself in the mirror.

All these days she'd been so desperate to remember her past. And now...

What if she didn't like what she found?

"Are you hungry?" Talos asked quietly when she came out into the bedroom. "Shall we have a quick breakfast?"

"That sounds fine," she said, careful not to touch him. Anything to get away from this place where, just as she'd found happiness at last, she'd been stabbed with pain.

Talos left his hands stuffed in his jacket pockets as they took the elevator downstairs. He opened the back door of the Bentley and helped her inside. But as he sat next to her on the short drive, he kept his distance. As if there were an invisible wall between them.

To think last night, he'd held her so tightly, whispering endearments to her in Greek, covering her body with hot kisses as he pressed his naked body against hers.

How had everything changed so much since then?

"What else don't I remember?" she whispered. "What if it's all bad? What if it's worse?"

He set his jaw. "What could be worse?"

"What happened to my father?"

He frowned, staring at her warily with lowered eyebrows.

"I don't know what happened to your father," he said finally. "We never talked about your family."

She stared at him in shock. "Never? In all the time we were together?"

He shook his head.

"How is that possible?"

"We didn't talk about the past," he said shortly.

"Never?"

"No."

"Then…what did we talk about?"

"We didn't talk. We just made love."

A cold trickle went down her back.

They'd never spoken about their pasts?

Their relationship had only been about sex?

The car stopped. Silently, Talos got out of the car and opened her door. Looking up, she saw a very elegant French restaurant in a glossy new building with coldly modern architecture. "This is your idea of a quick breakfast place?"

Talos gave her a smile that didn't meet his eyes. "It was your favorite restaurant in Athens."

Once inside, they were escorted to the best table, which overlooked the crowded street below. The fancy restaurant was elegant and chilly with sterile air-conditioning. There were many waiters but no other diners.

"It's not very popular in here on a Sunday morning," she ventured.

"I reserved the whole place," he said, sounding bored as he opened the menu.

"Why?"

"I wanted you to be comfortable." He closed the menu. "What would you like?"

With a sigh, she opened her menu. It was written in English and French. This place was entirely too coldly elegant, she thought. Looking out the window with longing, Eve saw locals and tourists thronging a colorful street market.

Outside in the hot Greek sun, she saw people smiling at each other, eating at outdoor cafés, bartering good-naturedly in the flea market.

The waiter came and took their order, speaking flawless English with a slightly British accent. After he departed, a different waiter brought them drinks. She took a sip of orange juice, then leaned forward with her elbows on the table.

"All right, Talos," she said quietly. "Tell me why we're really here."

His eyes were dark as they fixed on her. "This past summer, I almost lost my business," he said in a low voice. "A document was stolen from my penthouse which suggested I might be cheating my stockholders of a great deal of money. Of course, I wasn't. But it cast the company's finances in a sordid light."

She stared up at him, shocked. "That's terrible! Did you find out who did it?"

He looked at her, his eyes glittering. "Yes."

"I hope you put them in jail!"

He took a sip of black coffee. "That's not my style."

"But what does that have to do with me—and this restaurant?"

"This is the last place I ever saw you, Eve. Before your accident."

She frowned, shaking her head. "Right before I left for my stepfather's funeral?"

"You left me long before that. Almost three months ago."

"I don't understand."

"Do you recognize this table?"

She looked down at it. "No. Should I?"

"The last time I saw you, you were sitting here with Jake Skinner. Having breakfast with him, just hours after I'd made love to you."

"What?" she gasped.

His hands clenched on the white linen tablecloth. "Kefalas was following you—"

"Following me?" she gasped.

"*Protecting* you," he corrected. "During the one day I had an unbreakable appointment. He phoned me and I dropped everything. I rushed here like a fool to demand an explanation. You tried to laugh it off as nothing."

She thought of the American tycoon whom she'd met at the party. "So that's why you wanted me to dance with him," she said quietly. "To trick me?"

"I wanted to make you remember betraying me."

She shook his head. "I don't!"

"You disappeared from the city. The next morning, I woke to discover my company's name splashed across the newspapers, and my phone ringing incessantly with calls from press and angry stockholders. Skinner gave the document to the press. But the one who first stole it from my house—" he leaned forward, his eyes black and hard "—was you."

She drew back in shock. "Me!"

"And so I've been waiting for you to remember. Every place I've taken you, every memory I've hoped to reignite, was so you could tell me why."

Suddenly, she understood everything.

"Not just that," she whispered. "You wanted to punish me. It's what you've wanted since the day you found me in London. You wanted revenge—"

"Justice," he corrected coldly.

"But when you found out I was pregnant, that changed everything, didn't it?" She gave a choked laugh, then covered her mouth with an intake of breath. "You felt you had to marry me because I was pregnant with your baby. You never loved me. All you wanted— was to hurt me."

"I spent months trying to find you before you resurfaced at your stepfather's funeral. You're a wealthy woman, Eve, so you couldn't have betrayed me for money. So you must have done it for love. You're in love with Jake Skinner. It's the only explanation."

She thought of the playboy with his bleached-white smile and shook her head. "I could never love him."

"Then why? Why would you do it? What did I ever do to you?"

She took a deep breath as tears filled her eyes.

"I don't know," she whispered.

"Was it out of spite? Did I offend one of your friends? Did I ignore you or hurt someone you cared about? Why? Why would you give me your virginity—then betray me?"

"I don't know." She took a deep breath. "But…I'm sorry."

He stared at her, his handsome face the picture of shock.

"Just like that?" he whispered. "You admit your guilt?"

"I don't remember this restaurant. I don't remember betraying you. I can't even imagine doing something so horrible." Her eyes filled with tears and she blinked rapidly. "But I knew you had some reason to hate me. If you say I betrayed you, then I believe you. I must have done it." She shook her head. "I don't know why and can't offer any excuse. Except to tell you that I'm sorry, desperately sorry."

Talos just stared at her, wide-eyed, not moving.

No wonder he'd been so cold and distant after their marriage. No wonder he'd wanted to punish her. He'd hated her, but he'd felt he had no choice but to marry her because of the baby.

How would she feel in his place, forced to marry the lover who'd once betrayed her? Her heart ached just to think of it.

"You must hate me," she said softly.

His jaw tightened.

"No," he said in a low voice. "You're not the one I hate."

"Then—who?"

He turned away. "I thought you would remember Skinner if you saw him. I was sure you'd remember loving him."

"*Him?* No!" She shook her head fiercely. "If you say I betrayed you, then I believe you. But not for that man, no. Never!"

She saw the surprise in his face, the dawn of insecurity. "How can you be so sure?"

"He's dreadful!"

"Perhaps you didn't always think so. You've changed since the accident, Eve."

She bit her lip, looking down at her pink cotton tank top and simple beige skirt. She suggested in a small voice, "I was more attractive to you before?"

Unexpectedly, he reached his hand over the table, placing it over hers.

"No," he said in a low voice. "You were selfish and cold then, only focused on yourself. Now…" He took a deep breath. "You're different. You care about other people. You're loving and kind and sexy as hell. I've tried not to want you, Eve. Tried not to care. I've tried. And failed."

Her heart was in her throat as she looked up at him, tears in her eyes. She took a deep breath.

"I love you, Talos," she whispered. "Whatever I felt for you last summer—I'm in love with you now."

His hand trembled over hers. He started to pull his hand away, but she stopped him, pressing his hand to her cheek.

"And I'm sorry," she whispered into his skin, pressing her lips against the back of his hand. "Forgive me."

She felt his hand shake, but instead of pulling away, he suddenly took one of her hands in both his own. Looking up, she was startled to see the weight of emotion shimmering in his eyes.

Clearing his throat, he glanced around at the elegant, empty restaurant. "Let's go have breakfast somewhere else."

Looking into his face, she felt her heart leap in her chest. Suddenly, she knew everything was going to be all right.

She now knew the reason he'd treated her so badly— but now he'd finally told her the truth, it could be healed. He could forgive her. She wouldn't stop trying until he did—and until she remembered why she'd done it. And they could be a family.

Wiping tears from her eyes, she nodded.

Still holding her hand, he threw a large wad of bills on the table, then took her out into the bright sunshine.

The Greek sun was already starting to burn white. But as they crossed the busy street, the morning was fresh and new to Eve. Joy was everywhere.

Talos held her hand tightly as he led her through the traffic, protecting her body with his own. They hurried past ancient white stone buildings packed between new trinket shops. She saw young mothers playing with their children on balconies draped with clothes hanging out in the sun to dry, wizened grandfathers smoking as they played chess in the sun.

Palm trees waved above them, providing respite from the early heat as they crossed into the Plateía Avissynías, an outdoor bazaar rich with music, the sizzle and smell of souvlaki and loud, boisterous haggling in the market stalls over everything from jewelry to Turkish carpets.

And Eve suddenly knew happiness was waiting for them around every corner.

"I'm sorry I wiped out your fortune," she said once they reached the square. Talos stared at her in surprise.

Then he pulled her into his arms with a sudden boyish grin. It made him so handsome it took her breath away.

"You *tried* to ruin me," he pointed out. "But in the end, the press attention only revealed our integrity. My company is worth more now than ever."

"So really," she teased, "you should thank me."

On the sidewalk, he pulled her closer, his body hard against her own. Suddenly all the traffic and other people faded away.

His eyes were dark. Hungry. He pulled her close, stroking her face upward. "Thank you."

And as he lowered his mouth to hers, kissing her so deeply and purely, she knew she would love him—forever.

* * *

Nothing had changed.

And yet everything had changed.

As Talos looked down at her beautiful face in the busy outdoor market, her eyes were still closed. Her lips were swollen and bruised from his kiss.

As he lowered his head to kiss her again, he dimly heard his cell phone ringing from his pocket. He retrieved it and glanced down at it, cursing softly when he saw it was his assistant, no doubt calling about the Sydney deal. "Excuse me," he said with real regret. "I have to take this call."

Her beautiful eyes smiled up at him. Accepting him, flaws and all. Asking only that he accept her, as well.

She'd taken blame.

She loved him. How was it possible?

"That's all right," she breathed. "I'll just—um—look around the market until you're done."

"Stay where Kefalas can see you."

She bit her pink, bruised lip, and he could tell she didn't like the intrusion of a bodyguard, even from a distance. For a moment Talos was tempted to ignore his assistant's phone call, forget the billion-dollar deal and offer to be her own private bodyguard. Then she sighed. "All right."

Talos watched as she wandered toward the market. Even in the loose cotton skirt, he admired her backside. He admired her dark glossy hair, her perfect natural beauty. Her sweetly innocent love for him.

I love you, Talos. Whatever I felt for you last summer—I'm in love with you now.

The phone's incessant ringing finally penetrated his consciousness, forcing him to answer. "Xenakis."

"The Sydney deal is as good as done," his first assistant crowed happily. "Their board just voted in favor of the sale."

"Good," he said, but he wasn't really paying attention. He was watching his beautiful wife walk across the market, looking so happy, so interested in the world around her. He was about to hang up.

Then he suddenly paused. "Have Mick Barr investigate Eve."

His assistant's voice was too well-trained to register surprise. "Investigate Mrs. Xenakis?"

"Have him find out how her father died. See if there's any reason it might be tied to me."

As Talos hung up the phone, his gaze lingered on Eve, so beautiful and natural in the pink tank top and short cotton skirt. Instead of stiletto heels, she was exploring this city—exploring her life—in sandals that were clearly made for walking. Her bright, happy face, once so pale, was starting to tan in the sun.

He'd once thought to use her amnesia against her. He'd never imagined that her innocence and warmth would affect him like this. He felt knocked off-kilter by her tenderness, by her love.

I'm sorry. Forgive me.

He was blown away by her openness and vulnerability. She'd accepted blame for a betrayal she could not even remember. She'd chosen to believe him. To trust him, when all he'd done was lie to her, trick her, punish her. It was enough to bring any man to his knees.

Talos started to walk toward her, but he'd gone only a few steps before the phone in his hand rang. He saw his lead investigator's number and answered. "That was fast."

"I can tell you about your wife's father right now, Mr. Xenakis." Barr paused. "Does the name *Dalton Hunter* mean anything to you?"

Talos's entire body went hot, then turned to ice.

He was only dimly aware of the ebb and flow of people around him as his hand clenched around the phone.

"Dalton Hunter?" he repeated in a strangled voice.

"He died in a car accident when she was fourteen. A few months later, her mother remarried—to a wealthy British aristocrat. He adopted her. She took his name."

Talos's heart pounded in his throat. He saw black birds soaring in the blue sky above the city and for a moment he thought he was going mad.

Dalton Hunter—Eve's father?

"How was I never informed of this?" he bit out.

"We've known about this for months, boss, but you said you didn't want to hear anything about Eve. You just wanted us to find her."

Clenching his jaw, Talos stared at Eve across the market.

"The mother didn't live long, either. She died a few months after she moved the kid to England. Something about heart trouble."

Heart trouble, he thought. *Dalton's wife.*

And he knew just when Bonnie Hunter's heart trouble had started.

"Right," he said. "Thanks for the information."

He closed the phone.

He stared down at his hands, which had tightened into fists. All these months, he'd thought Eve had pursued him out of a mercenary desire for money—or out of love for Jake Skinner. He'd thought she was shallow and cold.

He'd been wrong.

Eve must have planned this since she was a fourteen-year-old girl. Talos thought suddenly of those books he'd seen in her teenaged bedroom in a newly chilling light. *How to Get Your Man.*

Her whole life since her father's death—the whole meaning of her life—had been to get revenge on the man she thought had destroyed her father, ruined her family.

She must have studied the models and actresses Talos had dated. She'd emulated them. It had all been a carefully constructed facade. She'd done it perfectly, down to the last detail. Except for one thing—unlike his other women, she'd always remained emotionally detached.

Now he knew why.

How she must have hated him.

Now, he looked at her across the crowd, watching the brilliance of her smile as she sifted through a selection of hand-knitted baby booties at a stall.

Dalton would have told his daughter that he was

innocent. He would have insisted he was the injured party, told her Talos had turned on him for his own gain. Dalton was charming and manipulative. It was how he'd swindled his own shareholders of nearly ten million dollars before an inside source had alerted Talos to the theft.

Would Eve believe him if he told her the truth?

Yes, surely she would forgive him.

He started to walk toward her. Then he stopped.

He would have to tell her the truth about parents she idolized, two people who were both dead. It would break her heart.

And would it even matter? If she ever regained her memory, she would still hate him. It wouldn't matter if he told her the truth. After a lifetime of loving her father, no explanation Talos could give would ever compete with that. And fairly or unfairly, she would hate him for destroying her most cherished memories and beliefs.

If she ever regained her memory, he would lose her.

Completely.

Forever.

It was simple as that.

Talos closed his eyes. The last time he'd seen Dalton Hunter, the man had been drunk when they'd run into each other in a New York hotel. "You've ruined me, you bastard," Dalton had cried out, staggering on his feet. "I taught you everything, saved you from the gutter and this is how you repay me."

"You were stealing from your stockholders," Talos had replied coldly. He'd left the man without guilt, knowing he'd done the right thing. The man had broken the law and now he was getting what he deserved. He hadn't felt guilty. Not even after Dalton had driven his Mercedes into the Hudson River. He'd cheated—and not just his stockholders.

Talos had believed it to be justice.

He'd never thought of the child Dalton had left behind. He'd never checked up on the man's broken-hearted widow.

Talos's first year in America, he'd gone to the Hunters' Massachusetts estate for Thanksgiving dinner. He remembered Bonnie's glow as she kissed Dalton, right before serving the turkey she'd lovingly prepared. Their daughter—Evie—had been just a chubby kid then, reading books and eating apples in a sprawling farmhouse outside Boston.

Eve had changed herself completely since then. But now that she was pregnant and her cheekbones had softened to a more gentle, feminine curve, he could for the first time see the resemblance to the girl she'd been.

Christ, he was the one who'd had amnesia—except it had been by choice.

In the scandal that followed Dalton's death, there must have been no money left. Bonnie Hunter had gone back home to England. Loving Dalton almost to madness, what would it have been like for her to marry John Craig after his death, to get security for her only child?

She died a few months after she moved the kid to England. Something about heart trouble.

Heart trouble?

No! *Thee mou.* He ran his fingers back through his dark hair, suddenly sweating in the cool morning. No one died of a broken heart anymore.

He looked across the market at Eve. No, they just took revenge.

For ten years, she must have molded her character, changing her appearance, remaking her identity to get close to him—all to repay him in kind. She'd attended the charity ball in Venice on his rival's arm just to get his attention. She'd purposefully set out to seduce him, so she could stab him in the heart.

It was a kind of hatred he'd never imagined in his whole life.

And now she was pregnant with his child.

No wonder she'd crashed her car when she'd found out she was pregnant. No wonder her traumatized mind had gone blank. It was like a severely injured person falling into a coma. It was for survival.

He watched her now at the outdoor market, laughing and haggling over two pairs of baby shoes, one pink, the other blue. Her face was beautiful and lit up. With the new feminine fullness of her pregnancy weight, he recognized the girl she'd once been. She looked so alive, so bright and innocent.

All this time, he'd thought this version of Eve was an illusion.

He'd been wrong.

This—*this*—was the real Eve. This was who she would have been if she'd grown up without grief or pain. This was the woman she would have become if Talos hadn't taken everything from her when she was fourteen years old.

Suddenly, he couldn't breathe. The air stifled him. He felt as if he was choking. He yanked off his tie.

If she ever regained her memory…

She would hate not just Talos, she would hate their child.

Eve suddenly turned as if she felt his glance. Their eyes met across the crowd. Joy suffused her expression. Her violet eyes shone with adoration and love, her cheeks were pink as spring roses.

She was the most desirable woman he'd ever known. The perfect lover. The perfect wife. The perfect mother. And at that moment, as Talos stood, he came to a sudden wrenching decision.

Slowly at first, then faster, he crossed the market. Taking Eve into his arms without a word, he kissed her fiercely. She kissed him back, then drew back with a laugh.

"What is it?" Suddenly frowning, she searched his face. "Is something wrong?"

"Not a thing." And he was going to make sure nothing was ever wrong for her again.

He held her tightly against his chest, cradling her as if he would never let her go, pressing a kiss against her hair.

He couldn't lose her. Couldn't bear to lose this precious, bright angel who'd burst into his life like a miracle. He knew he didn't deserve her. But he couldn't let her return to the person she'd been—another bitter, hardened soul in this cold gray world, seeking revenge, seeking payback. Calling it justice.

For the first time in his life, Talos didn't care about justice. Instead, he prayed for mercy.

Where could he take her? Where could he keep her safe, far from anyone who could remind her of the truth? What place could they hide where no old memories could ever ambush them?

Holding her hand tightly in his own, he pulled her away from the market.

"Where are we going?"

"Home," he said suddenly. "I'm taking you home."

"To the penthouse?"

"To Mithridos." He took a deep breath, and a cloud of fear lifted off him. "My island."

To save his family, to save them all, Talos had to pray she'd never remember—anything.

CHAPTER TEN

THE sunlight was bright, almost blinding against the palatial white villa.

Looking between the sky and sea, Eve thought she'd never seen so many shades of blue—turquoise, cobalt, indigo. As she stretched out on the lounge chair beside the infinity pool, the sky seemed to blend with the sea below. Putting down her pregnancy book, she watched the wild surf of the Aegean crash onto the white sands below.

They'd only been here a few hours, but she'd already happily changed into a new yellow floral bikini and pretty, translucent pink cover-up with a loose belt. She now had a closet full of comfortable, pretty clothes, brought here by her very own personal assistant. Curling her toes in pure bliss, she closed her eyes, relishing the feel of warm sunshine on her face and body.

And she wasn't the only one who seemed to like it. Her eyes flew open and she gasped, placing her hands on her gently swelling belly above the top edge of her bikini.

Had she felt…? Was that…?

"Good morning, *koukla mou.*"

She looked back to see Talos on the terrace. He was wearing only swim shorts, holding a tray with two glasses of sparkling water and two plates of sandwiches and fruit. She smiled at him, even though she wasn't terribly hungry.

At least not for food.

Talos was so handsome, she thought, with his tanned, muscular chest, his strong forearms and thick legs laced with dark hair. She still didn't quite understand the urgency that had brought them here from Athens, but he'd been so loving and charming, it had been impossible to refuse his need to take her home.

Since they'd arrived at the island that morning, he'd gone out of his way to make her comfortable here. Eve could hardly believe she was now the mistress of Mithridos, his lavish estate. The private Greek island off the coast of Turkey was accessible only by yacht, seaplane or helicopter. The many servants who ran the enormous white villa had already disappeared after having respectfully greeted her as Talos's new bride.

Now, her husband came forward on the terrace, setting down the tray and kissing her softly on her cheeks. "Do you like it?"

As if there were any way she wouldn't like it!

"It's like a dream," she said softly as he sat next to her on the lounge chair, his thighs warm against her legs. "It's a fairy tale. I love it."

"Good." There was something beneath his black

eyes, something she couldn't quite read, that exceeded mere domestic satisfaction. He took a long-stemmed rose from the vase on the tray and stroked the soft petals against her sun-warmed skin. As she inhaled the sweet, heady fragrance, he said quietly, "I want you to be happy. I want to raise our children here."

"Children?" She had the sudden image of making a permanent home here, creating a large, happy family, raising children with their father's smile. "How many children?"

"Two?"

"Six?" she countered good-naturedly.

He looked down at her, his dark eyes smiling. "We can compromise. Three."

"All right." She leaned against him with a contented sigh. "I'm so happy here," she confessed. "I never want to leave."

He flashed her a grin. "Then we won't."

"Just what do you have in mind?" she teased. "A honeymoon that never ends?"

He bent to kiss her lightly, tenderly on the lips. "Exactly."

He went to the white granite table, removing the two lunch plates from the tray. He set them out with silverware and linen napkins. He brought the two glasses of sparkling water to the lounge chairs and handed one to her.

He held up his glass. "To the most beautiful woman in the world."

Flushing with pleasure, she clinked the glass against

his. "To the most wonderful man in the world," she said softly. "Thank you for telling me the truth. Thank you for forgiving me. Thank you for putting it all behind us and bringing me home."

His dark brows creased, and he looked away. Tilting his head back, he gulped his water down to the very last drop.

Well, it was rather delicious, she thought as she took a sip. Sparkling and refreshing—just like him. Her husband was indeed a long cool drink of clear water beneath the hot sun. She took another sip, her eyes tracing over her husband's handsome physique.

Then she suddenly sat up straight in the lounge chair. With a delighted laugh, she put her hands on her belly. "I think I just felt the baby move!"

"You did?" He placed his hand on her belly over her translucent pink robe. He waited. "I don't feel anything."

"Maybe I was wrong," she said uncertainly. "I'm new at this." She frowned, straining to feel that little thrum that felt like music inside her, like champagne bubbles tickling within her belly. Then she did, and crowed with delight. "Did you feel that?"

"No."

She pulled off the pink cover-up. Pressing his hand against her naked belly, she watched his face as he waited, visibly holding his breath. As if there was nothing more important to him in the world than being with her, than waiting to feel his child move inside her.

Eve's eyes roamed over his handsome face.

Was any woman ever luckier in love?

Except, a voice inside her whispered, *he still hasn't told you he loves you.*

She didn't need to hear the words, she told the voice firmly. His actions showed he cared. Words were cheap. She could do without them.

Couldn't she?

"I still can't feel anything," he said, sticking his bottom lip out with a boyish scowl.

"You will," she said, hiding a laugh. "Although it might be a while. The book I was reading says it might be another month or two before you can feel it from the outside. But I love that you care about our child so much. I love…" *I love you,* she wanted to say, but she choked back the words. She couldn't say them again. Not when he hadn't said the words back to her. "I… I'd love some lunch."

"I exist to satisfy your every desire," he replied with a growl.

She ate all her sandwich and half of his, laughing with him, loving him. She felt hungry. Happy.

They spent the day kicking in the surf and walking on the sandy bay beneath the villa. Above them, the hills of the small island were rocky and sharp. The sand was hot on their feet, which were then cooled by the swift blue waves.

And every moment, she could feel his dark eyes on her. As the blue waves crashed over their ankles, he kissed her.

His lips were so tender, his kiss so passionate and forceful as he held her.

Holding her breath, she looked up at him through her lashes. The tanned skin of his naked chest gleamed as sea spray trickled down the valleys and hills of his muscular body. The hot Greek sunlight burned down on them as they stood on the edge of the blue waves.

"Don't ever stop kissing me," she begged.

Without warning, he picked her up in his arms, lifting her against his naked chest, skin to skin.

"I intend to spend my whole life kissing you."

He carried her up from the beach as if she weighed nothing at all, walking back to the villa. He took the stairs two at a time as he whisked her upstairs to the master bedroom overlooking the ocean. Behind her husband's handsome face, she barely noticed the high ceilings, the open balcony doors and the white translucent curtains waving in the hot breeze off the Aegean Sea.

She was shaking with longing, limp with desire. They never even made it to the bed. As they passed the balcony doors with its view of the wide blue sea, he kissed her. She twisted in his arms, wrapping her legs around his waist as the kiss intensified.

Pushing her against the sliding glass door, he slipped off her yellow bikini as her trembling hands pulled off his swim trunks. They kissed each other frantically, their hands touching everywhere, straining desperately to be close. As she kissed his naked skin, caressing his muscular body, she tasted salt and sun and sea.

With a growl, he lowered her to the soft rug. The

breeze cooled their skin as the sheer white curtains waved and twisted over their naked bodies. He kissed down the valley between her breasts to her belly, pushing aside her thighs to lick and suck her slick core. She gasped as he spread her wide, swirling his tongue over her taut nub until she thought she'd go mad. She clenched his shoulders, digging her nails into his skin.

With every flicker of his tongue, she grew tighter and hotter, until she was being swallowed up by dark heat. She felt him thrust his tongue inside her and writhed, bucking her hips, knowing she was about to explode, desperate to hold on just one minute longer.

"No," she gasped softly, tugging him upward. "Inside me."

He needed no further invitation. Rolling onto his back, he lifted her above him then lowered her against his shaft. For a moment she couldn't move. He filled her so deeply.

Then he lifted her again with his strong arms. His dark eyes were intense as he forced her to hold his gaze.

"Ride me," he commanded her, and she could do nothing but obey. She gasped with sweet ecstasy as she rocked back and forth against him.

She heard his harsh intake of breath, saw the stark need on his face as he allowed her—encouraged her—to control the pace. She held him tight, very tight, their bodies locked as one, both of them breathless and sweaty and panting. And with one last thrust, she exploded.

"I love you," she cried out. "I love you!"

* * *

"I love you."

Looking up at Eve sharply as she spoke the words, his body wrapped around and inside her, Talos felt embedded so deeply in her soul that he could not deny it any longer. Not even to himself.

I love you.

Making love to her in Athens had been explosive, mind-blowing. But this was more.

Watching her take her pleasure. Watching her beautiful face shine as she rode him, causing such agony for them both—and such explosive pleasure. When he'd heard her gasp out the words, he could hold back no longer, and he poured himself into her with a sharp cry.

Holding her afterward, he realized why this was like nothing he'd ever felt before. He hadn't just been making love to Eve.

He was *in* love with her.

Looking at his beautiful, pregnant wife, his heart lurched in his chest. *He loved her.* She had brought him back to life, made him feel and see things in his life in a totally different light.

He loved her.

He would die if he ever lost her.

And he prayed they would stay here forever, happy, hidden from the world, where he'd never have to be afraid she might remember—

She suddenly screamed in a hoarse voice that had nothing to do with pleasure.

Covering her face, she rolled away from him.

"Eve!" He cradled her back against his naked chest,

trying to see her face. When she finally rolled back to face him, her beautiful face was streaked with tears.

"I had another memory." Her voice was like a whimper.

The chill of fear struck through his heart. "What was it?"

She blinked up at him, her lovely eyes the chilling blue of ice. "I remembered stealing the papers from your safe. I gave them to Jake Skinner at that restaurant, just like you said. Then I ran away from Athens and kept running. I never wanted you to find me. I hated you." Her face looked shell-shocked, bewildered, her eyes filling with tears as she pleaded, "Why? Why did I hate you so much?"

His heart rose in his throat. He stared down at her, unable to speak.

"Tell me why I hated you," she cried.

"I…I don't know," he lied, wanting to protect his wife.

Covering her face, she pushed away from him, curling her body into a fetal position.

"It doesn't matter." He forced her to roll back. He looked down at her. "The past doesn't matter. Not anymore. All that matters is the future. Our baby."

Naked, she stared up at him.

"Do you love me, Talos?" she whispered.

He hadn't expected that question.

Yes, he started to say. *I love you.*

But the words got stuck in his throat. He'd never said them before to anyone.

I love you. And I'm terrified I'll lose you.

When he didn't answer, she sucked in her breath. He saw the misery on her face and knew he'd hurt her at the moment she most needed comfort.

"Eve…" he whispered. He leaned forward to kiss her.

Then stopped himself.

He'd thought by bringing her to Mithridos, a place she'd never been before, he could protect her from the memories.

But it hadn't been seeing the sights of Venice or Athens that had made memories return. She'd had her first memory after kissing him on the Rialto Bridge. Immediately after making love to him in Athens with such joy, she'd been crushed by dark memories of her father's death. And now, just as they'd made love a second time, she remembered hating him.

Memories returned after he kissed her.

Memories returned when he made love to her.

That night, he held her in his arms as she cried herself to sleep. He knew it was woefully inadequate, but he was unable to do more. He wanted to make love to her. He wanted to tell her the truth.

He could do neither.

Finally, after she slept, he could take it no more. Rising from the bed, he stared out the open French doors to the terrace, as the warm breeze whirled the curtains. He stared at the full moonlight floating against the black waves of the Aegean, like lost ghosts caught and trapped in dark, invisible webs to the earth.

He'd thought he could keep them safe here, hidden far from the world.

He'd been wrong.

If he wanted to save his family, he could never make love to his wife again. He could never even kiss her. Because if he did, she would remember everything and he would lose her.

Pain racked through Talos, catching at his breath. He gave one last longing look at his naked, pregnant wife sleeping in his bed. He reveled in her sweet beauty, even as his soul anguished over the tearstains on her face. He watched the pink of sunrise creep slowly over the room.

Then, with his hands clenched into fists, he left her to sleep alone.

CHAPTER ELEVEN

How had it all gone so wrong?

A month later, Eve still couldn't understand it. She lived in an amazing Greek villa on a private island. She was married to the handsomest man on earth and expecting his child. She was happy, healthy, living in blissful luxury beneath the Aegean sun as servants waited on her hand and foot.

But for the last month, Talos hadn't touched her. She'd been alone in her marriage. Alone in her life.

She'd never felt so miserable. Though they lived in the same house, they lived separate lives. Talos worked nights in the office, coming to bed only long after she was asleep, or worse—not coming to bed at all, just sleeping on the couch in his office. She spent her days decorating the nursery, organizing the house, taking the helicopter to the nearby island of Kos to visit the doctor.

She'd done everything she could think of to try and regain his interest. She dressed in pretty clothes, like the pink cotton dress she was wearing now. She'd learned to cook his favorite meals. She read newspapers to learn about his interests—basketball and business—trying to please him, to start conversations, to be available when he wanted her.

All in vain.

The problem was that he *didn't* want her.

Since the first day they'd come to the island of Mithridos, when they'd made love so passionately and exquisitely by the balcony overlooking the sea, he hadn't touched her. Hadn't hugged her. Hadn't come up behind her and embraced her, kissing her neck. He hadn't held her or kissed her.

He'd barely even *looked* at her!

After a month of being neglected and avoided, Eve's heart bled like an open wound. She'd outright asked Talos several times why he was ignoring her, asked him if she'd done something to make him angry.

At first, he'd brushed her off with an excuse. Now, he just avoided her completely.

What had she done to make him so angry?

She was almost afraid to ask one more time, because there was simply no further he could withdraw unless he physically left the island. At least as long as he was still in the house she could pretend they still had a marriage, pretend he was just moody or worried about a business deal, pretend their relationship could recover.

But how could they ever recover when he wouldn't talk to her? When he wouldn't touch her?

He was hiding something. Punishing her for something. What? What did he think he couldn't tell her?

She pressed her fingertips against her eyelids. As the

hot November sunshine poured in from the wide-open windows, the warm breeze filling the bright breakfast room with the salty tang of the sea, she was choked with despair.

"Good morning, Mrs. Xenakis."

Eve nearly jumped when she heard the housekeeper's heavily accented voice behind her. "Good morning."

The plump older woman set the tray of fruit, eggs, toast and pot of mint tea on the stone table. "Have a lovely breakfast."

Eve had a sudden flashback to the lunch she'd shared with Talos here on the terrace, the first day they'd arrived on the island. Where had it all gone so wrong? What did she need to remember?

"Where is Mr. Xenakis?" she demanded.

"I believe he is in the home office, ma'am. Shall I take him a message?"

Another message he could ignore? Eve shook her head. Staring out at the sea, she took a deep breath. Her last memory hadn't been a pleasant one. She was almost afraid to know what else she had to remember. What else could possibly be worse?

Talos wouldn't tell her. But his silence this last month spoke volumes. She'd done something else. Something he could not, would not forgive.

She had to remember! She had to make herself remember! Or she feared she'd lose him—and their chance of being a family—before her baby was even born.

She turned to the housekeeper. "Is there a spare computer in the house? With an Internet connection?"

"In the office, Mrs. Xenakis."

Eve licked her lips. "But I would not wish to disturb my husband. Is there another one elsewhere?"

The housekeeper gave a friendly nod. "There's one in my quarters, ma'am. You would be welcome to use it."

"Thank you," she said in relief. Picking up her breakfast plate, she rose to her feet. "Do you mind if I use it now?"

Sitting in the housekeeper's cozy suite ten minutes later, crunching an apple as she looked at the screen, Eve had barely started her search before she heard an angry voice behind her.

"What the hell do you think you're doing?"

Shocked, she swiveled her chair around to face Talos.

"Hi," she said, trying to act cool even as her heart beat faster in her chest. He looked more handsome than ever in his snug black T-shirt and dark jeans. She gave him a trembling smile. "I'm glad to see you."

"Mrs. Papadakis said you were here," he replied coldly. "You didn't answer my question. What are you doing?"

Her smile faded. "Since my memory still hasn't returned, I thought I would try and give it a kick start by looking up my name online, to see if I can learn—"

"I don't appreciate you sneaking down here."

Sneaking? "I didn't want to bother you in your office," she explained quietly. "The housekeeper was kind enough to allow me to use her computer." When he continued to glower at her, she tossed her head. "How can you accuse me of sneaking in my own house?"

She started to turn back toward the computer screen, but he grabbed her shoulder. His dark eyes looked grim, almost frightening as he said, "Don't."

"Why?" she demanded.

He ground his teeth. "You should be resting, not trying to research a past that doesn't matter. You should be redecorating the nursery, focusing on our future together and staying healthy for the baby."

"Really?" she said evenly. "If you'd shown the slightest interest in me or the baby for the last month, you'd know I finished the nursery a week ago. But you haven't. You've just been avoiding me, like you did after we were first married." She jabbed her thumb toward the computer. "And since you won't talk to me, this is my only option to figure out why!"

"It doesn't matter!" he said harshly. "Just leave it alone!"

"I can't!" she cried. "Not when you won't talk to me, when you don't touch me, when you won't even look at me!"

"I've given you everything any woman could ever want!" He looked down at her fiercely. "Isn't that enough for you? Can't that be enough?"

She shook her head as angry tears rose to her eyes. "I'm in a beautiful villa, I'm expecting a child—but I'm doing it all without you! You've left me here!" she cried. "Why? Why can't you just tell me the reason?"

He started to say something, then stopped. She could

see his tension pulse at his neck as he abruptly pulled away from her.

"You are getting yourself upset over nothing. I'm busy with work, nothing more."

"Is it that you don't think I'm attractive anymore?" She shook her head with humiliation and despair. Her voice trembled as she voiced her sudden fear. "Or is there another woman?"

He stared at her, his dark eyes narrowing.

"Is that what you think?" His voice was low, furious. "You think I would betray you that way?"

"What else am I supposed to think, when you—"

"You are the only woman I want," he ground out. "The only woman I will ever want!"

"Then why?" She shook her head. "I don't understand!"

"This last month has nearly killed me," he shouted. "Each day is worse than the last, seeing you right in front of me but knowing I can't have you. It's like falling into hell over and over again!"

"But I'm right here," she whispered. "Why won't you touch me?"

"If I do," he said in a voice so low she almost couldn't hear it, "I will lose you."

That didn't make any sense. Tears fell unheeded down her cheeks.

"Please, Talos." She looked up at him. "I need you."

Their eyes locked, held. She could see the rise and fall of his chest, hear the shudder and rasp of his breath.

Then with an explosive curse, he surrendered.

Sweeping her up in his arms, he kissed her, murmuring words in Greek. His embrace was hot and tender, full of anguished longing and regret as he kissed her.

"Eve, oh, Eve, I can't push you away," he whispered, looking down into her eyes with dark pain and yearning. "Whatever the cost—whatever happens—I can't hurt you anymore."

For a month now, Talos had been in anguish.

Wanting Eve but not being able to have her.

Loving her but not being able to tell her.

He could have lived through his own pain. He could have continued to endure it forever. But it was seeing the pain in his wife's beautiful face that had finally broken his will.

Horror had gone through him when he saw her in front of the computer where he knew she could eventually discover everything. Her tears pleaded for what should have been hers by right—his love and attention.

There was no place remote enough. Nowhere they could hide. No way he could keep her safe, not when by trying to protect her, he himself had caused her such hurt!

And finally he couldn't bear it any longer.

Scooping her up into his arms, he swept her upstairs into their bedroom. He tenderly set her down on their bed, the bed that they should have shared for the last month. She looked up at him, her eyes shining with tears. He could smell the sweet vanilla fragrance of her hair, feel the softness of her skin. He saw her hand shake as she reached up to caress his rough chin.

"Talos...."

Closing his eyes, he placed his hand over her smaller one, turning his face into her caress. He'd yearned for this for so long. For the last four weeks, he'd had to anesthetize himself—with hard exercise, with ouzo, but mostly with work—to try to fight off the constant desire for the woman down the hall, this frustrated desire that was always rising higher and higher until he feared he'd break apart.

Whatever happened, he could no longer resist her sweetness. He wanted his wife. Needed her. *Loved her.*

He pulled off the soft pink cotton dress with its innocent eyelet lace. Removing his own black T-shirt and jeans, he dropped them to the floor. His eyes greedily drank in the vision of Eve in her translucent white bra and panties.

Looking into her eyes, he finally spoke the words that had long ago been written across his heart.

"I love you, Eve."

She sucked in her breath, her gaze searching his. Wanting to believe. Needing to believe.

Then he kissed her.

Her lips seared him to the core. With every beat of his heart, he loved her. And all he wanted to do was make his vow of a month ago true; he wanted to spend the rest of his life kissing her.

She moved beneath him on the white blanket of the bed. Above him, he could hear the soft whir of the ceiling fan, hear the cry of the morning birds outside, feel the soft breeze against his naked body.

He touched her naked skin, bronzed from so many days spent outside. He stroked her body all over, worshipping her with his fingertips, with his hands, with his mouth. He was hard and aching for her.

"You love me," she repeated in wonder and joy. "You love me?"

"So much," he gasped. "You have my heart forever."

He kissed her forehead, her eyelids, her cheekbones, her mouth. With a groan, he caressed her body, pressing his legs between her thighs.

When he finally pushed himself inside her, he nearly cried out from the force of his pleasure.

He moved inside her slowly, savoring every second and every inch of his possession. Although—was he possessing her? Or was she possessing him?

She gripped his shoulders, throwing her head back, revealing her swanlike throat.

"I love you," he whispered as he pushed inside her again. He saw the light of joy in her eyes, and was astonished to suddenly taste the salt of tears—his own.

He held her tenderly, moving deeply and slowly inside her until he felt her tense. Until he felt her shake.

Whatever happened, he could not stop. Whatever happened, he prayed he could love her always.

Closing his eyes, he thrust into her one last time. He felt her coil around him, heard her gasp.

"I love you," he cried. And as the force of his words

slammed through his soul, he threw his head back and poured his seed into her with a shout of pure happiness.

Collapsing back on the bed, he held her tightly. She was his love—his life. He kissed her temple, pressing his hand against her sweaty face. Praying that somehow, they would be happy.

For one second, he thought they could be.

Then he felt her stiffen in his arms.

He felt her hands pushing at him, shoving at him.

"Get away from me!" Rolling away from him on the bed, she leapt to her feet. "Oh my God!"

He looked at his wife, the woman who had been so joyfully caressing his body just moments before. By the angry, furious, hateful look in her suddenly proud face, he knew his worst nightmare had come true.

Eve no longer had amnesia.

She stood naked in front of him, her dark hair brushing against her tanned skin as she quivered in rage. Her full breasts heaved over the slight curve of his child in her belly with every pant of her breath. Her blue eyes glared at him with such force he was surprised he didn't die instantly from the blunt icy dagger of her hatred.

Eve's beauty was perfect, and now—to him—it was forever unattainable.

He had lost the sweet woman he loved. He'd lost her forever.

When Talos said he loved her, Eve thought she'd die of joy.

After so many months of yearning, she'd finally felt

her husband's arms around her and heard him tell her what she'd longed to hear. She'd known happiness she didn't know was possible in mortal life. Then he'd made love to her so tenderly, with such deep, intense passion, her soul had soared to the dizzying heights of heaven.

Then he'd released her, and she'd come crashing down.

Down. Down. Down.

She'd hit the earth without a parachute. Little pieces of her had smashed into dirt and rocks. Her body and soul had shattered into a million pieces.

"You remember," he said quietly.

"Everything," she choked out.

She realized she was naked in front of him. And she'd just let him make love to her. How could she? *How could she?*

Shaking with a repressed sob, she grabbed her silk robe off the back of the bathroom door, wrapping it swiftly around her shoulders and tying the belt tight. She wiped away angry tears from her eyes before she whirled back to face him.

"Was it some kind of sick joke to you? You destroyed my family, then kept me here as some kind of pathetic love slave?"

"No! That's not how it was!" Rising from the bed, he grabbed her by the shoulders, searching her eyes. "You know that's not how it was between us!"

Against her will, memories rushed through her mind. The two of them running together beneath the rain in Venice. Making love against the backdrop of the

Acropolis. How he'd looked at her as he kissed her in the surf, their first day on this island. His laughter. His tenderness. His deep dark passion in the night.

Furiously, she pushed the memories away. She wouldn't think about that. She couldn't.

Misery flashed through her, misery so strong it nearly made her stagger. Just moments before in his arms, she'd been so happy. She'd been filled with joy that he loved her. She'd felt she finally had her place in the world—in his arms. As his wife. Carrying his child.

Now, all she felt was loss a thousand times. It was even worse than when she was fourteen, when she'd lost her father, her home and her mother in space of a few months. *Because of him.*

Because she'd failed.

She'd spent the last eleven years plotting to get revenge. To do whatever it took to take him down. Before he could ever hurt anyone again as he'd hurt her.

Instead, she'd betrayed her family's memory. She'd failed everyone she loved.

She'd always promised herself that she would be a better daughter to John Craig as soon as her revenge was complete. Then, in Istanbul, while hiding from Talos's goons, she'd been shocked—horrified—to hear news of his death. Her stepfather had died without knowing how she loved him.

And now it was too late. She swallowed, blinking back tears. A pity she hadn't been driving faster when her hands had slipped on the steering wheel of her Aston

Martin. A pity she hadn't crashed into a speeding train instead of the postbox.

She'd wasted eleven years of her life for nothing.

Talos had managed to keep his company in spite of her stolen documents. He'd tricked her into marrying him. And worst of all, she was pregnant with his child.

Her enemy's victory was complete.

She touched her belly in shock. "I can't believe it," she whispered. "Of all the men in the world—to be pregnant by the one I hate the most. The one I swore to destroy."

He winced, then reached for her. "Eve, please—"

"No!" She jerked away from him. "Don't touch me!" She turned away, heading for the door, desperate to get out of the bedroom, away from the soft, mussed sheets that were still warm from the tender passion of their bodies, away from the scent of him that still clung to her. Away from the happiness of the innocent, explosive joy she'd experienced but moments before.

"I don't blame you," he said quietly behind her, causing her to halt. "When I found out you were Dalton's daughter, I already knew I was falling in love with you. So I brought you here to the island." He took a deep breath. "I thought if I kept you safe and hidden from the world, you wouldn't remember. I prayed you never would."

She whirled around with a gasp, the breath suddenly knocked out of her.

"To punish me?" she said, wanting to cry. She lifted her chin. "To claim your victory?"

Talos bowed his head. "To be your husband," he whispered. "To love you for the rest of my life."

His words crept into her soul like mist, whispering echoes of past tenderness and love.

No! She wouldn't let him trick her ever again!

Wiping away her tears angrily, she lifted her chin. "Don't talk to me of *love*," she spat out scornfully. "My father gave you everything, and you ruined him without mercy. For your own gain."

"That's not true!"

"You never named your source. Who was it?"

"I gave my word I wouldn't reveal that," he said quietly.

"Because you forged those documents yourself!" She gave him a last, contemptuous glance. "My father should have left you in the gutters of Athens to die. And that's what I'm doing now. Leaving you—"

He grabbed her shoulders desperately. "He was guilty, Eve. I can only imagine what lies Dalton told you, but he was guilty. He stole almost ten million dollars from his shareholders. When I found out about it, I had no choice. The man deserved justice!"

"Justice!" Gasping, she slapped him across the face. "He deserved your loyalty," she cried, drawing herself up in a fury. "Instead, you betrayed him. You lied!"

"No!"

"After you ruined him, he drank himself to oblivion then crashed his car. My mother's death was slower. She went back to England to marry and make sure I'd be looked after. But within months of marrying my step-father, she took a whole bottle of pills to bed!"

Releasing her, he stared down at her in shock. "I heard she died of heart trouble."

She gave a scornful laugh. "Heart trouble. My step-father loved her. He wasn't going to let anyone speak ill of her or of the way she died. So he and Dr. Bartlett cooked that little fiction for the press. She was only thirty-five years old." She narrowed her eyes. "But you're right. She did die of a broken heart. *Because of you.*"

"Eve, I'm sorry," he whispered. "I did what I thought was right. Forgive me—"

"I will never, ever forgive you." She looked at him, cold and proud. "I never want to see you again."

"You're my wife."

"I'll be filing for divorce as soon as I return to London."

"You're pregnant with my child!"

"I will raise this baby alone."

He gasped, "You can't cut me out of my child's life!"

"My baby will be better off with no father than with a faithless, treacherous bastard like you!" Tears rushed into her eyes, tears she no longer even tried to hide. "Do you think I could ever let myself trust you? Do you think I could ever forgive myself if I did?"

"Your father was the one who betrayed and hurt your family."

"You have no proof of that," she said coldly. "You are the only liar I see. You said you loved me!"

"I do love you!" His voice was ragged, anguished.

"You don't know what love means."

She heard his harsh intake of breath.

"I do now," he said hoarsely. He reached toward her, inches from her cheek, and in spite of everything, her breath quickened as she recalled all the times he'd tenderly stroked her face. "When you lost your memory, you regained your lost innocence and faith. And somehow you made me find mine," he whispered. "Just give me the chance to love you. Test me as you will. Let me prove my love for you."

She thought she saw a shimmer of tears in his eyes.

Talos Xenakis, the scourge of the world—crying?

No. Impossible. It was another of his cruel, selfish games. She thought of how he'd ruthlessly wooed her in Venice, tricking her into marriage with romance and soft words only to punish her the moment they were married. Crossing her arms, she drew herself up stiffly.

"Very well," she said coldly, lifting her chin. "I will let you prove you love me. Give up this child and never contact us again."

He gasped. "Don't make me do it, Eve," he choked out. "Anything but that."

"If you don't do it, you prove you don't love me," she said with satisfaction. She started to turn away.

Without warning, he grabbed her. Pulling her into his embrace, he kissed her. His lips seared her with longing and wistful tenderness. It was a kiss that held the promise of love to last forever.

She trembled. Then even as her knees went weak, a cold sheet of ice came down over her heart.

Savagely, she pushed away from him. "Never touch me again."

Still naked, he clenched his hands, staring at her. When he finally spoke, his voice was low, guttural.

"I will do what you ask," he said thickly. "I will stay away from you and our baby. But only until I find the proof that your father lied." His dark eyes glittered at her. "When I have proof that you cannot deny, I will return. And you will be forced to see the truth."

She tossed her head, folding her arms.

"Then I am well satisfied, because you will never find that proof." Her lip curled as she gave him one last look. "But thank you. You've just given me your word of honor you'll stay away from me and the baby—forever."

CHAPTER TWELVE

FIVE months later, Eve stood alone by her mother's grave.

It was only the first week of March, but already the first blush of early spring had come to Buckinghamshire. The weeping willows were green and gold beside the lake, splashing the season's first color over the graveyard of the old gray church.

In her white goose down coat and green wellies, Eve felt hot and out of breath after crossing the hill from her estate. Not that it was terribly far, but at nine months pregnant, every move was an effort. Even bringing daisies, her mother's favorite flower, to her grave.

Eve glanced at the daffodils poking through the cold earth nearby. Just a few weeks ago, the ground had been covered with snow. How had time fled so fast? Her baby was due any day now.

Her poor, fatherless baby.

It had been such a long lonely winter. During the five months since she'd left Greece, she'd tried to forget Talos. Tried to pretend that her baby's father was a figment of her imagination, the remnant of a bad dream from long ago. But her dreams had insisted otherwise, and in her secluded, drafty mansion, she'd had one hot dream after another to make her sweat and cry out for Talos in her sleep.

She had tried to lose herself in the life she'd left behind, the whirl of social life, of lunch with friends in London and shopping trips to New York. But it had all just depressed her. Those people weren't really her friends—had never been her friends. She saw now that she had deliberately chosen shallow acquaintances, the kind she could keep at a distance. She'd never wanted anyone to really know her. It had been the only way she'd been able to stay focused on her goal of revenge.

Now what was left?

Even though she'd regained her memory, she wasn't the same woman anymore. Nor was she the happy, bright, naive girl she'd been before her memory had returned.

She almost wished she were. Eve closed her eyes, missing the happy, optimistic, loving person she'd been before. That she'd been with *him.* She missed loving him. She even missed hating him.

But it was all over now.

Her eyes swam with tears, causing the spring countryside to smear in her vision like an impressionist painting.

"I'm sorry," she whispered, placing her hand on her mother's gravestone. "I couldn't destroy him like I thought."

She knelt, brushing earth off the gray marble angel before placing half the daisies on her grave. "I'm going to have his baby any day now. And I forced him to promise to stay away from us." She gave a harsh laugh. "I guess I never thought he'd stay so true to his word. Perhaps he's not the liar I thought." She wiped the tears that left cold tracks down her cheeks, chilling beneath the brisk spring wind as she said softly, "What should I do?"

Her mother's grave was silent. Eve heard only the sigh of the wind through the trees as she stared down at the words on the gravestone.

Beloved wife, they said. She glanced at her stepfather's gravestone beside it. *Loving husband.*

Her stepfather had loved Bonnie since they were children. Then she'd met a handsome Yank in Boston who'd swept her off her feet. But John had still loved her—so much he'd taken her back willingly when she was widowed, even adopting her child as his own.

But her mother had never stopped loving Dalton—who had never loved her back with the same devotion.

Were all love affairs like that? One person gave—and the other person took?

No. Her throat suddenly hurt. Sometimes love and passion could be equally joined, like a mutual fire. She'd felt it.

The desire between Eve and Talos had been explosive, matched. She'd been so lucky and she hadn't even known it. For all her adult life, she'd been focused on the wrong thing. On revenge. On regaining a memory that had ultimately caused her nothing but grief.

A bitter laugh stuck in her throat.

She'd pushed away the stepfather who had loved her, spent time with people she didn't care about, learnt about fashion and flirtation and revenge. And for what? What did she have to show for it—for all her lost youth?

Nothing but the graves of the people who'd loved her, some money she hadn't earned and a coming baby who had no father. Nothing but an empty bed and no one to hold her on a cold winter's night.

"I'm sorry, John." She leaned her forehead against her stepfather's gravestone, placing a handful of the first daisies of spring on the earth. "I should have come home for Christmas. For every Christmas. Forgive me."

Hearing a robin's song from the nearby trees, she felt oddly comforted. She rose to her feet, rubbing her aching back and belly as she straightened.

"I'll try to come back soon," she said softly. "To let you both know how we get on."

And with one last silent prayer over those two quiet graves, she started to walk back home.

Home, she thought, looking up at the Craig estate on the other side of the hill. A funny way to describe this place. The only place she'd ever thought of as home had been her family's old Massachusetts farmhouse.

At least until recently, when every night she dreamed of a villa on a private island in the Mediterranean that was a million shades of white and blue…

She took a deep breath.

With her eyes wide open, she was left in darkness and shadows. She didn't know who she was anymore. She didn't know what to believe in.

She missed her old faith.

She missed *him*.

Eve felt her baby give a hard kick in response to the emotion racing through her. She felt another pain in her lower back as she wiped her tears fiercely. But obviously Talos hadn't missed her. If he had, he would have followed her here, promise or no promise. He wouldn't have stayed away from his wife and unborn child, searching for some stupid proof when their baby was due any day!

Don't make me do it, Eve. She heard the echo of his anguished voice. *Anything but that.*

She felt a sharp pain through her womb. With a gasp, she stumbled across the driveway and up the steps to the side door.

"Is that you, Miss Craig?" the housekeeper called from the kitchen.

Miss Craig. As if her marriage had never happened. As if she'd actually followed through on her ridiculous threat to divorce him. Hearing her maiden name still choked her—even though she was the one who'd insisted on it. "I'm fine."

The plump-cheeked housekeeper came into the foyer with a smile, holding a stack of letters. "I was cleaning out some of your stepfather's things, as you requested. I almost threw this envelope out with the rubbish but then happened to notice it had your name."

"Leave it with me," Eve gasped. Holding the envelope, she sat down on a hard chair in the dining room—afraid if she went for the cushy sofa in the parlor she'd never be able to get up again. Fake labor pains, she tried to tell herself. Braxton-Hicks contractions. But a moment later, as she leaned back into the chair, another pain ripped through her.

She took deep breaths as she'd learned in childbirth class—alone—and tried to control her sudden fear. Every nerve in her body told her that it was time. She was going into labor.

And she didn't want to do it alone.

In spite of everything, she'd somehow thought he would come back for her.

But why would he? she thought savagely. After everything she'd said? He'd been willing to forgive her cold-hearted betrayal last June, but she'd been unable even to consider the possibility that he'd been telling the truth about her father.

Her father…

Gasping, she looked down at the envelope written in her stepfather's hand. She ripped it open.

Dear Evie,

I found this letter among your mother's possessions after she died. I didn't know whether you should ever see it. Sometimes it's best not to know the truth. I will let fate decide. Your mother always loved you, and so did I. God bless you.

There was another smaller envelope inside. She sat up straight, ignoring another sharp contraction as she saw her father's sharp, faded handwriting. It was a love letter, dated the day before her father's embezzlement had been revealed to the press.

Bonnie,
I can't keep lying anymore. I'm leaving you. My secretary wants adventure like I do—like you used to. But don't worry, honey. You and the kiddo will be fine. I've managed to get a chunk of money, the bonus they should have given me over the years. I've left half the money for you.
Dalton

With a gasp, Eve crushed the letter to her chest. She'd thought her mother had died of a broken heart. She'd been wrong.
You never named your source. Who was it?
Sadly: *I gave my word I wouldn't reveal that.*
Her mother had betrayed her father. But within months, she'd been smothered by the coldness of her own revenge. It was the same chill that had frozen Eve over the last five months.

Eve had unknowingly modeled her life after her mother's. She'd given up love, selfishly thrown away her baby's chance for a father, for the cold, dead satisfaction of revenge.

Oh my God, what had she done?

Eve cried out as another pain ripped through her. And this time, it really hurt.

"Miss Craig?" The housekeeper suddenly appeared.

"Call me Mrs. Xenakis," Eve cried, rising to her feet. "I want my husband. Please—get me my husband!"

"Are you in labor? I'll call the doctor—I'll get the car around—"

"No," Eve panted, placing her hands on her belly. It couldn't be time, not yet. "We're not going anywhere—not until—he's here!"

She swayed, her knees nearly buckling beneath her as another pain ripped through her. Her baby was about to be born.

Eve looked around the elegant, cold, drafty mansion. She didn't want to be the woman she'd been, buried in the past as her mother had been.

Eve wanted a future. She wanted her baby to grow up happy and secure, in a home full of life and color and joy. She wanted Talos as her baby's father. As her husband.

She wanted to love him.

And she had the choice.

"Please get me the phone," she panted.

"You stay right there," the housekeeper pleaded, running to the nearby phone. She dialed the telephone number Eve gave her, then, after speaking, she held down the receiver. "His assistant says he's unavailable, traveling in Asia."

Unavailable? In Asia?

Talos must have decided he didn't want her, she thought miserably. He was done with her.

"Did you tell him I'm in labor?" she panted.

"Yes, and that you'd like your husband to come to London as soon as possible. Can I do anything more?"

"No," Eve whispered. There was nothing more to be done. Nothing more to be said. If he was in Asia, he'd never make it back to London in time.

Even if he wanted to.

Eve felt like crying.

As the housekeeper ordered the chauffeur to bring around the car, Eve covered her face with her hands. Why had she been so blind? He'd offered her his love with both hands, and she'd pushed it away. Now she was going to have their baby alone. She'd raise their child alone.

For the rest of her life she would be…alone.

And she would die loving him. A man she could never have. Her child would have no father, and it was all her fault. A shaky sob escaped her lips as she suddenly heard a loud noise, crashing, someone shouting.

"Let me in here, damn you, I know she's here!"

The dining room door banged open. She looked up in shock to see Talos, wild-eyed, pushing past the housekeeper into the house. He fell to his knees in front of her.

"I know you said you didn't want me, but if you send me away now—"

"No," she whispered, throwing her arms around his

shoulders with a sudden sob. "I'll never send you away again. You're here. I wanted you so badly, and you're here."

Exhaling in a rush, he closed his eyes and held her tightly. Her voice was muffled against his shirt as she said, "Your assistant said you were traveling in Asia."

"On my way here. I finally tracked down your father's old secretary to a convent in India. I have the proof that you—"

"I don't need that anymore," she said, and she gripped his hand as another contraction ripped through her. "All the proof I need is in your face. You're here. You came. Please," she panted, "never—leave me again."

"I never will leave you," he vowed, his dark eyes shining with tears.

She gasped, arching her back as another pain went through her.

"Oh my God, Eve," he breathed. "You're in labor."

He leapt to his feet, shouting for help. "Kefalas, get the car! My wife is in labor!"

Talos drove her to London, exceeding all speed records to reach the private hospital in time. They were too late for anesthesia. She'd just barely settled into her private suite, and Dr. Bartlett had just rushed in to check on her, before their baby was born.

Talos held her close as their son came into the world, protecting them. And in the instant their newborn baby was placed in her exhausted arms, both their lives changed forever.

Talos kissed his wife's sweaty forehead, then tenderly cradled them both in his arms. Their love was newly reborn in that single instant, brilliant and flashing like a comet illuminating the dark night, shining like a star that would always last.

EPILOGUE

"THEY'RE here!"

Four-year-old John was running up and down the hallways, screaming like a banshee when he heard the helicopter land on the other side of Mithridos. Eve smiled down at her son, even as she tried helplessly to hush him before he woke his two-year-old sister, who always got into everything when she was awake, or his six-month-old baby brother, who generally just sat on the floor and watched it all with his mouth open, drooling from his first tooth.

She'd meant to get dressed before the first guests arrived at their island, but she'd been so busy with the children that time had slipped away from her. Now, she realized to her horror that she was still wearing her white fluffy robe from the shower she'd taken twenty minutes ago. Pausing in the hallway, she glanced into the doorway of her bedroom.

Her ladylike party dress, white with delicate pink roses and twisting green leaves, a sweetheart neckline and a full skirt, was lying across the bed in wait for her.

As she stepped into the bedroom, she felt Talos come behind her, kissing her neck as he wrapped his strong arms around her waist.

"Are you ready for this?" he teased.

She turned around in his embrace, standing on her tiptoes to kiss his mouth. He hadn't dressed for the party yet, either. She was equal parts amused and exasperated to see he hadn't changed. He was still dressed in the casual clothes he had worn to take the children to the beach, shorts and a snug white T-shirt that revealed his muscular chest and legs and that always made her want to devour him whole.

Not a bad idea, surely, on their anniversary…?

She paused, looking up at him, her arms still around his neck. She saw the expression on his face suddenly change. With a wicked smile, he started to lower his mouth toward hers.

Then she heard little John knock something over downstairs, heard Annie cry, heard the baby start to wail as he was woken prematurely from his nap.

With a laugh, she gave her husband a wry look. "And our guests will arrive in about six minutes."

His dark eyes gleamed at her. "So we have six minutes?"

"Talos!" she said with a laugh, knowing what he was thinking. "We should welcome our guests to our home!"

"The kids are downstairs," he growled. "They can do it."

"You're incorrigible!" But still, she sighed with pleasure as he lowered his head to kiss her. They had a chaotic, crazy, artistic life full of friends and children and laughter, bright with color and warm with love. Exhausting, but oh, so happy. It was the life Eve had always dreamed of. Even on five hours sleep a night, she felt grateful every morning. She was lucky. *Blessed.*

After only one kiss, Talos drew back from her, his dark eyes twinkling. "I have a present for you. I wanted you to open it before the Navarres get here and the chaos really starts."

"For our anniversary?" she said in surprise. She looked around the beautiful bedroom, with its enormous bed where they made love every night, overlooking their private island and the wide blue sea. Every inch of the villa had already all been decorated with white lilies and orange roses for their party. Their home had never looked more lush and gorgeous. And Talos's four jets were flying in friends and family from all around the world to celebrate with a three-day, child-friendly party that was costing more than she liked to think about. "You've already given me so much. I couldn't possibly want more."

"Too bad. Open it."

He handed her a black velvet box. She opened it with an intake of breath. Inside, she saw a beautiful diamond necklace with six hanging emerald-cut diamonds, each as big as her fingertip.

"Lovely," she breathed, then looked up with chagrin. "But I didn't get you anything!"

He lifted his eyebrow with a wicked grin. "That's what you think." He slowly stroked her earlobe to her chin, making her shiver. Clasping the diamond strand around her neck, he ran his hands over the six large diamonds, caressing the warmth of her bare collarbone. "This necklace represents our family. One diamond for each of our six children."

"Six?" She frowned. "Have you been glugging ouzo? We have *three* children."

With a dark gleam in his eyes, he lowered his head to kiss her, whispering, "So far."

When the Navarre family came through the front door ten minutes later, they found only children to greet them, cheering and wiggling happily as the dog barked and danced around them amid a profusion of knocked-over flower arrangements. Fragrant orange petals floated softly down through the air.

"They'll be down in just a minute," the nanny told them nervously.

But Lia and Roark glanced at each other and smiled.

They didn't need any explanation.

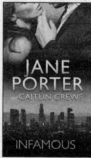

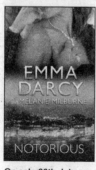
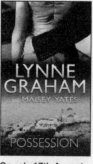

Happy ever after is only the beginning!

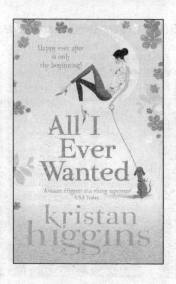

Callie Grey has got a great job, a great man and, fingers crossed, a whopping great diamond—then her boss/boyfriend gives her dream and her sparkly ring to someone else…

She's spent her life reaching for the moon. Now Callie's let go and, falling among the stars, who will be there to catch her?

www.millsandboon.co.uk

0712/MB

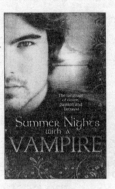
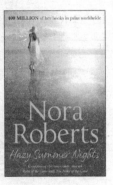

The World of Mills & Boon®

There's a Mills & Boon® series that's perfec
for you. We publish ten series and with new
titles every month, you never have to wait
long for your favourite to come along.

Blaze®
Scorching hot,
sexy reads

By Request
Relive the romance wit
the best of the best

Cherish™
Romance to melt the
heart every time

Desire
Passionate and dramat
love stories

Have Your Say

You've just finished your book.
So what did you think?

We'd love to hear your thoughts on our
'Have your say' online panel
www.millsandboon.co.uk/haveyoursay

- Easy to use
- Short questionnaire
- Chance to win Mills & Boon® goodies